Scales of Fire

The Five Furies of Heaven

Book 2

Ashley Capes

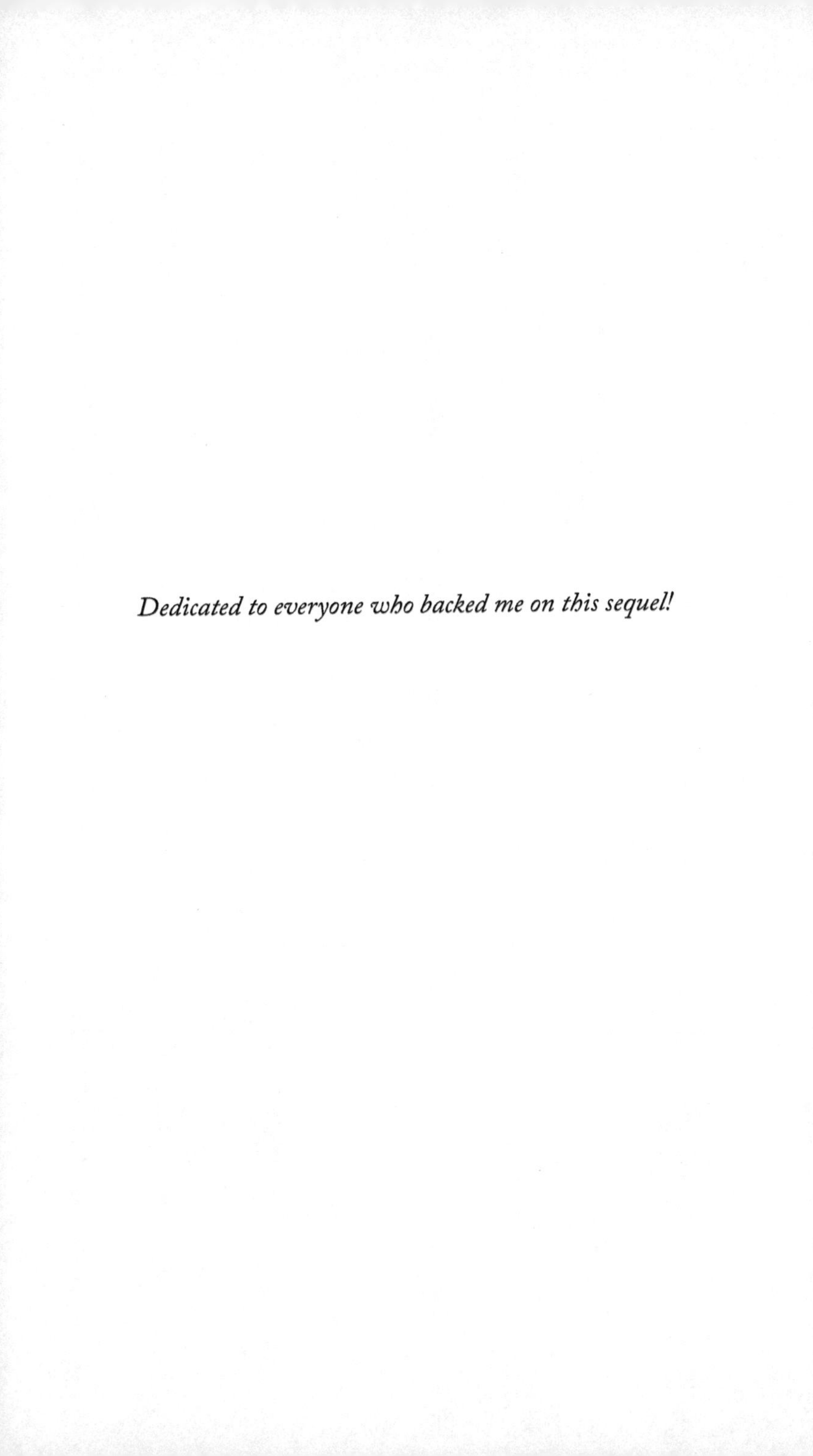

Dedicated to everyone who backed me on this sequel!

Chapter 1.

Kilek flinched as *Songs of Glory* thudded against the heavy carpet – a muted sound in the night.

His limbs were frozen.

Again!

Nakir simply stared, appearing very much at ease where he stood – torso bare, white collar at his throat, fingerless gloves gripping his blade.

Breath rasped in Kilek's throat and sudden sweat formed, as though his entire body had reacted to the flash of fear, reducing him to a coward once more. He ground his teeth, even as his limbs trembled. "No."

Nakir nodded slowly. "Yes, boy. Fight the terror. Come, raise your blade."

Kilek frowned. The man was... encouraging him?

Fear still coursed through his limbs; the twinge in his chest, the chill, the scent and taste of blood somehow, but he *had* to force himself to move. With or without Nakir's unexpected words.

Confusion made it easier. And though he clenched the

handle of his blade like a claw, he was able to lift the sword.

Nakir flashed forward, palm smashing into Kilek's chest.

Kilek crashed into one of the small tables. Books scattered and pain spread from his hip, but Nakir did not follow-up his attack, merely skipped back and sighed. "Well?"

Kilek glared. "You're toying with me." The realisation drew rage from somewhere deep within, a forge-fire sparking to life. He straightened. Nakir obviously thought so little of him that the assassin could afford to make a leisurely killing, not even bothering to start with his sword.

"For a moment, at least."

Kilek tried again, raising the point of his weapon as he took a stance that would lead to Dancing Spark.

"Good lad. Now, let's see what you can do with it."

Kilek met the Surrogate's dark eyes, ignoring a tremble that lingered in his arms. He did not lower his blade nor attack just yet. Instead, he raised his voice. "Who sent you?"

"That, I will not say. But you are, for some reason, quite high upon my master's list."

Nakir swung his sword.

Kilek deflected the strike, eyes wide, then skipped around to swing up from the side but Nakir swatted the attack away. Kilek circled further, twisting as Nakir feinted – once, twice, and three times before the assassin slid closer and flicked his blade.

Too fast!

Warm blood slid down Kilek's cheek. His knuckles must have been white but he kept focused on Nakir. The man was a dark shape beyond the circle of moonlight now, almost weaving in place. Kilek swallowed a surge of anger at being toyed with again, keeping his position. "You're not bored yet, it seems," he snapped.

"Not quite, no."

Kilek leapt forward before the final word issued from Nakir's mouth. He swung his sword fast, moving high then left, doing his best to control the slashes as he fell into the Dancing Spark pattern… only for Nakir to deflect or dodge each strike with only the simplest of movements.

And Kilek knew, the Anesca would be aware of every pattern, every possible stroke, every twist or surprise he might muster, especially as a novice. What damage could he possibly inflict upon someone that even Mathi's gift could only drive away, at great cost?

But giving up was not possible. Not now. Not when he was so close to finding the Song. Kilek swung hard, a curving slice.

Nakir spun away then fell into a crouch, sword swirling toward Kilek's legs.

Kilek leapt back.

Too slow.

The blade hit home... with a dull thump. Hard, but not the sharp bite of steel he'd imagined.

The man had used the flat of his blade.

"Bastard!" Kilek shouted. The last of his fear slithered away, replaced by outrage. If he was to die now, then at least let it be after a true fight, not as part of some game to satisfy the man's ego. "Do you have anything else, or is that all?"

Nakir shot forward and struck Kilek's wrist with his free hand. His weapon thudded to the carpet.

Kilek swung his own fist with a shout.

Again, Nakir was ready – almost a blur as he blocked Kilek's attack then pivoted, kicking out. Kilek's knee buckled.

He hit the floor with a grunt. Rolled, only to come face to face with the point of a blade, moonlight gleaming upon the steel.

Nakir's expression was lost to shadow, looming just beyond the circle of light.

"And now I am bored."

"Then kill me already," Kilek snapped. His heart crashed against his chest but it was all fury.

"Oh my, no – my orders are very different now. You're to be taken, not killed."

Kilek frowned up at the assassin. Blood from the cut Nakir had inflicted earlier now slid down the side of his neck. "Taken?"

"As I understand the matter, your potential has shifted from threat to asset," Nakir replied. "Now, you no doubt remember my collar – it will transport us to a safe place and then you're going to have to do a little walking. I won't promise you'll see your friends again, but you will survive at least until we reach my master."

"Until I'm no longer useful?"

"Quite possibly." Nakir crouched to place a gloved hand on Kilek's shoulder.

White blossomed at the man's throat –

Something dark crashed into the Surrogate. It sent him tumbling away, just as the collar burst into light, and then the assassin was gone. Now, a new figure was picking themselves up from the floor, moving into the moonlight.

"Kilek of Hasere."

Lord Inacien stared down at Kilek in his grey clothing, blond plait and bone clasp still swaying. He extended a hand covered in dark wrappings, helping Kilek up with a nod.

"Thank you, My Lord." Though relief eased the tension within his body, he found little cheer in his words.

Saved again.

Still unable to do anything for himself.

Not even his supposed Luck made a difference; Nakir would have killed him with barely a pause had he not wanted a hostage – or something else – for his master, whomever that was, exactly.

And it had been *very* close to a successful abduction.

"Phantom will arrive soon," the leader of the Knives said, speaking quickly. "I must pursue Nakir. Stay out of sight here."

Kilek nodded.

The man offered nothing more, only slipping back into the shadows on soundless feet.

Chapter 2.

And Florique did appear, calling from below soon after Lord Inacien left, but Kilek had not even moved; he still sat at the edge of the moonlight. He *did* now hold the *Songs of Glory* at least. "When did I pick this up again?" he murmured.

He hadn't opened the book.

Why bother? For all his foolish desire to make up for his cowardice, he had achieved absolutely nothing except to place himself in harm's way. And for what? To put his hands on *Songs of Glory* mere hours before everyone else would have arrived and done exactly the same thing?

The joke was only growing more bitter.

"Upstairs," Kilek eventually called back to Florique as he used one hand to push himself to his feet.

Soft footfalls soon brought the mage into view; his black cloak and calm expression revealed no hint of what he thought of Kilek's flight from the camp, though for some reason, he was not wearing his usual gloves. "It looks as though you at least have the correct book."

The man's words made his opinion a little clearer. "It's the

Songs of Glory. Nakir was here –"

Florique raised a hand, green eyes kind. "Yes. Now, in case you had an apology in mind, no need. I understand."

"... You do?"

He grinned. "Well, your motive, if not your method."

"I thought..." Kilek trailed off. It didn't matter; he'd already made another mistake. But maybe at least *some* comfort lay in having taken action this time. From not freezing up like a coward. *I fought Nakir.* "Should we help Lord Inacien? He seemed to know you were coming."

"Well, we can certainly trust the impressive Rian Inacien to deal with the obstacle of Nakir. For now, I believe we should talk, Kilek. Before everyone catches up to us, for I suspect there are things you might be more comfortable saying out of earshot of your friends, especially."

"Ah..."

"No need to hold back."

Kilek tried to hide his frown. Why was Florique so interested in him all of a sudden? Something to do with Surrogates? What had the man said before about wanting to stop the Cabeku due to his own goals? "What do you mean?"

"That being a Surrogate can be difficult. There are few to confide in, and all can see your frustration with the Goddess. At least with your friends, their Gifts are obvious, yes? And now at last, Paxoph has manifested a remarkable gift, while yours remains unclear."

"Well..."

The man chuckled. "You will not draw her ire if you complain aloud, Kilek."

"I *do* want to know. To do more," he said, voice rising

already. "I'm so *tired* of holding everyone back. I'm always being saved by someone else! Why couldn't she give me something that I know how to use? Or let me know what has changed, if I truly am Lucky? And what if it's something else? And I'm missing it! If only she'd tell me, so I could at least learn how to use the damn gift." He was waving the book around now.

Florique nodded. "Good lad. But don't forget, not so long ago, I told you that I saw something within you. That has not changed, but I will offer a caution, perhaps."

"About what?" Kilek said, lowering the *Songs of Glory*, a little shame bringing heat to his cheeks. How close had he been to hurling the book across the room?

The mage offered a slight shrug. "Of rushing toward change."

What was Florique trying to say? "Do you mean… that I shouldn't want her gift?"

"Did you have a choice, Kilek?"

"I... I did. I chose this. She showed me the future; I have to stop it."

"Commendable, of course," the mage replied. "Then let me ask another question. Could you have refused a God?"

"I..." He blinked. The question sent a chill through his body. Florique was right, wasn't he? Kilek shook his head. "I don't think so."

"Then you see my point."

"But I *did* choose." Kilek's voice rose a little in pitch once more. "She said she wouldn't force me."

Florique sighed as he stepped closer and placed both hands upon Kilek's shoulders. Up close, the lines and dark shadows remained beneath his eyes, as if whatever weariness had come upon him since facing the giant Cabeku was far from faded. "I am saying that if one day you came to regret your gift, for whatever reason, that such a fact would sadden me. More so, if you rushed toward a change that cannot be undone."

A chill settled over Kilek's shoulders, Florique's words somehow more troubling for their gentleness. In the time they'd travelled together, the man had rarely said a single thing that didn't have at least some trace of sarcasm. To hear such concern now... was there a deeper reason?

Was it in part due to the man's own unspoken regrets?

For instance, if Florique was a Surrogate and not just an extremely powerful mage...

Before Kilek could answer, the man smiled again. "In the meantime, we have the *Songs* now, finally. And if I'm not mistaken, the others aren't far from arriving. Why don't you show Dionarc our prize? Afterward, best we learn exactly what has happened in this place."

Chapter 3.

Dawn snuck through the windows, pale where it fell through the skylight to land upon the majority of his friends who now stood around Dionarc.

The bard smiled down at the book in his hands. "*Songs of Glory* indeed. While I can only hope Lady Wen has left the estate for some benign reason, if this is important to fighting off those Cabeku… creatures, then I must take heart."

Everyone seemed just as pleased; either too relieved at finding the book or too tired to question Kilek much about his flight from the camp. Pax, of all those gathered, had the least to say – his exhaustion clear from the way his head turned slowly when someone spoke to him.

Kilek covered the spots of his blood that remained on the floor with his boots, wiping at his cheek as he watched the bard open the book. Everyone leaned a little closer, though Alira was glancing at other books upon the shelves too, plenty of which had been knocked to the floor.

Dionarc flipped through several pages, careful with the tome, nodding to himself as he did. Finally, he exclaimed.

"Here we are." He held the book open for all to see, and a shiver of anticipation ran through Kilek's weary body.

Clarion Song.

Notes to the melody ran beside the words – three verses in total, the complete song!

The first verse Kilek recalled from the bard's room back in the palace, but the last was accompanied by something that was neither lyric nor note. Near the Song's final word – which was 'return' – rested an odd symbol. It was quite unlike the squarish Luargot letters and appeared almost as an open hand. "What does that mean?" Kilek asked as he pointed.

The bard rubbed his chin. "That there is more to the story. Historians and bards use such marks to urge one to read further."

"So, the Song is incomplete?"

"No, these are the three verses. The symbol means that whoever transcribed the Song had something to say about it."

"Orille perhaps?" Kilek asked.

"Well, I do not know. The symbol is a Herisman one and here it tells us to seek out the *Master Chorale*."

Tyar turned to the shelves, no hint of broken bones in his movement. "Does Lady Wen have it?"

Dionarc nodded. "All bards do – I have a copy in my own room."

"That's a relief, then."

The bard raised a hand, a sheepish expression coming over his face. "There is one complication, however. I am not much of a translator, you see."

"Oh." Princess Zenia appeared crestfallen. Like Tyar, it

was impossible to tell from her bearing and movements that she had only yesterday suffered a near-mortal wound. Only the bloodstains upon her clothing remained. "Then we can't find out why the symbol was put beneath the Song?"

"We will, but it may take me a little while." He glanced up to the brightening morning. "Perhaps we'd better organise a meal; I can let everyone know about this tiny setback, and I'll dig up the *Chorale*. Why don't you gather everyone in the sitting-room, Kilek?"

"Right." Kilek strode from the library, a new purpose to his step, almost running down the stairs. There, he found Mathi and Sir Eciven returning from a search of the grounds. Light from tall windows fell across them, their boots muffled by the carpet, golden dust motes stirring as they approached.

"Dionarc wants us to meet in the sitting-room. He needs to translate something about the Song."

"You really found it?" Mathi asked.

"We did."

Sir Eciven smiled. "Joyous news. In contrast, we have found little evidence of life here. Lady Wen and her staff look to have been gone for some time."

"Troubling," Florique added as he slipped out of a nearby room, where he had been searching for clues as to why the mansion stood vacant.

"Well," Mathi said, "the stable is empty and other buildings are too. No signs of any sort of panicked flight either."

Sir Eciven tilted his head in thought. "We might find answers at another mansion or one of the villages. Or perhaps the Ocean Palace itself."

Florique nodded. "As I am sure Dionarc would attest, Lady Wen is not so disorganised as all this. I do hope that when the truth is revealed, she will be found alive and well. For now, let us solve the mystery of the Song."

When all had gathered in the sitting-room, Kilek found a soft armchair by the window but did not sink into its cushions; he leant forward as his pulse quickened. How nice to feel another rush of excitement instead of fear. Surely now, they were close to calling forth the dragons. *Just how big are they, really?* It was difficult to imagine. Supposedly, their scales could cast sparks and some could heal by reflected light…

He glanced around. It did not have enough seats, and while Pax took a footstool at first, it was not for long – Alira smiled as he exchanged his larger frame for hers upon the stool. Sir Eciven had to stand but offered no complaint.

The room was not unlike the others – the faint taste of dust and stale air was somehow more present than swirling patterns on the upholstery or the small ornaments of musical instruments that lined the mantle. Even a clean fireplace before them with its neat stack of firewood, its promise of warmth, seemed to have greyed beneath a layer of dust.

Something had happened in the mansion, but the mystery receded once more when Dionarc lifted the first from a small stack of three books. He handed one to Florique and another to Kilek, then took his own chair. "I'll need some help with this, if you please."

"Do you want extra light?" Tyar asked.

"Or some tea?" Zenia suggested as she moved to a sideboard where a teapot shaped as a bluebird waited.

"If you handle the wood, I'll start the fire," Florique

offered. "I don't care much for splinters."

Tyar arranged the firewood into a steeple then stood back. Florique snapped his fingers and a spiral of flame spun through the air to splash across the wood, and though sparks bounced around the hearth, none caught within the soft carpet.

Warmth, light, and the crackle of flames soon filled the room, a pleasant scent from the wood rising as Zenia and Tyar set to work on the tea.

Dionarc blinked down at the *Chorale,* which he'd opened across his lap. "That is better, yes. Now, when Supreme Orille transcribed the Song all those years ago, the bard left a mark for future generations. It urged them to read more about the Song."

"Because he knew it had something to do with the dragons?" Zenia asked, turning from the fire.

"Possibly. The obvious concern is that if we perform the call without being aware of all factors, that it will fail. Or something worse may happen."

"Makes sense."

"Very well. I think it's time to begin. Now, to help you each, I have given Kilek a Herisman symbol key and Phantom holds a phrasebook. And here is a *Master Chorale,* something of a reference book."

"I'll do my best to help," Kilek said.

"Splendid. Now, the *Chorale* collects stories about the composition or even uses of Songs from the past, and that is what we will translate."

"I am ready," Florique said with a wave of his book.

Dionarc nodded. "Kilek, there is a swan-like symbol upon a lake – does it speak of a place?"

Kilek ran his finger across the page, skimming over symbols with more densely arranged shapes. And there, a swan-like curve to one of them. "It means 'ancient lake'."

"Just so. The swan as a symbol of Herisman eternity." He nodded to himself, mouthing words a moment. "Florique, is this phrase present? *Firab ko lihmes.*"

Florique flipped through a few pages. "Can you give me any more context there, old chum?"

"Ah, the first and last symbols are mirrored – I think this has to do with the dragons themselves."

"Right." The mage kept searching, stopping here and there, but soon shook his head. "I'll need a touch more time, I think."

"Of course." Dionarc tapped his page. "Kilek, I have a symbol here that I have never seen. It is mostly horizontal lines, not unlike an anvil, though I doubt that is what it represents."

Kilek turned the pages of his own book until he found something similar. The room was quiet with anticipation. Even the handing out of tea had paused, but his pulse was still charging along. "Here it is. The book says it is an obligation... ah, like 'must', I think?"

"Hmmm."

Florique clapped his hands together – not too hard, thankfully – and looked up. "Found it."

"Yes?"

"Simply this: 'so they believed'."

The bard exhaled. "I see. Very well, one more now for Kilek – though I think I have a better idea of what has been written already. A circle above a horizontal line."

Kilek flipped through, and though the book was slender,

it took a moment to find the correct section where several symbols of a similar design lay. "There are three that might be the one you mention. Is the circle... more like an oval?"

"No, it's a true circle."

"Right. If the circle is high above, it means 'shining bright' and if it's closer, it means 'shining' only."

"Thank you both." Dionarc stood. "Here is the full passage, translated roughly, and so I'm sure you'll forgive me. It says: 'So the people of Deluargot believed the long-absent dragons might return if the Song were used as a call, though its popularity in battle would suggest otherwise. Yet it is reported that the Clarion Song must actually be performed upon the ancient lake of High Rios and more, that no simple choir will suffice. Instead, it must be played upon the Luminous Clarion, shining treasure of the Eastern Queens'.""

Silence filled the sitting-room.

Finally, Zenia lowered her cup. "Then it's true, what the dragon told Kilek."

Tyar frowned. "So we have the Song but we need a special instrument?"

"So it seems," Dionarc replied. "Not to mention a special location."

Sir Eciven moved to place a hand on the bard's shoulder. "Fine work, Dion. And we need not be so dejected, Tyar. Queen Liana's line has resided in the east for generations now. We will ask the former Queen – Liana's descendent – if she knows where the Luminous Clarion can be found."

"I'm surprised I've not heard it mentioned," Zenia said.

Sir Eciven shrugged. "Considering the bad blood between Moranlier and your father, perhaps not? It is vaguely familiar to me. Described as an heirloom, I thought."

"And the ancient lake of High Rios?" Alira asked.

"I think I know where that is," Kilek replied.

"You do?" Zenia asked. "Tell us, Kilek."

"Well, it sounds like the mountain lake that's mentioned in the Myth of the Silver Dragon."

Florique stood with a grin. "Ah, the hunt has another leg!"

"This isn't exactly good news, is it?" Mathila asked. "Do we have time to find a legendary instrument *and* a mythical lake? What if more of the giant Cabeku come for us? Or if they attack one of the cities?"

The mage nodded. "Of course, you are right to fear such things, though I can shed some more light on the Cabeku. But first, I believe we should prepare a meal that will far surpass the scent of somewhat stale tea, as I for one, find myself quite famished."

Chapter 4.

Kilek blinked throughout their late breakfast; the chaos of the last few days finally catching up with him, transforming the armchair into something close to a bed. He wasn't the only one hiding yawns as they ate their travel rations. Even as Florique started to explain why another giant Cabeku was unlikely for now, and that there was still time to prevent the hordes, Kilek found himself missing words here and there.

At one point, it seemed the mage sat as he spoke, yet between one blink and the next, Florique was standing before the fireplace, still explaining.

And then nothing but a sweet, soft darkness as Kilek closed his eyes once more.

***

He woke to the sound of creaking wood.

Dying embers in the fireplace were the only things lighting the sitting-room... which was now empty. He straightened. Where was everyone? "Hello?" Darkness loomed beyond the window. *When did night fall?*

The creaking of wood continued, drifting down from an upper floor.

But it wasn't the only sound.

Music echoed. A somewhat wistful tune, tinkling as if played upon a delicate instrument. And though the song swelled and fell in a soothing rhythm, there was an urgency too – he had to find the source. And unlike his bewitching by the Prisawi woman, the sense of danger was clear now.

Kilek stood. *We're all in danger.*

But from what?

He strode from the room, reaching for his sword... and finding nothing at his hip. Kilek paused, one foot half-raised. *Am I even awake?* Had the song plunged him into some inescapable dream? The wooden stair, the walls with their evenly spaced but darkened lamps, everything seemed real; and reaching out to touch the wood, to push against it, offered an unyielding panel.

He started up the staircase, now steeped in cobwebs and dust.

Each step stirred the webs, rising and floating as if caught within invisible water. Was it the song that created the dream-like state? His own steps were not so light, and every other footfall still won a creak.

At the top, the source of the music became clearer – waiting behind the first door. It, too, stood covered in icy-looking webs, along with scraps of grey leaves and twigs that fluttered slowly in place. Kilek pushed his way inside, strands breaking with soft sounds of resistance, revealing a sunlit room.

Sunlit?

Inside, floorboards were bare, and old carpet had rotted away to the corners of the room where yet more cobwebs gleamed. The fireplace stood empty and beneath the window, a harp of jade rested upon a stand – though no hand caused it to play. Instead, the song continued, sounds still seeming far too delicate to come from the instrument.

But he was not alone.

A shadowy shape wavered in the centre of the room. It was becoming solid, not to mention quite familiar where it stopped before the harp – Alira! Her head was tilted as if listening.

"Alira?"

She stopped, staring down at the harp but did not turn. Instead, she began to move her arms, as if pulling at the empty air.

Leaves, twigs, webs and even dust were all drawn near.

Alira kept working, dragging everything closer until it hung near the harp. Finally, she shuffled around so that when she moved her arms, it was to push the debris she'd gathered to smother the harp.

And the song dimmed!

"It's working, keep going," Kilek called.

Though she did not appear to hear him, Alira continued hauling more detritus onto the harp until the song was actually difficult to hear.

Kilek glanced around the room but nothing else had changed yet.

Even so, Alira's magic was working.

A sharp crack echoed.

Kilek flinched. One of the harp-strings now floated

free from the murk. Before Alira could act, another string snapped, and then another. The song changed, discordant notes filling the room.

He faltered where he stood. The melody was no longer music but a hideous clashing of sounds. Worse, it somehow caused a tightness within his chest.

Alira had fallen back, hands clamped over her ears.

Was she screaming too?

Her mouth was open but Kilek heard nothing as he crumpled to the floorboards, limbs twitching with panic.

Then Florique appeared.

He wore a deep frown and his hands were already spread wide.

When he swung his arms, thunder clapped.

***

Kilek woke, unharmed, and everything had changed.

The jade harp's song had returned to 'normal' and he reclined in a *bed* and not the armchair. The air was no longer… thick. It was also dawn now, according to the gentle light that pushed gently through the curtains. Soft voices, ones he recognised, conversed in the hallway outside, and when he sat up, Alira turned to face him from a second bed, blankets wrapped around her knees where she rested.

"You're awake." She was smiling.

"I am. What happened? It was almost like being underwater. I could see you but I couldn't help."

She tapped her fingers together. "Well, I could hear your voice but I couldn't see you. Did the song wake you, too?"

"I think so." He rubbed at his neck. "What about Florique?"

"Well…" Alira looked away. "After he saved us, he and Dionarc created a song to counter the harp's melody. Dionarc has to sing or hum it fairly often, but the way Florique's magic works to replicate the song is really quite magnificent. I don't know how he did it."

"That sounds like good news."

"It is, but Florique collapsed right after." Concern was clear in her eyes. "No-one can wake him, so we need to make a stretcher before we leave."

"Oh."

Alira sighed. "I'm hoping we can find answers at the Ocean Palace."

"I'm sure we will," he said with a smile, though it was difficult to include much cheer in the expression.

Chapter 5.

They rode through the wooded hills with expressions of concern, the harp's song not only following, but seeming to stalk them – humming between the leaves, down from the very sky even, an ever-present reminder beneath the *clop-clop* of hooves.

And while the horses were not bound by the harp, Dion's own song was still needed to hold off the spell for everyone else. Thankfully, his voice remained stronger as the bard maintained the echo Florique had created.

Kilek couldn't enjoy the respite; Florique had not improved.

The mage slept upon a stretcher rigged behind Sir Eciven's gelding, peaceful-seeming, unperturbed by any bump or dip in the road, but his hair was a little too close to white, his cheeks gaunt.

Sir Eciven and the princess were not as concerned, claiming to have seen him go through similar periods of powerful exhaustion in the past. But Florique's words from last night – his warning about the cost of being Anesca rang louder to Kilek than either the song that haunted the road or Dion's humming.

More so if you rushed toward a change that cannot be undone.

Just what was the truth about the mage?

"I trust that he'll recover, Kilek."

Alira smiled across at him from where she rode nearby. The others had split into familiar groups or pairings, with Mathi and Tyar together, led by Sir Eciven and Zenia just behind, and Pax bringing up the rear with the bard.

"He's changed a *lot*. What if he doesn't wake?"

"He once told me that he could survive almost anything, though the cost was 'not insignificant' as he put it."

"I hope he's right."

Ahead, the trees began to thin, their smooth, grey bark giving way to smaller shrubs or spreading grounds with neat lawns. And set off from the highway, another mansion soon appeared, bright circle of the sun hanging behind it as the afternoon wore down. Like Lady Wen's home, no signs of life; no staff roaming the gardens, no carriages or visitors in the entryway, stillness in the stable.

"Whoever is behind this song is far more powerful than first thought," Sir Eciven said. "Princess, have you heard of trouble here in the east? Riders or messengers not passing through or perhaps failing to return?"

"Nothing, no," she replied. "But Peycu would know better. Over the last few years, little of substance has passed between the two palaces."

Another clue that something was amiss between the royals. "Why is that?" Kilek asked.

"Former Queen Moranlier has long since shut herself off from King Hadeon," Sir Eciven said, glancing at the princess.

Zenia did not respond, though it seemed a little tension entered her posture.

"Oh." Kilek kept his gaze elsewhere. *That was stupid, wasn't it?*

Onwards they rode, and still the homes and buildings nearby – some larger than Lady Wen's mansion – appeared utterly empty. As the afternoon sun continued to fall, it was all but confirmed they would not pass a single traveller, nor see anyone moving upon any of the grounds.

Not while the song held dominion over the land.

Powerful, indeed.

"Someone had to have passed this way recently." Sir Eciven's frown was so deep now that it turned his moustache down, changing the shape of his scar. "A messenger, merchant, anything! Didn't His Majesty send a force for a cooperative training exercise just a week ago?"

"Let's ask," Zenia suggested, pointing ahead to where a Wayfarer's Inn rested. Its three storeys were differentiated by stone for the bottom two, then timber for the third. The *Home in the Woods* included a large stable and even a nearby sporting ground of coloured grass, stained by some unknown means, and arranged in large diamonds.

Sharps was a game popular in the south, but at home, Kilek had never seen it played. Even after reading the rules, it had been difficult to imagine the game itself, with so many varied movements and commands.

Yet this, too, was a quiet, empty place.

"Will there even be anyone inside to tell us?" Mathi asked. "Or will the song have gotten to them, too?"

"Either way, it may reveal something." Zenia glanced to the stable, which seemed to be empty of all but old straw.

Next, she tried the inn's front door, finding it locked.

Kilek peered in through a window, Tyar at his side, but the glass had been covered by cloth from the inside. "What's happening here?" he whispered.

Tyar's expression was grim. "It can't be anything good."

The princess rapped on the wooden door, its large handle and lock carved as a wreath of leaves. "We are travelling on the King's business and seek admittance!"

She received no response.

Clouds passed over the sun, though the warmth hardly vanished.

Kilek left the window as Sir Eciven withdrew something from an inner pocket and leant over the handle. Tiny sounds of steel against steel followed and within moments, he'd nodded to himself, rising to push the door open.

Beyond, Kilek caught only a glimpse of the room, wherein there waited something soft and faintly blue, something that rested against the furniture...

And then...

...and then, up ahead, Kilek could see a stretching bridge. It led to the Ocean Palace, their destination for days, ever since Florique recovered and saved everyone at the *Home in the Woods*.

Luckily.

It had not been easy, of course, but everything worked out in the end.

Didn't it?

The flicker of doubt vanished quickly; an important task waited. They had to cross the bridge and reach the Ocean Palace in order to uncover who or what lay behind the song. The palace buildings waited at the far side, a distant shimmering of blue, green, and white. But the glass-covered bridge itself was equally eye-catching – perhaps more so than the sparkling ocean, a vast wonder itself.

Effortlessly, it seemed, the bridge stretched out and above the peninsula's stony sand and restless waves, its breadth enough for half a dozen carts. The span had been split along the centre courtesy of a ridge-like division, so that visitors could flow into the palace-city on one side, while those leaving were free to use the other.

At least, so it was according to Zenia.

But the bridge stood empty.

And now they were closer, it seemed the place was starting to decay. *Like Lady Wen's estate.* Posters on the green, brine-bitten arches were faded and tattered, some speaking of visiting or local performers and even chefs… but all were from years gone by.

Overhead, too, an occasional crack or hole waited in the mighty glass that sheltered visitors.

"That's a lot of glass," Tyar said as he rode, reins held only loosely.

"I don't think any will fall," Pax replied.

Kilek had already glanced from the clear ceiling and its sturdy frame, which was supposedly strengthened by the glass-wrights of the city, for there was a dark figure slumped against the dividing stone ahead. Too distant for much in the way of detail, but they did not seem to wear armour. Someone from nearby? Or the Wayfarer's Inn? "Do you see them?"

Sir Eciven nodded. "Do not rush, but we will help whoever it is, if possible."

"Are you expecting some sort of ploy?" Alira asked, her

expression one of concern. "Should someone stay back with Florique?"

"No. But let's not make any mistakes."

Kilek twisted in the saddle. The mage still lay stretched across his sled, wrapped securely in blankets. Dion rode nearby, humming along to maintain their protective song. His voice was not weakening, but his eyes revealed more weariness compared to how he seemed back at the inn… didn't they?

"Hmmm." Kilek frowned to himself. Details about leaving the inn were unclear in his memory.

But it had been impressive, what they'd achieved there, that much was absolutely certain.

And they owed Florique, too.

"Well, this one's not a threat." Sir Eciven's voice broke Kilek's reverie.

Everyone had stopped by the figure.

The slumped man bore a worn cloak and no visible weapons, but the yellow wax that covered the entirety of his one visible ear was far more noteworthy. Sir Eciven rolled the fellow gently onto his back, revealing no wounds but skin very much the pallor of the deceased.

"We'll take him back, won't we?" Alira asked, her voice soft.

Sir Eciven nodded, face grim as he rose. "Once we learn the truth about what is happening here. And that will be no mean feat, since I suspect that whatever is waiting for us in the palace is well-aware of our approach."

Chapter 6.

"It has to be another Surrogate." Mathi's arms were folded, letting her mount follow Sir Eciven and Zenia. "We know that, don't we?"

"Then hopefully we have the advantage of numbers," Kilek said.

Tyar shrugged. "Only if there's just *one* Surrogate in there. And no army of insects."

"We don't know what waits inside," Zenia said from over her shoulder. "But we must face and overcome it. Can I rely on you all?" Her tone gave the words an expectant air rather than that of a request. Not only the friendly young woman Kilek had sparred and travelled and fought with, but also the *Princess*. The set of her jaw seemed to suggest concern for the people who relied upon her station.

Did she also have family and friends within the city? So much about the former Queen was not clear – the King's mother, or a one-time wife that had for some reason been… banished?

Whatever the truth, any and all within the Ocean Palace

were under threat.

"You can rely on us, Your Highness," Paxoph said, and the others nodded or added their own assent.

"Thank you all," Zenia replied with a smile.

The rest of their trip across the bridge passed in silence, save for hooves against stone and the thump of waves below, until before them at last, the walls of the Ocean Palace rose from the enormous island.

The masonry had been patterned in rising triangles, as though green waves charged up blue walls. It was an astounding work of art that continued upon the palace itself. Columns of similar shades rose, with banks of arched windows and towers bearing rooves shaped almost like the wings of a bird. Even the gate bore the image of twin, frost-tipped waves on each side. Such waves met at the centre, gleaming in the light, and signalled a gate that was very much closed.

All quite dissimilar to what was built farther west, but it was not the architecture that brought everyone to a halt this time, even though Kilek knew he and the others had been staring like the villagers they were during the approach. No, it was the huge grate beneath their feet, one which had now replaced the bridge, leaving the churn of waves visible below.

Kilek pulled his horse back a few steps.

Sir Eciven chuckled. "Sorry to laugh, lad. This is one of the palace's more inconvenient defences – if you're on this side of the bridge."

"Do we enter here?" he asked.

The knight captain looked up to the gate and the walls, which stood empty of archers, soldiers, guards or anyone. "Not without some effort."

"There's something else," Alira said. "The harp's song is stronger."

Dionarc nodded from where he still hummed – unable to answer with words. His voice was yet to fail but his hair was damp at the temples now, and sweat beaded his brow, even beneath a chill ocean breeze.

Kilek closed his eyes to listen for the dangerous strains, then stopped. *Foolish thing to do.*

"Dion won't be able to keep this up forever," Paxoph said. "I think we need Florique."

Tyar dismounted to kneel before the grate, reaching down to touch the steel. "Can we break in somewhere else? Sneak in via the sea somehow?"

Sir Eciven had folded his arms. "None that I know of, and the wharf is on the far side of the city."

"Maybe I can try something," Alira offered. She had withdrawn the two feathers from the Goddess – colour like fire and azure – and with them, four more feathers of varying size. Three were black and one white. "Before I do, will a trap be sprung if I succeed? Like the grate falling away, to dump me into the sea? Or if there are watchers inside, will it happen even if we approach the gate itself?"

Her concern made sense, since crossing close enough to try her magic upon the huge gates would mean standing in danger the whole time.

"We could use rope to anchor you," Tyar suggested.

Sir Eciven rummaged through his saddlebags, soon producing a long coil. "Without a better idea, I think we should try it. Anyone?"

Kilek shook his head, as did everyone else, and so the knight turned to Alira. "Expect a jolt if the grate does fall away – but just remember, I'll have you."

She nodded. "It's a risk I must take, so thank you, Sir Eciven."

The knight tied a harness then, hands moving swiftly, before fastening it around Alira's waist. Next, he aligned the rope across both shoulders, handing off the excess to Paxoph, whose grip was just as tight. "Tyar, draw that bow of yours in case anyone tries to interfere from the wall."

"Right."

Alira strode across the grate, the rope seeming to have plenty of give and her footing solid – so far.

Kilek found himself holding his breath.

But she reached the mighty stone gates without falling, lifting her arms to place feathers on the wall – one black feather for each side. Then, she held Avendria's feathers up and they shimmered in the light. An answering glow came from the dark feathers, as both sank into the stone.

"How goes it, Alira?" Tyar asked without taking his eyes from the walls.

"It's working, Ty." And then, as with the entry to Daciael's resting place, the stone moved.

The gates swung inwards on a faint rumble. Kilek had a hand on his sword hilt, yet naught but a courtyard was revealed. Empty of people, it stretched off toward the main buildings, chief of which boasted a broad stair with generous landings. There, each handrail became an ornate sculpture. They seemed to depict sea-creatures, things that lay somewhere between dolphin… and a lizard? Did it bear just a faint resemblance to the lizard that attacked them in the cave?

To each side, the courtyard gave way to overgrown lawns.

The breeze tossed thin leaves across stone and into the grass, across the marble benches, and sent them swirling around quiet fountains and stretches of narrow pools with dark water, too.

Other than the wind, not a single hint of movement.

"We'll search in pairs," Sir Eciven said as he drew his greatsword, gesturing for Kilek to follow him up the first flight. The knight glanced over his shoulder to where the others fanned out through the gardens, some heading for a nearby guard post and connected stable. "Someone keep an eye on Phantom. And stay within earshot."

Dionarc lifted his voice, singing at volume now – it was firm enough but a little raspy at the edges as he fought the song.

"Do you think everyone is hiding somewhere, like at the inn?" Kilek asked. *That's what was happening back there, before we saved them.*

"It's possible," the knight replied with a nod. "There is a small town beyond the palace itself. People could have withdrawn there."

"And why haven't we been attacked by whoever is occupying the palace?"

"My concern, also."

They had not made much progress when Kilek came to a halt upon the first landing, his own blade in hand. There, beside a tiny pool that had been carved into the base of a dolphin-like statue, waited twin piles of Cabeku. At least a dozen. And each and every one of them drained of colour, nearing translucence as they sat in absolute stillness.

"What could do that to them?" he asked.

Sir Eciven exhaled as he nudged one with his blade. The

insect toppled free, clacking softly against the stone. "No idea, lad. It is not like the magic I know, that is for certain."

"Should we…" Kilek trailed off.

On the next landing, a figure was sliding up from beneath the stone.

Dark eyes stared down from her sad expression; the woman wore a layered robe the colours of a muted rainbow. Frayed at the edges, it seemed to be responsible for the glittering echoes in her hair. She extended her arm toward them, palm open.

Kilek whipped his blade upward, but there was no attack…

"Climb no further." Her voice was not a whisper, but it was fainter than he expected… as if reaching him from afar? Somehow, it remained audible over the harp's curse and Dion's singing.

And then she was fading away, leaving only a tiny glimmer in the air.

Who was that?

Aside from whatever magic she possessed, something else was noteworthy about the strange woman, as though she hailed from a distant land. She did not bear the tanned skin of the Prisawi, nor the pale skin of home, and nor was she so dark as Pax. Instead, her hair had been pale, tinted blue.

Kilek glanced to Sir Eciven, who stood with narrowed eyes. "Time to regroup," the knight said.

"Who was that? She tried to warn us."

"On the surface, she was a woman from Dhanhek. And a mage, obviously."

Distant Dhanhek, where they rode all manner of

creatures in their jungles and where the people had no king or queen, according to rumour. Instead, they had an enormous collection of priestesses. "Then she must be the one responsible for all of this?"

"Likely, but we don't know for certain."

"Then why warn us away? She could have attacked."

Sir Eciven rubbed at his jaw as he led Kilek back down toward the others, lifting his voice to call for their return, before answering. "A fine question, lad. One possibility is that she is not so powerful as she seems."

"And another?"

"That she is sincerely trying to warn us, and that she *isn't* behind the disturbance here," he replied. "However, that I doubt."

"But what would a Dhanhekan be doing here?"

"Precisely."

Everyone soon returned to the foot of the stairs, where Alira had watched over Florique with Dionarc, who'd resumed his humming. The others had found no evidence of any remaining people, and so Sir Eciven explained about the drained Cabeku, the woman in the robe of dim rainbows, and her warning.

Silence descended over the group. Zenia was the first to break the hush. "I really do wish we could ask Uncle about this."

Paxoph glanced over to the stairs. "It seems likely that she is Anesca, right?"

"But for who, is the next question," Mathi said.

The princess and Sir Eciven exchanged a glance before she asked something of everyone. "Can you tell, for certain? I did not think Surrogates were so plentiful."

Mathi explained that they could not, and a little on Avendria's rules that bound them. "I don't know if we mentioned any of that to you before, but I don't think I could tell if someone was Anesca. It's just a guess, based on this place."

"A fair guess, most likely," she replied.

"Are we safe to assume that the woman isn't working for Javoteth?" Kilek asked. "The Cabeku up there seemed to have been drained by magic – who else could that have been? I don't know much about Dhanhek. Is that what their mages can do?"

"It is," Sir Eciven said. "They leech the very life from their targets. But we shouldn't rule Javoteth out, despite a Dhanhek deity being more likely."

Alira held the two large, coloured feathers. "I could try using these to contact Avendria? I know that is a risk of a different nature; we might be giving the strange woman more help from her own God."

Tyar shrugged. "Does she need it? Considering this place, I say go for it, Alira."

Clattering footfalls echoed from the entryway. Kilek spun with the group, one hand on the hilt of his blade.

Cabeku.

Just one. But the thing was man-shaped beneath its torn cloak. Many-chambered eyes gleamed from an angular face. No skin, it instead bore a shell coloured near to lilac, the whole thing all the more grotesque for its closeness to human. Even with a frozen expression, where only its eyes moved and ichor leaked from a wide mouth.

Unlike the thing that had captured him, this one did not move so fast. It was considerably bulkier, moving on two strong legs and bearing talons on three sets of arms.

"Protect Florique," Alira said as she charged.

Kilek nearly stepped after, but her hands were already glowing – bright feathers of green appearing just beyond her grip. Nevertheless, each one seemed connected to his friend, matching her movements and hissing where they spun.

She flung her arms at the creature. Green feathers blazed forth. Most thudded into the Cabeku with sizzling accuracy. It stumbled but did not fall.

An arrow flashed by next, only for a jagged talon to swat it aside. Tyar swore, circling with another arrow nocked to his string.

"Surround it," Sir Eciven commanded as he charged, greatsword held aloft.

Kilek ground his teeth. *This isn't going to be like the last time.*

But he'd barely taken two steps before a new figure appeared, clothed in her robe of various colours.

The woman from the stair pointed at the Cabeku.

It collapsed with a screech, arms scraping against the stone as it twitched. The thing was already turning pale, shadows and lilac alike fading, even the stolen cloak… And then, the creature moved no more, leaving only a transparent lump in place of something that had once lived and moved.

The woman's robe boasted vibrant colours now but for whatever reason, it did not seem to grant her strength, as the mage fell against a marble bench. Unable to remain upright, she slumped, rolling onto her back with a gasp. Her breathing was ragged, quite loud in the silence that followed…

Silence?

The harp's call had vanished!

The absence of both the song and Dion's humming, sounds that all-too-quickly had seemed to have followed Kilek half his life, was most welcome.

But when the woman spoke, Kilek's relief soured.

"I ask that… you kill me. Now... quickly."

Alira lowered her hands, the shimmering green feathers dimming. "Who are you?"

"I wonder. Do you mean… whom do I work for?"

"That too," Zenia said as she and Sir Eciven neared.

By the time everyone had gathered around, weapons still in hand, the Dhanhek mage had caught her breath, though she did not try to rise. A tear, or perhaps sweat from her brow, ran down her cheek. "Gianh… is my name."

"And your master?" the princess asked.

"Dayen, Lord of the Seven Jungles, of course."

"It seems you stand against Javoteth," Pax said.

"Yes, but we seek the same thing. For different purposes," she replied, and her voice softened. "To no avail."

Kilek frowned. "The Luminous Clarion."

Gianh nodded, closing her eyes.

Zenia knelt on one knee, but did not move closer to the mage. "It's here, then?"

"As you know, yes."

"Why?" Zenia asked. "Why didn't you take it, if that's what you sought? Why linger here? Why enslave everyone with your song?"

"Is it not obvious, Your Highness?"

The princess frowned. "You know me?"

Again, the mage nodded. "Each of you. So Dayen willed

it."

"Will you tell us?" Alira asked, her expression now somewhat softer than that of the others.

"Not unless you promise to kill me."

Zenia frowned. "Why?"

Gianh opened her eyes now, meeting Alira and then Zenia's gaze with what seemed to be more than merely frustration. "Because I can no longer fight; I am useless."

"No," Alira replied. She glanced at everyone else, and Kilek found himself nodding to her, despite his own doubts. Was there a chance that Gianh was a true enemy of the Cabeku? She obviously held useful information… and above all, simply killing her now seemed wrong.

"Tell us what we need to know, and we will decide," Sir Eciven said.

The mage closed her eyes again, but did not answer.

"You fear something worse than death," Zenia said. "Failure. Shame, perhaps?"

"No." She shook her head. "I feel no shame – I accomplished more than I imagined."

"You and your God obviously have no love for the Cabeku. We could be useful to each other."

"Only if you kill me. Please – I saved you here; I would appreciate my wish being fulfilled."

Pax knelt beside her. His golden hands glowed, but his expression was stern. "If you will not share what you know, I will heal you instead. You will have to face the rest of your life."

She lifted a hand, perhaps to push him away, but could barely extend it. "You don't understand!"

"Do your best to make us," Dionarc said, his own

expression troubled. And while his voice rasped from long use, he was understood.

Gianh seemed to find a little strength, which she used to cover her face with both hands. "Then I ask that you make me a different promise, then."

"We will listen," Zenia said, her tone still wary.

"Take me from this place when you leave. Stop those who will follow me."

Again, there was a pause of confusion before anyone else spoke, and it was Sir Eciven. "You are raising far more questions than you answer, mage. Is this a surrender? Are you offering yourself as a prisoner in exchange for sharing what you know, and what you have done? Are you in fact asking for our protection?"

"So it seems, since you will not kill me."

"Not in cold blood, no," the knight replied. "Though the king may wish to execute you, should you return with us to Alaycron."

She nodded. "That is acceptable."

Zenia folded her arms. "Then I give you my word. Speak now."

"Very well." She paused to take a breath. "While the Surrogates of Javoteth seek to destroy the Luminous Clarion, I came here seeking the horn for the same reason as you – I wished to call the dragons back."

"Why?"

"Simply – because a tide of filthy Cabeku do not threaten only those here, or those to the west."

Of course. Kilek waited for her to continue.

"We cannot hold them at bay forever. Another will be sent to take my place, but for whoever succeeds me to triumph where I have failed, they will need to add my magic to their own. That is a process that I would not survive."

"But…" Kilek trailed off. If what she was saying was true, it surely meant that her death would actually thwart Dhanhek's attempt to stop the Cabeku? And before, she'd asked to die… but didn't she want to be in service to her homeland?

"You understand," she said, as though she'd read his mind. "It is an act of incredible selfishness on my part to ask that you kill me, but I will not share my reasons."

Another moment of silence passed.

Zenia seemed to be choosing her words carefully. Or perhaps she was deciding whether to push for the very reasons mentioned by their captive. "Can not your God send a stronger Surrogate, instead?"

Gianh smiled. "I was the strongest."

"Then why did you fail?" Eciven asked.

"Because the Luminous Clarion cannot be used by one such as I."

"No?"

"I have come to believe that it chooses whether *and* with whom it will leave this place. It chooses for whom it will sing," she said, and glanced to Kilek for just a moment before turning back to the knight.

Chapter 7.

"Meaning, what?" Zenia asked, and she too, had given Kilek a look – one that seemed part curiosity and part... understanding?

The mage sighed. "Meaning that when I realised I could not prevail upon my own, that I had been discovered, I played a final card."

"The glamour of sleep," Alira said softly.

"Yes. Then, I communicated my failure, and waited for a replacement to arrive, in case they would succeed where I had not."

Sir Eciven stared down at the mage. "But the Cabeku interfered?"

She nodded. "Likely, yes. My successor has yet to arrive and I can no longer reach Dayen. Whether the insects are responsible for that or not, they did attack the sleeping villages, and the palace too. I have been draining them for weeks."

"You left the people vulnerable." Zenia's eyes narrowed.

"Not all have died – I did what I could," Gianh replied.

And though there was no apology to her words, Kilek did not feel she had lied. "Even so, a new hive is in place; I cannot dislodge it. Not while splitting my magic across so many tasks."

Again, quiet followed her words. Doubts lingered, but was there a way she could become an actual ally? If she could be trusted. And yet... *Does she deserve to join us?*

Mathi said, "Then, now that the song has been broken, you can help us more easily, can't you?"

The woman did not answer right away. "With knowledge only. I cannot yet manage to drain another. Not without rest."

Zenia raised an eyebrow. "When you recover, you will help us as we deem necessary. There will be more to drain."

Gianh nodded. "Even the Cabeku can be of use, in this way."

"Let's focus on the Clarion for now," Sir Eciven said. "I assume this hive you mentioned blocks access to the horn?"

"Hidden beyond the queen's chambers above." She lifted herself into a half-sitting position. "It is not far, but I fear I will have to be carried. I trust that is acceptable within the frame of our agreement?"

Princess Zenia's expression showed little in the way of pity or even compassion. "It is. What of the queen? And what will happen to those who were put to sleep? Are they waking now? Where are they?"

"Yes, they are soon to wake. All will feel unwell, including the queen. Some may have gaps in their memory. The very elderly may not wake – yet setting aside however the Cabeku interfered for now, most should have survived. Here and across the land."

"Most?"

"I see no reason to lie to you, Your Highness," she replied. "You will be able to see for yourself; a great number have taken shelter beneath the city."

"Why?"

"I was able to convince Her Majesty of an impending disaster before putting them to sleep."

"Even that, I doubt."

"I did not need an entire palace's worth of people in my way while I worked here – be they corpse or slumbering."

"Hmmm." Zenia motioned for Kilek and Sir Eciven to follow as she started across the floor. "Watch her," she told the others, speaking over her shoulder.

"Of course," Pax and Alira replied, almost speaking in unison.

Once out of earshot where they stood beside one of the pools, Zenia lowered her voice. "What do you think? I don't trust her. Not in the least after what happened to the people here."

Kilek hesitated. Why would the princess ask for his opinion? Unless... That look from Gianh, earlier. *Does the mage really think* I *would be chosen?*

"Her claims will be easy enough to verify," Sir Eciven replied. He nodded to Kilek. "And I think we all saw her look your way. The implications seem clear, lad."

"But how? The Luminous Clarion has no reason to choose me."

Zenia spread her hands. "You met Daciael in his glade, remember?"

"I did... but, I don't know." And yet, what if it were possible? *Because I'm Lucky?* Either way, Zenia was right.

Daciael had told him to seek out the song. And Alira's words about the Goddess, from when they'd travelled with Lady Clara, echoed in his mind. *She's seen something in you and when it finally becomes clear, things will be better.* He exhaled. "Maybe Gianh is telling the truth. It doesn't seem likely, but I'll do whatever I can."

Zenia smiled. "That's what I thought you'd say."

"Pax will carry Gianh, Alira to watch," the knight said. "I'll arrange the rest of us around that grouping. How does that sound, Your Highness?"

"Perfect." Zenia led them back to the others, where she addressed the Dhanhek mage. "I expect more detail about those to follow you, and why you are turning away from your people. But if you lead us to the Clarion now and pledge to assist when recovered, you will be given shelter in my city."

"Thank you, Princess."

"Paxoph and Alira will assist you."

Sir Eciven motioned for Mathi to lead the way up the stairs. "With me, if you please. Kilek and Zen, take rear guard. Dion and Tyar, you've got Phantom. Everyone, eyes open – other Cabeku could still lurk about."

"I sense only those in the hive," Gianh said as Pax lifted her. "But I am not at my strongest."

Kilek let them pass, Alira keeping a close eye on the Dhanhek mage, then followed with Zenia at his side. Her jaw was set, and she frowned ahead, her footfalls quite hard against each step. Kilek kept his hand near his sword, glancing over his shoulder often on their way to the top of the staircase.

The halls soon became wide, statues more frequent – mostly of people rather than sea-creatures now, and most created in glass. The artistry of the glass-wrights, no doubt. Broken pieces strewn across the floor crunched underfoot, but surprisingly, only a few had been toppled.

He saw no intruders, and no waking inhabitants stumbling from other rooms or passages as they passed. Yet the nearer they drew to the Queen's chambers, the more transparent Cabeku corpses could be found, strewn about in various frozen poses. One creature even lay half-crushed into a potted plant where it rested beside a narrow stairwell.

And while the number of smaller creatures was not insignificant, more impressive were several of the larger Cabeku – their harder shells and more human shapes equally see-through, and equally impervious to Gianh's power.

"Could we have stopped her, if she wasn't weakened?" Kilek asked, keeping his voice low.

Zenia nodded. "Together, yes."

He smiled. "You know, I thought you'd say that."

She punched his shoulder, not too hard, and she was smiling as she did.

"The hive is ahead." Gianh spoke from where she rested within Pax's arms. "In an antechamber, blocking the resting place of the Luminous Clarion. Any Cabeku you injure, I should be able to drain. At that point, I will no longer be a burden but I first need to lower a barrier."

"Noted," Zenia said as she led them into the queen's rather spacious chambers, where dark furniture dominated. Kilek followed her to an opening in the wall obscured by shimmering light. A bookcase lay in ruin nearby, tomes spilling from the shelves, pages twisted.

Beyond the barrier waited the Cabeku nest, standing between them and a closed door of stone. The door featured wave-markings similar to those found at the palace gates, though he could not be sure, since a dark mass obstructed his view. The thing took up half the antechamber, purple ichor oozing from irregular openings in the nest. Inside, things… wiggled, and pressed against the sides. *Stretched* the sides.

"They're smaller. I think I can destroy them," Alira said. Once more, green feathers spun just beyond her grip, moving in concert with her limbs as she strode closer.

"I will lower the seal," Gianh said.

The Dhanhek mage did not raise an arm, but colours glittered within her gaze and then the barrier flickered out of existence.

The Cabeku stirred, clicking sounds rising above the squelching.

Alira flung her hands down – the movement bringing Florique to mind – and green feathers flashed to the nest. They flew deep with wet, slicing sounds. The Cabeku fell still. Though plenty began to move again, perhaps only twitching in death, Alira was not finished, casting more and more feathers into the mass.

How does she make them appear?

But the question was forgotten when Alira finished, leaving behind only a shredded pile of insect bodies and tattered hunks of the nest. Her legs trembled, and she reached out to Paxoph, gripping his shoulder for balance.

"Do you need healing?" he asked.

She waved her hand, gesturing to the alcove with a nod. "Go on, I'll be fine."

"Are they guarding the door?" Zenia asked. "And if so, for who? The human-like one from downstairs?"

"Most likely someone else," Gianh said.

"Nakir, perhaps," Zenia said, almost to herself.

"The door itself will open at anyone's touch," Gianh advised. "But like me, none of them could move the horn, be they insect or somewhere between insect and man."

"But maybe you." Zenia smiled at Kilek. "Lead the way."

He stepped over the nest, the corpses and spreading pools of ichor, to push upon the stone and its wave-symbol. The door split down the centre. It swung inward, revealing a chamber with walls lined by huge scales. Silver, green and blue gleamed at every turn. Most were shaped almost like shields, tapering toward a point, but others seemed to have been cut to fit into the smaller spaces between.

"Amazing," he said, softly.

And in the centre, a small stone pillar held the Luminous Clarion. Despite its name, it was a dark horn, slender, with an engraved bell and no glow, no brightness. The engravings could have been words in unfamiliar script, or they could have been something else entirely.

A sense of age lurked within the musical instrument.

Older than even the War Heart that hung against his chest?

He moved closer. The stand bore a single silver scale; words had been carved into its surface also, but he could not read them either. Nor did they suddenly make sense when he reached out to trace the strange letters. *Fool, why would they?*

And yet, something *did* feel different, just from standing in the room. A new awareness, but of what exactly? The scales seemed to respond to his gaze, now offering a slow, blinking twinkle...

Are they welcoming me? It hardly made sense.

Others had joined him now, their eyes drawn to the Luminous Clarion. "Do we need to test it first?" Mathi asked. She reached out, taking a hold of the horn. But when she tried to lift it and could not – not even when her eyes glowed blue a moment – she soon gave up with a shake of her head. "Guess you were telling the truth," she said to the mage.

Gianh nodded.

"Kilek, why don't you show us how it's done?" Sir Eciven suggested with a grin.

"If you say so." He lifted his hand, resting it atop the smooth, cold surface and paused.

Had there been a sound, back in the antechamber?

Foe.

Rage coursed through him, as if not his own. Kilek spun, jaw clenched as he pushed through his friends and then the slimy antechamber, charging into the queen's rooms where he leapt over Florique's stretcher.

Cabeku.

A hulking form this time, like *two* of the human-esque ones smashed together. It had only one working eye, and five arms instead of six. And something seemed to have given it pause, by the way it flinched upon seeing him, its expected speed not at all present.

Kilek roared.

Silver mist burst from his lungs. It shot across the space between them, enveloping the unusual Cabeku. And despite the sheer power of the mist, the rush of triumph with it, the glimmer faded quickly, to reveal the Cabeku still standing in place.

Frozen in place, since it was not moving at all…

No. Frozen in *stone*.

Everyone joined him, their questions clamouring over one another, but it was Alira's voice that seemed clearest. "Kilek, how did you do that?"

"I… don't really know."

He turned and her eyes widened. She grasped his shoulders. "Kil, your teeth!"

"What about them?"

She frowned, one hand half-raised now. "No. Sorry, I thought… For a moment, it looked like they were fangs."

Just like Daciael. Kilek lifted one hand to his mouth and found only his normal teeth. *But what just happened wasn't normal.* Somehow, he'd spat a silver mist from deep within his chest, and it turned the Cabeku to stone. In an instant.

What am I?

"If Kilek did this…" Tyar was examining the stone creature, nudging and even slapping the surface.

"We all saw it," Sir Eciven said. "And are all grateful, too."

"I hadn't heard it approach," Zenia said, a slight frown on her face.

Pax was smiling. "Now you know, Kil."

"Now I know what?" But the question was almost a reflex, for the answer was wonderfully, disturbingly obvious. *So, I'm not Lucky?* "That's what the Goddess gave me?"

"Chosen by dragons," Gianh said with a nod, almost to herself, as if she'd received confirmation of a guess. And perhaps she had.

Everyone seemed to be smiling, but Kilek looked back to the Luminous Clarion. *It's true isn't it? I actually have a gift!* His heart was racing but a tiny splinter of doubt kept true joy at bay. "I have to know. For sure."

He strode back to the inner chamber of scales, then reached out to take the cool, smooth darkness of the horn – and lifted it free.

Chapter 8.

Kilek paced an expansive balcony not too distant from the queen's rooms, night air welcome against his skin. He'd finally found a moment to himself, spending it with potted plants and darkened lamps that lined the rail, and behind him, three arched entries leading back into the palace – all empty, thankfully.

Since freeing the Clarion and learning that he *had* been given a gift after all, learning that he was now quite dangerously powerful, and realising that he could finally release some of his bitterness was confusing enough. Only to then be overwhelmed by questions from his friends, from everyone – one thought had begun to scream within his mind: escape.

Peace and quiet so that he could sort through a tangle of emotions.

And so, while he was supposed to be helping everyone find and gather inhabitants of the palace – many of whom could already be seen wandering the darkened grounds in a daze – Kilek took a chance to sneak away. Offering the simple lie that he needed to relieve himself, he'd left Tyar in the gardens below and found his way to an empty, shadowy place.

Something was not yet right. It wasn't only shock and surprise – he could not seem to unclench his fists.

Why? Why don't I feel better?

Was it because… no, it couldn't be that. Kilek gripped the rail, squeezing. A crunch followed. He flinched back, lifting his hands to reveal a long crack in the stone.

"Kilek?"

Gianh stood within one of the arches. Her form was not unlike mist, colours muted once more as lamplight from inside poured through her figure.

He straightened. "Yes?"

"I have come to ask something of you." She did not move any closer. "Would you consider lending my people your aid?"

"How would I do that?" While Gianh showed no signs of aggression, it seemed odd that she was alone. Zenia would still have someone watching her, even with all the promises Gianh had made. Unless… *Of course.* The figure that stood before him was more like a spirit, similar to her first appearance on the stair.

Still, could the mage do that, while moving and talking and working in a different location? Perhaps she could, now that she'd restored her power by draining Cabeku corpses cut down by blades rather than magic.

"You could assist by sending the dragons to help my people."

"I… sending?" He frowned at her. "Even if I can call them, even if they arrive, how could I *send* dragons anywhere? They wouldn't listen to me."

Gianh smiled. "Come now. You know you have been chosen – who else has any chance of doing such a thing? Please do consider my request. Even if you were to send them after you attend to your own people, it would be better than nothing at all."

And then she was fading, gone before he could answer.

Kilek ran a hand through his hair. Another problem. He turned back to the grounds below, with their growing light courtesy of torches or freshly lit lamps. *So much for the peace of being alone.*

No sooner had the thought left his head, approaching footsteps reached him.

This time when he turned, it was to find an unfamiliar woman standing very much in the flesh. Her blonde hair was touched with grey and her fine gown of green bore wrinkles and creases, faint bloodstains too. "Are you Kilek of Hasere, perhaps?"

"I am… My Lady," he said, unsure of exactly who had come to seek him.

"Wonderful. I am Queen Moranlier, and I have come to offer you my aid, regarding the Luminous Clarion."

He blinked. "Forgive me, Your Majesty. I didn't realise."

"You need not concern yourself, not in the least because I owe you and your friends a debt." She smiled, raising a hand before he could continue. "No need for modesty, either. And that goes for what I am about to say, since I'll be lending you the *Silver Fin* with my prayers for success beyond your voyage."

"Do Zenia and Sir Eciven know?" he asked, then flushed. "I mean, thank you, Your Majesty. That's very generous."

"Of course, Kilek. But I have one further item I must entrust to you, specifically. While my family have long-guarded knowledge about the Luminous Clarion and its mythical purpose, there was never any indication of when or even *whether* it may be needed. Or if it would work. Those… insect creatures are sign enough for me, even had you not been able to lift the horn."

He glanced at the dark instrument where it leant against the balcony railing.

"It's all still a little hard to believe, I imagine," she said as she drew near and handed him a scroll, something he hadn't realised she'd carried. "This is a copy of an old map that I am sure will assist with your passage to High Rios."

He unrolled it slowly, being careful with the worn edges, though it was a thick animal skin; aged but not at all fragile within his grip. Spidery handwriting that remained legible showed directions through a mountain pass with various markings that appeared to be Herisman, or at the very least, something that might be translated via the materials they'd gathered back in Lady Wen's mansion.

What if I lose this? "Is the map something I must carry?"

"Tradition dictates that I hand it to the Burdened One directly, but that is all. Certainly, others might carry it, if that is your concern," she added with a smile. "Or make a copy, even."

"I see." He had to laugh, turning his gaze back to the animal skin. "I'm certainly easy to read, aren't I?"

"Having an honest face is no crime," she said. "Not unlike your parents."

His head snapped up from the map. "You knew them?"

"I met them a few times only. Many years ago, now. They

were… undertaking something important for the king."

Then, they *were* spies, it seemed. "Do you mean they were Knives?"

Her expression grew sad. "You did not know."

"No." Again, Camilea had shared *far* too little, over the years. *I need to pin down Lord Inacien, if he ever stays in one place long enough.* Everyone knowing more than he, and no-one willing or able to say much at all… something was being hidden.

"I'm sorry." She lifted her hand and paused. "I would offer you a moment of comfort, should you wish it?"

He nodded, almost a reflex, despite not knowing exactly what she had in mind. A brief embrace? *That would be really unusual for royalty, wouldn't it?*

But instead, she placed her hand upon his cheek. "I can only imagine hardships ahead, for a great burden has been placed upon your shoulders. Should you ever need respite, the gates of the Ocean Palace will always be open to you."

His eyes filled with tears. The warmth from her words… and more, that someone had offered them to begin with. It was unexpected enough that his emotions nearly overcame him. "Thank you, Your Majesty."

"You are welcome. Now, I believe that Phantom wishes to speak to you; he is gathering the liberators within the minor kitchen below."

Florique had finally awoken – welcome news. "Is that what we're being called?"

"It is no lie, after all," she said as she started from the balcony. "I will arrange for a servant to guide you, Kilek. Please wait just a moment."

"Thank you, Queen Moranlier."

Little time passed before a young woman in white and blue livery appeared. "This way, please."

Kilek lifted the Luminous Clarion and followed.

The servant led him out of the queen's chambers and down through a different palace; a place now alive with voices and movement as other servants, soldiers and nobles alike worked to clear away the Cabeku or to help one another, putting things back to order or setting up small spaces for healers to work.

And when he was directed down a final, dim corridor to the kitchen, it was to find that the now-recovered Florique had arranged for a rather large group to gather in the space; its walls of green and blue tiles lit by lamps and great ovens alike. Warm but empty, it seemed the queen had her staff working elsewhere.

"Why are we meeting here?" Tyar asked from where he stood beside Mathi, toying with a pan. Neither appeared too concerned about the choice, more curious, but nearby Pax was frowning. He did not add his own concern, whatever it might be. Only Alira and Dion were absent, probably watching over Gianh.

"Convenience, mostly," Florique replied with a smile, and it seemed he had recovered well, considering the time it took to do so. But why not? He'd used so much power to save everyone back at the inn…

Tyar raised an eyebrow. "Then, you're telling us that you're hungry?"

"Often," the mage replied. "But that can wait. I want to propose a division of important tasks."

Zenia nodded. "I believe I can guess at the most pressing one – Gianh."

"Precisely." Florique assured everyone that Gianh was being watched by his own gaze, along with Alira. "She is a valuable source of information and power. Both of which we may need. Yet whoever escorts her back to Alaycron may face one of her brethren, a fresh Surrogate, for lack of a better phrase. At the same time, Gianh's escort will be expected to keep a close watch on her for signs of treachery, notwithstanding her noteworthy assurances. I would argue that some diplomacy will also be required for arrival at the capital."

"I would hear your suggestion, Uncle," Zenia said.

"It is thus; that Dionarc and I escort her to the city, while the rest of you continue on to call the dragons."

A quiet met his words. Kilek exchanged glances with the others, noting equal concern. *Can we succeed without him?*

Sir Eciven spoke first. "I would include the princess in your party. Failing that, I'd take your place within the escort home, Phantom."

"I think I'll decide for myself," Zenia said with a frown directed at Sir Eciven.

"Of course. But I have responsibilities to your parents. And my nation, of which you are an important part." He smiled then. "And don't tell me that you're 'only a spare'. I think we both know what your father would do if I failed to protect you."

"I'll have plenty of protection here," she replied. "You will be with me, for one. And then there are the heroes of Hasere. One of which appears to be part dragon, if you recall."

"I do, My Lady."

Kilek glanced away. Was that the truth? *It is, isn't it?*

"What of Alira and Dionarc?" Pax asked. "They ought to

be here, too."

Florique nodded. "I agree. Dion wishes to head west, so that he can check upon his old master, but I have asked Alira to join whichever party she deems best. I believe that she wishes to seek out the dragons."

"Then it is decided," Zenia said. "Florique and Dion will escort Gianh. The rest of us will take up the queen's offer and head for High Rios. Uncle, I suggest we all prepare and take some rest."

"Of course, Your Highness," he said, and caught Kilek's eye. "Kilek, please stay a moment. I would offer some advice."

Kilek nodded. *About my new powers or something else?*

Once the others had left, their footfalls echoing down the stairwell, Kilek joined the mage, who'd stepped closer to one of the ovens. He extended his hands toward the coals. "Before you leave, you should ask Dion to give you some help with the horn, since I assume you cannot play?"

Kilek shook his head. "I don't know how, no."

He waited a moment.

Up close, it certainly appeared that the mage had recovered, but his eyes held a weariness that Kilek had come to think of as normal. Something that the man's flippant nature could not always mask.

"There is something else. Your awakening."

"Awakening?"

"I assume Avendria would term it as such. More importantly than any naming arrangements, I sense that it is incomplete. That is probably how it feels to you?"

The mage was probably right.

It could have been part of Kilek's lingering frustration, too.

Despite the surge of power earlier, despite the faint tingle deep within his chest suggesting his new ability remained within, even if it was not wholly his own power yet, there was no way to call it forth. He'd only tried to do so twice, standing alone on the balcony, but each time, he'd achieved nothing. Had barely known what it meant to 'call' for the power. For whatever the Goddess had hidden deep within him and, for some reason not seen fit to allow manifest until now, was not something he could simply reach out and use.

She could have been waiting for him to touch the Clarion Horn…

But if so, why? *Why put us all through that suffering, when I could have helped my friends sooner?*

Or was Daciael more involved, somehow?

"I have an idea that may help," Florique continued. "Something I wish to leave with you for the next part of your journey. For I suspect that, once you call and meet the dragons, everything will be easier for you."

"You sound confident."

"A benefit of age, my boy." He reached into an inner pocket and withdrew a long fang. Its age did not seem to come from its colour, for it was a bright white. "You might find it easier to discover what's within you when holding this."

"How…?" Kilek accepted the fang. The smooth surface against his skin was quite warm, and as he held in his palm, power *did* stir inside…

Out of reach for the moment, but definitely closer.

"Before you ask, I have long collected all manner of curious items. This one from a now-nameless land beyond the southern ocean. A land, sadly, of ruin."

Kilek thanked the mage, then hesitated. While it seemed a good time for his next question, he couldn't be certain it *needed* to be asked. And yet, a little doubt did linger. "Florique. I… wanted to ask you about something."

"Of course."

"About the *Home in the Woods*."

"We were quite lucky to succeed," the man replied, his voice exceedingly reasonable. "Almost as if the Gods were smiling down upon us."

Kilek nodded slowly. "Right…"

"Wonderful. Why don't you get some rest, Kilek? You have certainly earned as much," he said with a kind smile.

"Oh, well… thank you. Good idea," Kilek replied as he turned to leave the kitchen, where he'd have to go looking for someone to help locate an available bed.

After all, tomorrow was going to be another long day.

Chapter 9.

Queen Moranlier waved to their ship from the docks. She was a small figure now, still surrounded by other nobles in bright finery, by soldiers with their graceful armour and sweeping helms, and also by servants and villagers, as though folk from all stations had been given the chance to see off the Liberators of the Ocean Palace.

Soon enough, their smiles and cheers no longer reached Kilek where leant upon the rail. He could imagine them still, sounds racing across the small peaks of dark blue waves.

Not all the Liberators were staring out across the ocean with him. Some were not too far away – Paxoph for one. He walked beneath the snapping sales overhead, neck craned. Not in wonder, precisely, but there was something a little… boyish to his delight, in spite of his apparent age.

A lie that continued to fool most, of course.

Is that what continues to bother me? That I'm still young?

Beside him, Zenia sighed.

Kilek turned from the coastline to focus on the princess. Her dark hair had been tied into a top knot, wind tugging at the loose strands. Her expression was pensive and for just a moment, his heart seemed to slow. She really was beautiful… And she made it far easier to ignore the rocking of the *Silver Fin*, large though the ship was, with its twin masts and swarms of sailors in blue stripes.

Or the vastness of the ocean, which seemed to contain absolutely nothing…

"Is something wrong?" he asked.

"Not precisely." She frowned across the water. "More disappointed in myself. I ought to have spoken with Moranlier."

"Ah, was that… I mean, had you planned to?" he asked, changing what he had been going to say.

"I should have. But I told myself that I would when we returned, because despite the bad blood between her and my father, I should have conducted myself as a princess."

"I see," he said, even if he did not – at least, not specifically.

Zenia smiled, as though she knew he was merely answering in a way that he hoped would be suitable. "And what of you, Kilek? I see that you're not seasick, unlike Tyar and Alira, poor things – they didn't last long, at all."

"No." Both had appeared quite green in complexion, and were now below decks in the care of the ship's healer. And standing before the ladder leading down, was a small group made up of the captain, who was a gruff man with a long beard and bald head, Sir Eciven, and Mathi.

Discussing the weather, no doubt, as the moment they set off on their journey, Captain Jeadu had announced a rainstorm was due to hit before long.

"Then, you're feeling well?" she asked. "Considering everything that has happened."

"I think I am."

She moved a little closer. "I think I disagree, Kilek. You seem troubled. Don't make the mistake I just made back in the palace – tell me. I will keep whatever you say to myself, you have my promise."

"Well…" He trailed off. Even believing her as he did, it was difficult to begin. *I don't even know everything that's bothering me… just the obvious things.*

"I can probably guess some of it, at least."

He nodded. *Maybe that would be easier.* "It seems like I'm not doing a very good job of keeping it to myself."

"You don't always have to hide things from your friends."

He couldn't help but smile. "Is that your guess?"

"One of them," she replied. "It's a bad sign if you don't feel that you can turn to them for help. And it's not as though you've thrown some tantrum… but you know, I feel like I haven't seen you speak to anyone, really, except Florique. Not since the giant Cabeku attack."

She was probably right, for the most part. Reluctance clung to him. *It's not that I don't trust them.* Was shame still holding him back? Probably. Resentment too. Not for *all* his friends, surely? "I don't know."

"You've been given an enormous responsibility," Zenia said. "That's not easy."

"You handle it well," he said, meeting her gaze now. Was it improper to compliment a princess? But not continuing seemed a little dishonest. "I think it's impressive."

"Well, I've been dealing with it since I was a child, so I'm used to it," she said with a smile. "But think about it. You have new worries on top of what you were already dealing with, being one of Avendria's chosen. Now, *you're* the one who has to call the dragons too, right? And everyone is expecting you to succeed. Because we've all seen what you can do now. Which is another thing you have to come to terms with. Your body has changed, Kilek." The princess put a hand on his shoulder. "You're more than human now."

He swallowed. Another fact he was yet to confront. His body didn't actually feel different in any kind of disturbing way… and yet nothing was the same. Nothing would ever be like it was before. *I am still me, aren't I?* He turned back to the ocean – which was suddenly not so troubling, not in comparison. Even if the waves were beginning to grow larger, thudding against the ship's hull. *Is this how everyone else has been feeling since they were changed?*

"Your friends will probably understand, if you decide to talk to them," Zenia added.

"I think you're doing a better job than they would," he said, and there was a little bitterness to his tone. More than he'd meant to reveal.

"Are you certain of that?"

Kilek sighed. "No."

"Then promise you won't rely on bad assumptions, if you're looking for someone who might understand," Zenia said with a small smile as she left.

Chapter 10.

"Why are we meeting here?" Tyar asked from where they'd gathered in the dim hold, a bright lamp swinging gently. "Something I'm sure I asked only yesterday about a kitchen." He looked better than earlier in their trip, as did Alira, thankfully.

The location was perhaps an odd choice, crammed between boxes and barrels of spices, but Kilek was happy to escape the weather. Not long after his conversation with Zenia, the rainstorm sent them all below, at which point Sir Eciven called the meeting.

"Captain Jeadu had no other space." The knight captain grinned. "But you can enjoy the patter of rain above and the scents of spices while we're here."

"What are they?" Alira asked. "They seem awfully potent… almost magical. I think I could actually use them, if needed."

"Do you mean as weapons?" Mathi asked.

Kilek nearly commented himself, but something struck him – had a little shift in attitude occurred? Before Alira's destruction of the Cabeku with her burning feathers, her question could well have been considered frivolous. Mathi herself might have even rolled her eyes.

But not now.

"Perhaps," Alira replied.

"Most sailors call the barrels on the left Fire-spice," Sir Eciven replied. He pointed to a higher stack, strapped to the hull. "Those are Beans of Bliss. They all have local names, of course, but we probably cannot afford to buy any from the captain, so we'll have to settle for our existing strengths."

Alira nodded.

"To our task, then. Three more days until we reach Agenac. It's one of the mid-sized eastern ports, but one that offers a direct path into the mountain marked on the queen's map," Sir Eciven explained. "However, we may well face resistance from the Baron."

"Why would that be?" Tyar asked. "I thought Agenac was a vassal?"

"It is," Zenia replied. "But an independence movement has been growing for some time now."

Paxoph frowned. "So much that cooperation will be somehow conditional? Or are you expecting violence?"

"Perhaps something akin to your first concern."

"We will not know until we arrive," Sir Eciven added. "But that is not the only threat I want to bring to your attention, and there are several. Firstly, it is clear various Surrogates are involved. The count may rise again, now that we're in possession of the Luminous Clarion, and now that its bearer is revealed."

"Surrogates like Nakir," Kilek said. Thankfully, merely saying the man's name was not enough to cause even a quiver in his limbs. Not anymore. *I will be ready for you, Nakir.* Even if he didn't yet understand his gift.

The alternative was no longer an option.

"Yes. I can only assume that Lord Inacien is still on Nakir's trail, but that doesn't mean Nakir won't attempt to capture you once more, somehow. Further, Javoteth will doubtless send more creatures, with or without other Surrogates involved."

Paxoph's frown grew deeper. "I have wondered if Nakir is the only Anesca the Plague God has sent into the world. We are five, after all."

"And what about Inacien?" Kilek added. "If he is working for Yaende, do their goals align with Avendria?"

"No reason to doubt him, lad."

Kilek nodded. Hopefully that was true, considering what the man said during their first meeting.

"We don't know much about Gianh's successor, either," Alira added. "What if they're somehow able to search for the *horn*, instead of her? We'll still be a target."

"We would be, yes," Sir Eciven said. "Guarding against that is another threat we must consider."

Zenia tilted her head. "We'd spot any Dhanhek ships easily enough, wouldn't we? Since they're supposedly all pirates."

"That's an exaggeration."

"I know, I know."

"Finally, there's someone else I believe worth mentioning, for the sake of a complete account, perhaps," Sir Eciven said. "He may well turn his gaze this way, though I am not sure how likely that is."

Pax shifted where he sat upon one of the larger barrels. "A new threat?"

"An old one. I cannot confirm that Prince Yan of Minjao is a Surrogate of Javoteth at all, but I still wonder, will his obsession with the Night Thorn change once word spreads that the Clarion has been discovered?"

"What of him, then?" Mathi asked with a frown. "Did Inacien share anything with you, Sir Eciven? He would not give me much when I asked."

"All I know about Yan at present is that Inacien's Knives have been tracking all the conscripts they can, sending information to the king for their next move."

"Being?"

"I won't guess that far, but I wouldn't be surprised if troops were already stationed west – in place to support us, when we have the dragons."

"I see," Mathi said. "Then what is our plan for all these threats, *before* we have the dragons?"

"Depending on our reception in Agenac, we may have to take on or hire a guard. On the other hand, we have five Surrogates of our own, don't we? Our vigilance should count for much. Specifically, I'd ask Alira to use all that she has learnt through study or from Phantom, to watch for approaching dangers."

Alira nodded.

"Kilek, I expect your gift will be equally useful, as it develops," the knight captain added.

"I hope so," Kilek replied. How was not clear, but he had the fang. And if using his gift became simple as the Clarion accepting him, it would be more than welcome after so long with nothing. At present, the horn was packed away in the room he shared with Pax, ready for use when they found the ancient lake.

Paxoph leaned forward. "Can you tell us more about this Baron you believe will impede our progress?"

"Baron Gigene is the grandson of the first Kiore leader to accept Luargot governance," Sir Eciven explained. "The most recent negotiations for a return to independence have not been going well."

"Father relies upon access to the mines for their gold," Zenia added.

"Hmmm," Pax replied. "It really does sound as though we're passing through a tinderbox."

Sir Eciven sighed. "I cannot say. But I do not mean for us to become involved."

"We could bypass the city," Kilek suggested. "If Captain Jeadu sent us ashore on a longboat, somewhere nearby?"

Zenia shook her head. "I don't believe the situation is so grim as all that. I won't be announcing our arrival, in any event."

"Do we need disguises?" Tyar asked.

"It would not hurt," Sir Eciven said. "But an equal concern may be the mountain itself, since one of the key disputes between King Hadeon and the people of Agenac is the allocation of resources to deal with wolves in the mountains. The Baron has requested more support and Hadeon cannot provide."

Zenia frowned. "This pre-dates the Minjao attack, as Father knows."

"And now we must deal with the consequences."

"The wolves must be a significant problem," Pax said.

"They are. For the Baron, it interferes with certain shipments from neighbouring Sassehim, which means he must rely more on Luargot goods."

"Unlike access to the Kiore mines," Zenia said, "which remains clear. And so Father has not rushed to assign more troops. It's something he and I have argued over before."

"He'll find a way, in time," Sir Eciven said.

"I hope so."

"For now, local soldiers, guards and mercenaries work with Sassehim, but it remains a dangerous crossing. The most direct path takes us through those passes, according to Queen Moranlier's map."

"We can't afford to waste time circling a mountain," Mathi said. "What about these wolves?"

The knight captain nodded. "Larger. Faster. More aggressive and, supposedly, their fur is always the colour of blood."

"That's not a detail I was expecting," Tyar said with a frown.

"There are still guides in Agenac that agree to escort travellers," Sir Eciven said, "since the attacks are not constant. They are mostly aimed at large groups. However, part of what makes the attacks unsettling is that none appear related to warnings around territory or protection of cubs. They merely kill and then vanish, their trails never lasting long. That is what we will face once we begin our climb."

"We'll prepare as best we can once we reach Agenac," Zenia said. "Until then, we should try to rest."

Chapter 11.

The rain had passed into a storm that rocked their ship long into the night. Not enough to trouble the sailors, but Kilek certainly found himself tense. By morning, it had eased, and the next few days soon slid by in a haze of blue sky and blue waves, until the *Silver Fin* was at last nearing the port of Agenac – due to arrive by dawn, according to the captain's estimation.

And Kilek could not sleep for waiting.

Not due to any misplaced excitement but because Alira had asked to meet him on the main deck before the sun rose. All she said was that she needed his advice, yet… *Will I even be able to help her?*

He stared down at the dark water where foam swirled.

The mass of white bubbles were tinted yellow from the ship's lanterns, seeming almost restless. As if moving independent to the waves… He squinted. *Was* the foam moving by itself? He wrapped one arm around the rail and leant over. It was already spread thin enough to dissolve, pulled apart by the waves.

"Kilek, what are you doing?" Alira hissed at him.

He straightened to find her standing nearby, eyes wide. "Just waiting."

Alira joined him with hurried steps, even taking his arm in a gesture of worry that contradicted her smile. "We need you on this side of the ship, you know."

"Of course. I was just watching the waves." He'd have to check again, to be certain that the foam hadn't been *crossing* the waves, rather than riding them. Just in case.

"Good."

"So, what did you want to ask me?"

"It's about the Goddess," she said. "Now that we know what your gift is, I think we need to speak with her. It's overdue, actually."

"Even with the risk that poses?"

"I think Tyar said it best when he suggested that the other Surrogates have obviously received plenty of assistance."

"It does seem that way." Was the reason for her question that she wanted him to suggest it? "You know, everyone will listen to you if you bring it up, Alira."

She smiled, and it seemed a little sad. "You mean, 'now', right? Now that I've used my magic as a weapon?"

"Well, I meant that you used it to protect us…"

"Is that all I have to do? Protect everyone so that they'll listen to my suggestions, Kil?"

He raised his hands. "No, I didn't mean that."

Alira let free a long sigh.

He nearly reached out to give her a hug – she still held doubts, even though she didn't need to. But he didn't lift his arms. *She's upset, so she might feel… ashamed to accept comfort from me?* He settled on words. "I'm serious, you know.

Everyone should listen to you anyway, *especially* when you're certain. I trust your judgement."

Alira shook her head, her expression sombre. For a fleeting moment, it seemed not just sombre, but *despairing*, as though two expressions existed simultaneously. Yet before he could be certain, it was already gone. *No, I imagined it.*

"I'm sorry, Kilek. I know. It's just that sometimes I'm not sure anyone else does."

"They do. And it's not your fault if it took them this long."

"Well, when you put it that way." She was smiling again. "I do feel a little better. But I still want you to make the suggestion. You should ask Avendria questions about yourself, too."

He nodded slowly. "Right. She's all I have, without someone like Daciael to give me advice." Or Florique. *And wasn't there something I needed to ask him?* Something about the Wayfarer's Inn. Especially since a few details still didn't seem right. Or were missing.

"Kilek? Something else on your mind?"

"There is. It's the Wayfarer's Inn. Do you remember exactly what happened there? I know everything worked out fine, just not the details."

"Oh, well. I remember that Florique saved everyone and then we kept travelling until we reached the Ocean Palace. I remember Dionarc's relief that Lady Wen was well."

"Right." He nodded. "But when I try to remember *how*, I'm not sure."

"I thought…" She tilted her head slightly. "You know, I'm not sure. It must be too early, because I can't really remember the details, either."

"Isn't that strange?"

Alira joined him at the rail, glancing across the water. "It is. I wonder what everyone else can recall, because…" She trailed off with a frown.

He turned to follow her gaze. Foam was approaching the ship. It fought against the push and pull of the waves, drawing closer, growing swiftly and showing no signs of slowing as it stretched for the hull. Already it was five times as large as earlier.

"What is that?" she asked.

"I saw it before. But it was a lot smaller."

Clacking sounds came from the opposite side of the ship – something hard and small hitting the boards. He turned, but the far side was mostly clothed in shadows. *Something definitely fell to the deck.*

Kilek exchanged a glance with Alira. "I think something's wrong."

He reached for one of the lanterns, and together they approached the rail where the clacking continued. Kilek lifted his light and gasped.

White foam was climbing over the rail.

It scaled the ropes too, twirling and gleaming, new shapes becoming apparent, not unlike scores of little ovals… that bore fins. Even as Kilek watched, the foam darkened, deep as soot.

A sound best-described as soft bubbles being popped filled the air.

Something else fell, bouncing across the deck to settle in the space between them.

Alira knelt to flick at the dark shape.

It did not move in response. It seemed to be two ovals melded together, fins gleaming. He looked up, where the black foam continued to slide up the ropes. *New creatures? They're not like the Cabeku…*

"Kilek, feel this," Alira said. The melded ovals rested in her palm.

He took the shape between thumb and forefinger – and had to add a second and third finger to his grip; the thing was far too heavy for its size! Would the sheer number of the creatures, a number that was not showing any sign of slowing, actually threaten the ship? "We have to stop them, somehow."

"Wake the captain," Alira suggested. "Maybe he knows what they are."

He nodded. "What about you?"

She took the lamp. "I have an idea."

Chapter 12.

Kilek stumbled down the ladder, ducking under beams and dodging swaying lanterns as he ran toward the rear of the ship, aiming for a black engraving of an anchor that marked Captain Jeadu's room.

An urgent cry from a horn echoed from above, muffled by the decking.

From the crow's nest?

The warning continued, insistent enough that the captain's door flung open before Kilek reached it. The bald man wore the same red coat as earlier in the day, as though he'd not been asleep at all. "Lad?"

"Captain! There's some sort of sea-creature attacking the ship. It looks like foam, but it's climbing all over everything."

Jeadu took him by the shoulders, a look of concern clear. "Black or blue?"

"Ah, black," Kilek said.

The man swore.

Footsteps thundered closer, and the first mate appeared, his white hair in disarray. "Pirates?"

"Worse," Captain Jeadu said. "Creeping Death. Get the Two-Salt."

"There ain't much left."

"It'll have to do. Quickly."

"What are they?" Kilek asked. *And what is a Two-Salt?* "Alira's trying to stop them, I think with fire."

Captain Jeadu drew Kilek after, charging down the passage. "That can slow the pale ones, but once they change, it's too late," he explained as he climbed the ladder.

The answer didn't help much, but Kilek followed onto the *Fin's* decks keenly aware of the captain's concern. Which only served to have his pulse racing faster – considering he and Alira had already touched the Creeping Death.

Light burned. Not only on the deck where Alira swung her burning feathers of green, and sailors swung their burning brands at the Creeping Death, but also from above. The lookout was now firing arrows into the slowly-lightening sky, each one bursting into trails at their zenith. A signal fire?

Everywhere Kilek looked, the Creeping Death had covered more of the *Silver Fin.* The ship even seemed to be groaning, creaking wood audible beneath the shouts. The fire was working, the pale creatures vanishing in little puffs of steam, but darker ones were not harmed, nor did they even fall.

"Where's that salt?" the captain roared.

Just what sort of threat did the Creeping Death pose? *Can it actually sink the ship? Or suffocate us?* "How can I help?"

"Once the Two-Salt gets here, take a few handfuls and hurl it at the Creeping Death. It dissolves them."

"What if there's not enough?"

Captain Jeadu frowned. "Then we hope the Port Watch has seen our call for help."

The first mate returned with a large barrel in his equally large arms. He was trailed by other sailors, along with Mathi, Tyar and Paxoph. From Sir Eciven's voice, it was obvious the man and likely the princess were not far behind.

"All free hands to me," the captain called as his first mate set the barrel down and ripped the lid free. "Take as much as you can carry."

All those gathered peered within.

The barrel was only a third of the way full, the Two-Salt gleaming almost purple in the dim light.

Kilek grabbed a handful and ran to the nearest rail, where the Creeping Death had already found the water barrels. He skidded to a halt and hurled his Two-Salt. It hit with a sizzle. The Creeping Death dissolved like dust – not only the section of foam he'd hit, but the Two-Salt burned farther, racing like silent flame.

He spun for another handful and something caught his legs.

He hit the deck with a grunt. Before he could even turn, he was being dragged toward the rail! "Help!" Kilek twisted where he slid, finding the Creeping Death wrapped around his calves. It pulled him toward the rail and the water beyond, sliding faster and faster.

But he did not crash into the wood.

Instead, the ship, the pre-dawn sky and the fire all spun, as somehow the Creeping Death whipped him up and over the rail. For a bare moment he was floating – then cold enveloped his limbs.

Kilek thrashed, straining toward wavering lights of the

ship as they grew distant, smaller and darker. The Creeping Death dragged him down, surrounding him like a seamless wall of bubbles with tiny fins. Panic clawed at his lungs – but somehow, the closer the sea-creatures pressed around him, the more his pulse slowed. *I can actually breathe?*

Whatever the reason, he was sinking deeper but didn't seem to be in immediate danger of drowning.

I hope.

Even so, breaking free to swim for the surface was still impossible, considering the force that continued to draw him into the inky depths.

He tried to take steadying breaths but it did not help much. His body trembled no matter how he tried to tell himself he was not in terrible, terrible danger. *Alira is still up there. They'll all be working on a way to find me.*

Once they freed the ship…

The captain might even have an idea, since he seemed to know a lot about the Creeping Death. *Or maybe the Goddess?* He swallowed, clenching and unclenching his hands. *If I've really been chosen, she'd think of something, wouldn't she?*

And on, sinking deeper into the chill darkness.

No changes bar the light above shrinking so small that he could not be certain he wasn't actually imagining the tiny point.

There was no way they'd be able to find him.

Not now.

Kilek screamed.

Chapter 13.

Kilek opened his eyes and pushed himself upright from where he'd slumped against the Creeping Death. He'd passed out from the fear. Either that, or something had been done to him. Whatever the truth, his thoughts no longer raced and his pulse was steady.

Steadier, at least.

Thankfully, he'd calmed enough to notice circles of red light blooming in the dark above, faint and spreading, as if across a sky. Of course, it was only the endless dark of the ocean above, but it was a change.

Each ring seemed to stretch toward one another from opposite ends of the horizon, and smaller circles drifted down from within, like rings of smoke that grew brighter as they fell ever-so-slowly.

Kilek turned inside his cell of bubbles – a cell that somehow seemed to provide him with air.

Exactly what did they fall toward? Through the clear bodies of the Creeping Death, little was visible, no sense of an ocean floor of sand, stone, or whatever else. Just more darkness as he drifted, matching the red's descent.

In time, Kilek passed through one of the falling lights.

And it was not a light at all, but a cloud of glowing creatures, smaller than the Creeping Death, their bodies little more than a bright strip of something wrapped around… something else.

When several bumped gently against the surface of his cell, they spun away, going dark, and eventually winking back into colour, drifting down again. There was a beauty to it all.

At first.

The cloud's centre finally brought enough light to illuminate his surroundings; a world tinted in blood, wavering in the water. Huge veins, each tall as a house, ran alongside him, twisted into lumps and snags in places, but generally moving forward, like tubes that had been imbued with bright lights. The lights pressed against the veins from within, blooming and fading like pink brush strokes as he passed.

The Creeping Death slowed its passage when it reached a depression that stood ringed by more of the veins – a wall of them, really. And while Kilek had decided on the word 'depression' as a description, the ocean floor was still not visible, merely a darker patch before the red.

Here, the red pulsed.

Slashes of pink still passed through, but they ended where some of the tubes were open, where they became shapes not unlike poppies. And above it all, the red mist continued to descend… drawn *into* the wall?

Sucked down into whatever unfathomable thing lay before him.

What is this?

If nothing else, its age could not be denied. Something had spent a *vast* time lurking – like a mountain, resting far, far beneath the surface. And somehow, the bloody veins were able to draw in those it sought. Via the Creeping Death? If the two were not actually one and the same.

Kilek tensed when he finally stopped moving.

His cell had not changed; merely held him in place. The great wall of twisted veins with its poppies and streaks of pink simply loomed over him, expectant. *Is it waiting?* And just as importantly, *what* was it? *Why bring me here?*

Something stung the side of his neck.

He swatted at it, only for his hand to snag on something that was *not* dislodged. A bubble-like shape had attached itself to his skin! The Creeping Death? He ground his teeth as he reached up again, but a piercing chill drove him to his knees.

Please use your gifts to aid us.

The pain faded. He looked up from his hands and knees, but no-one had joined him within the cell, and no-one stood outside… which left the Creeping Death itself. Or the wall beyond.

Kilek exhaled, letting his pulse slow. If nothing else, he faced no immediate threat, no visible hostility.

Instead, he was needed.

"What are you?"

A long moment of silence followed his question. *Here.*

"No, I mean…" Kilek stopped himself. Would it understand if he asked again? Considering its first answer, perhaps not. "You know me."

Yes. Please devour the Forgotten One.

"Devour?"

With a mind blinded by age – or worse, it lashes out at any and all it encounters, wasting all that it destroys.

Still, he could only answer with another question, since it all made so little sense. "Wasting?"

It should eat what it kills.

"Is that what you do to ships?" Kilek asked with a frown.

We all eat.

Kilek's frown did not ease. "Are my friends safe?"

Yes.

"How can I believe you?"

Please remain focused. We have no ship in our maw. Will you aid us? Will you aid the ocean?

"Will you send me back to land?"

Of course.

No trace of hesitation in its answer. Hopefully, a good sign. "This Forgotten One is threatening the entire ocean?"

In time. You can prevent the worst. We need you.

"How?"

Become what you must and return to the ocean. We will know you.

"And then what?" Kilek couldn't keep his voice down. "You haven't told me anything! All you've done is bring me down here to speak in riddles."

Devour the Forgotten One, as only you can.

"I need more than that."

The pink brushstrokes shifted throughout the tubes again. *We will explain when you are better able to understand.*

He was moving again.

The cell of Creeping Death shifted as if caught on a sudden current. Another sting as something tiny and sharp was withdrawn from his neck. "Wait," Kilek called. The red began to recede all too swiftly. "If you're returning me to the surface, where will I end up?"

No answer.

"I need to reach the port of Agenac."

But what chance did the wall of veins have to understand him without the Creeping Death attaching itself to his neck? Kilek rubbed at the little wound; blood – quite black – upon his fingertip. It soon became invisible as the dark of the ocean swallowed the very last light below.

Chapter 14.

Kilek stumbled through the foam and onto wet sand with a series of gasps, coming to a halt with both hands upon his knees. Overhead, the noon sun beat down upon his head and shoulders, but it was welcome after the chill of the deep dark.

The Creeping Death had spat him out somewhere near the shoreline, leaving him at the mercy of waves that were only too happy to dump him in the shallows. But despite the water and sand in his ears and eyes – and mouth – he found his feet easily enough and walked free with a single backward glance.

What was *that thing?*

Somehow, despite the immensity of the creature he'd just encountered, it was not so different to everyone else. *After all, it wants something from me too.* Avendria, Queen Moranlier, King Hadeon and Gianh – they all wanted him to help, didn't they? He knelt in the sand, taking a further moment to catch his breath, clothes and hair dripping.

Nearby, sand soon gave way to stringy shrubs with purple

flowers. Weaving paths headed up into uneven dunes, but he found no immediate sign of a road or homes or jetties – exactly how far was Agenac?

A raised voice reached him.

Someone appeared at the top of a dune, waving their arm, fishing pole in hand.

Kilek rose as the fisherman set the rod and a bucket down before tearing across the sand with excited calls… and it wasn't a fisher*man*, but a boy. A local boy, considering his unfamiliar words. Perhaps nine or ten years old at most. He was grinning when he arrived, eyes bright with excitement. "Were you swimming?" he asked, now speaking in lightly-accented Luargot. "Do you need help? I can help you, if you need it."

"I do need help," Kilek replied, unable to stop a smile. "A storm struck my ship before we could reach Agenac."

"Oh, I didn't hear of any wrecks."

A relief. "That's good to know. Could you take me there?"

"Not all the way to the city, but my mother could," he said, and set off again. "Come on," he called after.

Kilek followed at a rather uneven jog, catching up soon enough despite the way sand gave way beneath every step. It continued to plague him until they reached the boy's home, which was a hut resting on stilts. The building was actually three rooms connected by short, covered walkways, and not the only one to be found within the dunes, even if the other homes were somewhat distant.

At his call, the boy's mother stepped out with a frown.

She wore a white tunic with sandals and her eyes narrowed upon seeing him, but the boy spoke quickly in the Kiore language. She answered with a sigh before gesturing for Kilek to approach.

"Help here. Then to Agenac."

Her accent was strong, but Kilek understood. "Thank you. How can I help?"

She climbed down and led him behind her home to a modest vegetable patch fenced by driftwood. Fine leaves were a pale blue and large shells of black and yellow had been spaced between.

A sharp scent met him as he neared – from the vegetables or the shell?

Less than half the crop had been harvested, and so when she pointed and mimed removing the plants, Kilek nodded. The boy smiled beside her. "You can start. I'll bring a basket."

"Right." Kilek knelt in the sandy earth and got to work.

The leaves were only delicate-seeming, since they provided a firm hand-hold as he pulled something free – a root-like vegetable of deep blue. It had dense ridges across its surface, making it quite unfamiliar. The scent did not change as he held it, which suggested it came from the shells – something to ward off hungry animals, perhaps.

He made a pile as he worked.

The boy soon returned with a basket. "Just fill it up, and then Mother will take you to the city."

"How far is it?"

"You'll arrive before nightfall, if you work fast," he said with a grin, then set off for the ocean again. "I hope you find your friends!"

"Me too," Kilek said with a brief smile, returning to work.

The afternoon wore on, but before he finished – with a quarter of the crop remaining – the mother appeared with water. "Good." She bent to grip the side of the basket and, for the first time, he noticed her hand was bandaged. She also had a bag slung across one shoulder. "You carry."

Kilek drank, then stood and lifted the basket. The weight was not unbearable, and depending on how far the port was, it might not be such a problem. Yet the longer they walked, the heavier it grew… until something changed deep within his chest, a familiar tingling that grew to warmth as his gift reappeared in a subtle way this time. Then the basket was no more a bother than if he had to carry a single apple.

Or, a handful of the vegetables he actually *did* carry, whatever their name. He lifted one free. "Can you tell me what this is called?"

The woman did not seem to understand.

"Ah, the name of this?"

She nodded. "Chetyo."

"Thank you," he replied. Had it been possible, he would have asked about its taste but doubted his ability to successfully communicate much more.

And so they walked in silence, footfalls loud against hard-packed, sandy earth of the road, the dull roar of the ocean on one side and dunes and thin shrubs on the other. They only occasionally passed other Kiore on the road, but Kilek did see plenty of them fishing.

When Agenac came into view dusk was falling. The city's stone walls were ringed by slender trees with pale bark and its wharves stretched out into the ocean – some far longer than seemed normal, but then, how would he know, having seen only one harbour in his life? As yet, no ships were recognisable beyond the fact that some had coloured sails and were of varying sizes.

And then path curved, leaving only the city walls visible.

There, large open gates offered glimpses of movement inside, guards in Luargot armour, horses and wagons, people in clothing similar to that of his guide, only with more colour for the most part.

Once waved inside by the guards, his guide pointed to a nearby market, then reached out for the basket with a nod.

He handed it over and she seemed to thank him, before giving a second nod, this time in the opposite direction. There, the road sloped down between buildings of white and grey stone, toward the muted crash of the sea.

Kilek thanked the woman and started toward the harbour at a jog, passing murals on the walls as he did. Many were chipped or stained, but they caught his eye, even in their few colours – mostly grey and purple, some few bearing a similar blue to the grasses and shrubs in the dunes. *Focus!*

He needed a plan if the *Silver Fin* was not actually docked. Few ideas came to mind, save for somehow trying to convince another captain to start a search for the ship. But once he stood at the edge of the harbour, making room for a small family that had lined up for food from a stall, Kilek smiled.

The *Silver Fin*.

Docked only a few jetties away, its sails were a little worse for wear but the ship was definitely in one piece.

Next, making sure everyone else was, too.

A heavy hand fell upon his shoulder. "We meet again, young man."

Chapter 15.

A shaven-headed man wearing an orange coat with circular blades hanging from his belt stood smiling down at Kilek.

He's familiar…

The Prisawi merchant from Trisoma's market!

Kilek stepped back and bumped into someone. He spun. The Prisawi enchanter. She wrapped her arms around him with a smile, and once again, he found himself nearly face-to-face with a swan-shaped brooch of pinkish red.

"You seem tired, young man." Her accent bore the same clipped sound as before. "Can we help you?"

He blinked at the sudden heaviness to his eyelids… and his limbs. He tried to speak, but his words were a garbled mess.

"We'll take you to your inn, of course," she said.

The man nodded from above, his shape blurry. "Don't fret, you're not in danger."

No words could have evoked more doubt but Kilek found himself unable to resist.

Together, the Prisawi carried him away from the harbour

and through several dim streets, into a building with a brightly-lit room. It could have been a skylight above or it could have been a chandelier.

Still, he could not move, but something was stirring deep within, even if it remained out of reach. While the light didn't help with his vision, he could hear well enough, at least. They'd set him down on some sort of table, and the man now drew a blade to cut through Kilek's tunic. Next, he began to work on the leather armour.

I hope I can get another tunic with the two poplars from Sir Eciven. The thought drifted across his mind. Part of him knew it was an odd thought, knew that more important things were afoot, but it wasn't a large part...

"I cannot believe our luck," the woman was saying. She ran a hand across her own shaven head as she smiled. "This is astounding – and he still has it."

"We are blessed by Ariwade."

The tone of her voice changed, and it seemed her relief was great. "We can finally be free."

"We can."

Something snapped at Kilek's throat, a faint sound only – the War Heart being torn free?

No!

Warmth rushed into his chest, somehow shoving the spell the woman had cast to one side. "The *sum-an* can only be given, not taken," Kilek said. His voice was strong, commanding, as if he were not actually their prisoner. And more, it seemed that he was aided by... some knowledge from an unknown place.

"For an immediate transfer, yes," the man replied after a moment of hesitation, and it seemed he held the pendant up to the light. "Herismen artefacts hate to lie dormant, you see."

"You cannot survive the five days it will take to forge a new connection." Again, Kilek found himself speaking with more confidence than he felt. Back in Alaycron, Amil *had* told him plenty of facts about the War Heart but it seemed he knew more now. Or at least, was more certain.

"You are alone in Agenac," the man replied. "Lisya?"

She appeared over him, murmuring soft words… but the enchantress soon trailed off. "It's not going to hold anymore."

"What?"

"I don't know… but he's actually already under a glamour. And it's *far* stronger than anything I've ever seen." Concern entered her tone. "I think it's interfering with mine."

Kilek blinked as his vision cleared.

He lay in an unassuming room, save for the skylight above. The splashes of orange from his captors remained bright where they'd moved aside to discuss their discovery, slowly becoming more detailed. And what the woman said *was* concerning, even with an obvious answer, one that had to be probed later. *Once I'm out of here. Then I'll figure out what Florique has done. And why.*

But for now, with his limbs twitching, he used the chance to reach for his weapon… and found nothing. Kilek kept searching – not even a belt knife. Yet there *was* something in one of his pockets; something small and hard, not unlike stone.

The fang!

Kilek reached in. Skin touched smooth bone. A spasm shot along his body, power coursing through him, searing outward from his chest. He sat up, lifting a hand to find deep emerald scales and sharp claws, gleaming beneath the skylight.

As it should be. Nothing at all to fear.

"Thieves." He stood and pointed with one claw. "Return the *sum-an*, if you value your remaining days."

Both fell back with a cry. The War Heart clattered to the floorboards, bouncing toward him. Kilek bent and lifted it, again using his claws, before setting it down on a nearby chair.

The man had drawn his weapon but did not attack, while Lisya was speaking in a soft, soothing tone – yet from her slight tremble, and perhaps the fact that she was speaking Prisawi, the words had no effect.

For even if he'd been able to understand it wouldn't have made any difference.

Kilek flashed forward. He caught both thieves by the throat, lifting each to shove them against the wall. The man's blade bounced off Kilek's scales, useless, but he fixed a glare on Lisya first. "When you leave this place, you will locate my friends. They sailed upon the *Silver Fin*. Go."

He released her. The woman stumbled free, eyes wide.

"I'll be keeping this man here until you return. Work swiftly, and he will not die."

"What are you?" she managed.

"Impatient." He squeezed, and his prisoner began to beat at Kilek's grip – a futile act. "Return well before darkness, if you wish to see him alive again."

Lisya ran from the room.

He turned back to the Prisawi man, who continued to struggle. "Save your strength – you will have a task of your own to complete soon enough."

The fellow could only blink.

Kilek eased the pressure, enough that his captive could speak – fear quite clear in the question. "Who are you?"

"Call me Fang, if anything." Doubtless, it was not the answer the thief sought. "What is your name?"

"Dutepka."

"Very well, Dutepka. You have work to undertake while we wait."

"What work?"

Kilek wrenched the remaining weapons from the man's belt. "What is your purpose in this place? Why do you seek Herisman talismans?"

"You know they are valuable."

"I do."

He hesitated. "I don't know what else to tell you. We will sell them, if we find more."

"Find?"

Now the thief glared. "I won't justify the choices I've had to make in order to survive to a monster."

"Nor could you, even if you attempted as much." Kilek carried the man to the table and slapped him down. "Catch your breath."

The man gasped for air a moment, before glaring up at him.

"Why Agenac?"

Dutepka rubbed at his throat. "Someone found something in the mountains above. Part of a lost Herisman city – the markets have been full of artefacts."

"But none of true value, I assume."

"Some *are* impressive. But nothing like what you carry."

"Where?"

"They call it the Weeping Face of Oramaki. There's a closed path between the peaks; the baron controls it now."

"And the Blood Wolves are not a threat?"

"The encampment is close enough to the city that it's not attacked as often. They're well-provisioned."

"Ah. So, that is why you cannot engage in a little grave-robbing, as you'd prefer."

"The dead stay dead, no matter actions of the living."

"Some, perhaps."

Heavy footfalls interrupted Kilek's next question and a door flung open.

Lisya, breathing hard, as though she'd ran the whole distance. And maybe she had.

"You are empty-handed," Kilek said as he stepped forward.

"I know where they are," she said, her eyes wide. "They've been detained by the baron's men."

Kilek frowned. That changed his plans, somewhat. "Each of them?"

"Yes. It's the talk of the harbour."

"Well." Again, moving too swiftly to be stopped, he caught the woman by the arm, then gestured to Dutepka. "Your turn. Bring meat from a market. Plenty of meat."

The man rose, climbing down from the table, his expression still one of anger. Yet his movements were wary, and he exchanged glances with Lisya. She no longer trembled but her jaw was certainly clenched. "Our funds are not inexhaustible."

"I assume that's why you are thieves. Go."

"What about –"

Kilek gnashed his teeth. "Lisya will be explaining more about her failure – that will help you work, I think. And you must work fast, as I am hungry."

"I'll be fine, Du," she said, her voice tight.

The man strode from the room with a short nod. Kilek pushed her into the empty chair, then leant against the wall beside her. "What else did you learn? I need specifics."

"Their ship survived a storm but it seems that the moment they met with port authorities, the princess and her companions, including the captain and crew, were detained. Baron Gigene supposedly holds them in his mansion, not the prison," she said, her expression becoming doubtful. "I am surprised that you travel with Princess Zenia."

Kilek waited.

She muttered to herself before continuing. "I don't fully understand the local politics, but this could end up being a serious scandal."

"They will find a way to deal with whatever political ramifications exist. Where is this mansion?"

"On the river, in the northern part of the city. Why?"

Kilek folded his arms. "Because we'll all be leaving soon, and I need directions. You and Dutepka will make useful guides and assistants."

She stood. "Wait. That is madness."

"You are not unskilled."

"It's far too dangerous. You're asking us to help you break a royal from detainment in one of her vassal's buildings?"

"That's a problem for Baron Gigene. You need to consider how you will save your own skins."

She met his gaze, and doubt seemed to war with defiance. For just a moment, Kilek caught himself on the cusp of sympathy, yet it was difficult to hold. After all, the two thieves were hardly paragons of virtue.

"Do you have a complaint?" he asked.

"Several."

"Is it about being approached as a young man in a market by a pair of predators intent on stealing something precious from him?"

She folded her arms, and by her expression, his barb had struck home. "No."

"Then air them once darkness falls, and once we have completed the task at hand."

"What is your plan then? How are you going infiltrate the mansion then escape the city with such a large party?"

"No-one can stop me entering. And I guarantee that Gigene will not be able to refuse my commands once we have spoken."

She did not answer – a welcome change.

And so Kilek remained in silence, thinking as time passed, and yet it was not that much longer before Dutepka returned carrying a bulging sack. The scent of meat was exceptionally easy to detect. Much was salted but enough remained warm, too.

"Arrange it in a row upon the table," Kilek said.

Kilek waited for the thief to finish, then caught the man's free hand. He pressed it to his lips – allowing just a whisper of silver breath to escape between his fangs, then released.

Dutepka cried out, clutching his hand as Lisya overturned her chair to reach him. The man's face was twisted in pain, but he remained upright. Lisya glared at Kilek. "What have you done?"

"Something that only I can undo." Kilek sat before the meat. He lifted the first hunk of beef, drawing a breath of anticipation.

"Half my hand is stone!" Dutepka shouted.

Kilek took a bite. "Not your throwing hand."

Delicious. The next piece was saltier, but he finished that in a single bite, the taste and even the weight of it in his stomach *very* welcome.

"What kind of monster are you?" Lisya demanded.

Kilek lifted the next piece of meat – this time, chicken. Another single bite. He took the next hunk and ate that too, tossing it into his maw. And then another. And all without rushing.

Instead, he simply enjoyed his meal.

Chapter 16.

Moonlight glinted upon soft ripples in the moat, able to compete well enough with torchlight shining down from walls across the way. Baron Gigene's mansion and its grounds were fortified, but few guards walked the parapets. Most of the defence seemed to hinge upon the stone itself, along with the closed drawbridge.

But it would soon come crashing down.

"You still don't know their precise location," Dutepka said. He and Lisya crouched nearby, wearing expressions of concern. "Not to mention, how obvious it is that you aren't human, even with that cloak and hood."

Kilek glanced back from where he leant against the alleyway's stone.

Wedged between an inn and the style of indoor-market common to Agenac, it was a fine vantage point offering a view of patrols in the street, Kiore and Luargot men armed with swords and short spears, along with merchants and other people simply out to enjoy the night.

So far, no-one had paid Kilek and his 'assistants' much

heed, but Dutepka was probably correct about the brighter interior of the mansion. *Speed will count for much. And fear.* "Someone will know. Lisya can enchant where needed. Failing that, I will convince them to speak, once they see me."

"And the drawbridge?" she asked. "The guards on the wall? I don't fancy catching an arrow in my back."

"Listen well," he said then, turning to face them. "The drawbridge will open for one of the guard, since you will bewitch someone to lead us within. Once inside, I will create enough havoc to not only draw arrows, but for you to gather the information I need. Then, we will storm the cells or rooms, free everyone within and use superior numbers to fight our way free from a disorganised defence. My travelling companions count powerful warriors and mages, as I trust you are aware."

"I am not going in there to kill indiscriminately," Dutepka said.

"No?"

Lisya frowned. "We're not mercenaries."

"Kill, incapacitate, or deceive as you see fit," Kilek said with a wave of his clawed hand.

Dutepka hesitated, then shook his head. "What about after? How do we escape the city?"

"Lisya will convince several witnesses that you drowned in the moat, and that the rest of us fled toward the harbour."

"But you won't return to your ship?"

"Some may."

"And you'll restore Du's hand, before that?" Lisya asked.

"Yes," Kilek replied. "Now, find us a likely guide – they can describe us as prisoners, when it comes to the drawbridge."

"Fine. What if that doesn't work?"

"Then I will swim the moat and break in."

Dutepka raised a hand – the fleshy one. "Why doesn't Lisya convince whoever she finds to hand over their uniform? You can be the prisoner then and we might be able to get some information *before* you need to make a mess of the place."

"Very well." He nodded to Lisya. "Go."

The night continued to pass – without conversation, which again, suited Kilek.

When Lisya returned, it was with armour and tunic enough for both the Prisawi. Neither set represented a perfect fit but it was good enough for them to lead Kilek across the street and up to the moat's edge.

"Let's see if they bite," Kilek said when they stopped. He kept his claws out of sight as best he could, his hood pulled low.

Dutepka raised his voice, and suddenly the faint accent was gone, and he spoke Luargot as if a born citizen. "Open up. We've got another prisoner Baron Gigene should see."

A hatch in the wall opened, and a man with silver stubble looked down at them a moment before grunting. "Bring him, then."

Chains rattled and the drawbridge soon thumped down with a boom, revealing a bright courtyard. A portcullis in turn offered glimpses of a dimly-lit garden path beyond. Two guards approached, with two more leaning against an empty wagon, speaking softly.

Lisya stepped forward. "You must be looking forward to taking a break, I bet?"

"We are," one said with a slight frown – it was the man with the silver stubble.

The other only nodded, his eyes a little glazed already.

"If you wish, we'd be more than happy to escort this one the rest of the way. Save you having to do it."

"Well, that would be welcome," the glazed one said.

"What's he got to do with his Lordship and the 'guests'?" Silver asked as he squinted up at Kilek. His question was not one of suspicion, but perhaps curiosity.

"We're not sure, but he was caught asking after the *Silver Fin*."

"I thought the captain and crew had been released."

"Best we let the baron decide."

"Fair, fair." Again, he squinted up at Kilek. "Big one, isn't he? Looks a little odd, to be honest."

Lisya smiled, her voice becoming yet more soothing. "That he is. Ugly fellow, truly."

"Hmmm. He is, at that."

"Forgive me, but this is my first time within the grounds," Dutepka said. "Where do we take him?"

Lisya rolled her eyes, but Silver was only too happy to oblige. "Straight through and then to the barracks on the right. Hand him over there."

"Many thanks."

Together, they walked for the gate, which was being raised. Lisya waved to the men at the wagon, suggesting that they enjoy their night. And as before, her words carried power enough that the guards merely nodded in response, gazes rather incurious.

The garden path was broad, room enough for wagonloads of supplies or luxuries. It soon split into multiple directions, breaking around a large, circular garden-mound covered in flowers. A giant, fountain shaped as a shell waited at its centre, lit by several lamps.

Above and to the left waited the mansion's main buildings, where a warm glow spilled from arched windows, but their destination was a building near as large, only far darker.

The barracks.

Three more guards waited beneath scant torchlight of the garrison and stable, while another guard paced the various outbuildings. Not unlike the layout of King Hadeon's palace.

Which made sense, considering Agenac's position as vassal.

"If you still want me to attempt an enchantment relating to our escape, I must conserve my strength now," Lisya said.

"Leave it to me," Kilek replied as they drew nearer to the guards.

"What does that mean?"

"That the survivor will agree to lead us to the princess."

Dutepka stopped. "What if they raise the alarm instead? Can you take on an entire garrison?"

Kilek shrugged. "Easily."

Lisya's steps faltered too, and it seemed she had more to say but a call from the guards reached them. "Is something amiss, over there?" The lone guard had joined his fellows.

Dutepka caught Kilek's arm. "What would the princess think about you slaughtering her subjects?"

Perhaps a valid point.

"Fine." Kilek shot forward, hood flying back. His speed was once again quite unnatural but most welcome. The guard were drawing swords or readying their spears, but Kilek sucked in a giant breath and sprayed three with his stone-breath.

They creaked into stillness, perfect statues.

It left one man cowering in fear, his spear thudding to the earth beside him, where he'd collapsed to the dirt.

The Prisawi pair caught up, eyes wide.

"Take us to the prisoners, and I will restore your fellows," Kilek growled.

The guard scrambled to his feet with a whimper but took them inside and along a short corridor then down a flight of stairs. At the bottom, two more guards waited.

Kilek encased them in stone before they could finish their first question.

Their guide was trembling. "Ah… the key was on Kirra's belt."

Kilek lifted a knee and kicked the door. It clanged across the floor. Shouts echoed from behind cell doors in response, but he focused on the thieves. "Stay here. If any come, convince them that you have seen a mage on the loose in the grounds. Fail, and die," he added for the benefit of the soldier, who was only able to nod in response.

Inside, a dozen darkened cells with narrow bars on tiny windows waited, lit only by a single lamp in the centre of the room. He strode to the first cell and lifted his voice. "Princess? It's Kilek."

Joyous assent echoed from nearby cells, and his heart seemed to swell a little but it was not time to bask in happy relief. *Not yet.* One voice had belonged to the princess, and from another cell, Sir Eciven called encouragement. Kilek crossed the room to stop before Zenia's door. "Stand back. I'm going to tear through."

"What do you mean?" Zenia replied.

He glanced down at his clawed hands. "Avendria's gift is a little more than stone-breath."

"Oh."

"Ready?"

"We are," she said.

Kilek lifted an arm and punched through the steel, shattering the lock as though it were a mere twig. He dragged the door open and flicked it aside to reveal Zenia, Alira and Mathi standing in a large cell with two cots and even table and chairs. Upon seeing him, their expressions of relief became uniform in shock.

"Kil?" Mathi took half a step forward.

"Right. Just let me free the others." *How much have I changed?* He moved to the next cell and offered another warning, receiving the same surprise from Sir Eciven, Tyar and Paxoph when he freed them.

"What happened?" Tyar asked.

"This is my gift," he said. "No time to talk. What now? Why did Baron Gigene do this?"

"As leverage," Zenia said. "Once he knew we'd made landfall, he arranged to have us meet him. Eciven and I didn't take kindly to the way he went about things and the situation… escalated," she said, finishing with a somewhat sheepish glance to Sir Eciven.

He chuckled. "Nothing to worry about now. He's overstepped and he knows it."

"Good," Kilek said, doing his best to ignore the few glances he still received. *How unpleasant do I look?* "That means he can't complain when I tear this place apart on the way out."

"How much longer?" Dutepka called from the entry.

"Who is that?" Zenia asked.

"Two Prisawi that are helping me. Let's hurry," Kilek

said, and led them back to where his unwilling allies waited beside the second set of stone statues.

"Can they be saved?" Alira asked.

"Yes, but they will not be conscious for some time." Kilek exhaled before them, and without knowing how, only that he could, this time his breath was softer, and tinted with faint traces of gold.

Colour returned to the guards swiftly, though each crumbled to the ground where they then appeared to be merely sleeping.

Kilek gestured to the thief. "Dutepka, your hand."

Dutepka lifted his half-stone hand, and Kilek exhaled again, just a small amount – and the thief's flesh was restored. "Lead on. Spread confusion about our escape. And be convincing, unless you want me to hunt you down."

The Prisawi pair charged up the steps without a word from either, though Dutepka did cast a final glance to the War Heart, where Kilek had made him tie both it and the fang around his neck before they'd left.

Sir Eciven was returning from a storeroom with their possessions, which he explained did not include their copy of the map, but thankfully *did* include the Luminous Clarion. The baron had confiscated the map as something relating to his lands but cared not for an 'old horn of no value to any but a bard'.

Good and bad luck. "We don't have time to steal it back. Let's go," Kilek said as he led them out at a run.

"Can they really do what you said?" Zenia asked from where she charged along beside him.

"She can. Her enchantment won't last indefinitely, but the guards will believe that those two drowned in the moat and that we fled to the harbour. At worst, it will confuse and delay any pursuit."

"Perfect."

At the entry to the barracks, Kilek paused to breathe life back into the other guards, then glanced ahead. It seemed Lisya was already speaking to the small group of soldiers in the courtyard, all of whom were all nodding along to whatever she was telling them.

"The mountains are waiting," he said as he resumed their escape.

Both Prisawi were gone by the time he reached the courtyard, passing through with barely a second glance, his clawed feet scraping against the drawbridge as everyone followed him into the streets and the waiting darkness.

Chapter 17.

The Oramaki Mountains were blooming through iron.

Be it the stony trail or the jagged peaks around him, the rigid shrubs clinging to the walls or towering mountain ash – all were coloured grey and even silver as the sun rose, no matter that the shades lasted for a fleeting moment only.

Greens and browns followed gently.

A wonderful sight, but not enough to distract Kilek from his concerns. Or his hunger from where he sat upon a log, staring up along the trail ahead. Not even the triumph of their escape was adequate. Hours had passed with no sign of pursuit, whether any had been organised or not. And considering what his friends had said about the baron, perhaps he would not send anyone at all.

Kilek was also yet to come across signs of any encampment near the lost Herisman city, though perhaps one of the other trails led to its location, and not those needed to be trod upon on their path to High Rios.

A creature shifted in the undergrowth some distance away; not so far that he couldn't reach it quickly if he tried.

But from the scent, it was small. A rabbit or one of the tree-foxes he'd seen on the climb.

Not enough, really. *I need deer. Or boar, at the least.*

More important was the unnatural scent mixed in with wolf that he could sense. As promised, somewhere in the mountains the Blood Wolves lurked. It was difficult to be certain, but it seemed they numbered in the scores.

Gathered around a particular set of caves… north and… east.

But they had not moved yet.

Were their own senses enough to sniff *him* out?

Yet another scent joined that of rabbit, leaves and budding flowers, and the distant Blood Wolves.

Human.

He turned to find Tyar, the man's step faltering slightly as he approached. "How goes the watch, Kil?"

"Surprised?"

"A little," he replied as he drew near. "I know you said you'd be fine to take the watch, but I thought you'd ask one of us at some point. How long have you been awake?"

"I don't know. But I'm not sure it's safe."

"Why?"

"I can smell the Blood Wolves. I think they're aware of us but they haven't approached."

Tyar's hand moved as if to reach for his bow, but he hadn't brought it with him. "How close?"

"Not at all. It's a system of caves to the north-east."

"Well, how long can you stay… dragon-like?"

"I don't know that either."

Tyar sighed. "Then we really need to find someone who can give you advice. Or help."

"Oh." A sudden rush of affection hit, only somewhat muted by his dragon-form. How long since Tyar had said something like that? *Since I felt this close to my friend?* In fact, the longer he'd spent with everyone, the easier it was to feel 'normal', even while transformed. There had been something terribly cold and impatient about his actions, his words and thoughts, after turning the tables on his captors back in the harbour city. "I guess so."

His friend nodded. "Someone like Florique or Daciael."

"Well…" And that was another concern, brought to the forefront – one the Creeping Death and everything after had interrupted. "You're right, but that reminds me of something I need to ask you. And the others."

"What?"

He leant forward. "When we saved everyone at *Home in the Woods*, what happened? Exactly. Can you remember?"

"Why? I mean, are you having trouble?"

"Yes. Can you try, anyway?"

"Of course. But there's not much to say. Once we got inside, Florique saved everyone and then we left for the Ocean Palace."

Kilek nodded. "Alira and I remember about the same. But nothing else. Tell me what Florique saved everyone from? Who was in the inn? Can you remember a face or a name? Can you describe Lady Wen herself? How did Florique save us? With fire? Chains of smoke?" He spread his hands. "A magic light of blue or pink?"

"I…" Tyar frowned, and he did not speak for some time. "You know, I can't answer any of those questions. I've got no idea. When I try to remember, there's… nothing. But I just *know* everything worked out."

"Me and Alira, too."

"So, what does it mean?"

Kilek sighed. "To me, it seems like Florique has hidden something from us for some reason."

"Why? That doesn't make sense."

"Perhaps."

"Couldn't it be some side-effect of the harp song? I mean, I know he's a little strange, but he's on our side, right?"

"I suppose so."

Tyar glanced back to the camp with its cold fire-pit and circle of tents. "What about everyone else?"

"I haven't had a chance to ask."

"I'll check with Mathi once she's awake." Then he shrugged. "You know, we should just ask everyone at the same time."

"Good idea. We can all compare what we know. Or *don't* know."

Tyar grinned, only for it to fade quickly. "Kil, there's something I want to ask you, too. And now that we're alone, it seems like a good time. It's about Mathi. Do you… know?"

Kilek nodded. Quite wonderfully – despite the flash of pain he thought was buried a little deeper – his face would not have given much away, considering his transformation. "For a while."

"And you're not upset?"

"Only if you end up hurting each other," he said. And it was true. Jealousy did linger a little. It did. But not enough that he'd be bitter. Perhaps a greater surprise was that the fang or the transformation, or time itself, had allowed him to come up with the kind of answer an actual adult might have given.

Tyar chuckled. "We're taking care of each other."

"Good," Kilek said with a smile, and hopefully the expression didn't create a mess of fangs and saliva.

His friend pointed. "And what about you?"

"Huh?"

"You have feelings for both Zenia and Alira."

"What are you talking about?" Had his voice came out a little high-pitched?

Tyar raised his hands. "All right. No need to be so sensitive. Give me a week, and I'll guess."

"What?"

"If I'm right, you owe me."

Kilek stood and folded his arms, claws scraping against scales. "Even if you were right, the girls would get a say, don't you think?"

"Of course." The man was still grinning.

"Shut up. And we should talk to the others," he said, starting back toward the camp. "Come on."

Chapter 18.

Everyone recounted their memories over a breakfast of toasted bread, dried fruit and the last of Zenia's tea, taken from the *Silver Fin*. Kilek assured his friends that he could not sense any pursuit, and further, the Blood Wolves were quite distant.

But their relative safety ended up being the best news of the morning, since not a single person could recall even a single specific detail about the *Home in the Woods*.

"I don't understand," Mathi said with a groan as she leant toward the fading flames, elbows resting on her knees. "He's been helping us this whole time."

Sir Eciven exhaled heavily as he lowered his bowl. "I have known Phantom half my life. He is no villain, but he does not always share his purpose or method. This must be one of those times."

"But why?" Kilek asked.

"That, I do not know, yet I trust him still."

"As do I," Zenia added softly. Alira nodded from beside her, though her frown had not faded.

Paxoph was pacing nearby. "It would be no surprise if he is Anesca, like us. Right?"

"Then which God?" Mathi asked.

"A good question. A Luargot God, then?"

"Someone benevolent, enough," she replied.

Tyar added, "You know, I don't remember him trying to force us into anything."

Kilek found himself nodding along. The conversation with Florique in Lady Wen's library returned. *I am saying that if one day you came to regret your gift, for whatever reason, that such a fact would sadden me. More so, if you rushed toward a change that cannot be undone.*

The words of someone who cared.

But why the deception?

"I think we might be asking the wrong question, for now," Alira said. "After all, why would he make us all forget a good thing? That's more confusing to me."

Silence fell over the group.

"Then, are you saying that we *didn't* succeed at the inn?" Tyar asked.

"I'm not sure."

Zenia frowned. "I don't think that is true, but I cannot say why. Although, it's certainly nothing from my memories giving me that belief."

"These might be questions for Phantom when we next see him – assuming he is still minding Gianh and not off on some other task, by now." Sir Eciven tossed a piece of crust into the flames. "Nevertheless, we should continue our search. I only wish we had a guide."

"If nothing else, I can sense the Blood Wolves," Kilek said.

"That will make a difference, true," Sir Eciven replied. "It still leaves the lake at High Rios. The right path is unclear. I remember enough this close to the harbour, but the map was vague for what looked to be the final leg."

Kilek nodded. "The Myth of the Silver Dragon describes a four day climb, but not many other specifics." Though the loss of the map was significant, there was a tiny thread of confidence within him, somehow. "There is mention of a fading stone wall and a ring of shadow. Nothing else really relates to possible landmarks."

"For now, we'll have to rely on that, whatever it may mean."

And so they broke camp and climbed on, certain of little more than the fact that they had days of travel yet before them.

On the first night, a cold wind wreaked havoc with their campfire, but they managed; the bigger problem, as far as Kilek was concerned, being his appetite. He found himself unable to ask for more than a single serving and unable to hunt his own game… shame had finally reached him, after what happened with the Prisawi.

But he kept a tight rein on his hunger through the next two days and nights, climbing higher into the mountains, passing only one merchant and her guard, eating only what was served of an evening, until finally, on the last night before their supposed arrival at High Rios, Kilek could take no more.

The moon was full and the flames low when he sat upright, as if torn from sleep by hunger.

And from the gnawing emptiness in his stomach, perhaps that was no lie.

He rose to his feet.

Pax was on watch, not too distant, and everyone else seemed to be asleep. *Good.*

Kilek slipped into the trees and started down a slope, drawn by the scent of animals. Close enough, especially at his pace. Though he was not ghost-like with his movements, it was easy to avoid the biggest obstacles, since even faint moonlight slipping between the branches was enough.

He slowed before his target; the opening to a burrow, half-concealed by a fallen log.

Rabbits within?

Not all that deep, either. Tearing his way through the soil would not be difficult. Kilek stalked closer, bending to one knee and raising a clawed hand. Below, at least six heartbeats… parents and their children.

It would not be a feast, but it would be better than nothing.

Fresh.

His hand hovered above the earth, talons glinting – and he could not stop. Fangs creaked as he fought himself, fought a desire that howled within.

Soil and stone sprayed.

Breaking through was easier even than he'd expected, revealing rabbits huddled together, their grey fur muted.

He clamped a clawed hand over the animals, holding them in place. Dark, liquid eyes stared up at him, little bodies twitching.

His mouth fell open, drool slipping free.

No!

Kilek stumbled back with a hiss. He pushed himself away from the animals, stumbling through darkness, shoulders crashing into branches, feet tearing the earth. He did not stop until he came across a small clearing where moonlight sparkled upon a small pool a mere few feet wide.

He scooped water as he knelt, splashing it across his face. *As though I were still human.*

It did not ease his hunger.

And when the ripples eased, an unfamiliar face was reflected upon the surface: dark green scales, horned ridges above glowing eyes, horns grown from his head, a mouth too-wide, fangs visible… Kilek shuddered.

He smashed his fist into the water.

No joyous laughter now. He had a gift, at last, but it was nothing like the realisation had been for his friends when they'd changed, back in Avendria's temple.

Doesn't mean you give up.

Kilek grunted. "Fine."

Chapter 19.

Morning and noon had already passed when they stopped at a fork in the mountain road. Overhead, sunlight was weakening under the slow passage of grey clouds but rain had not started to fall.

Of more concern, the fork offered *four* paths.

Two led higher up the mountain, one to the east, and the other pair turned westward… with no outward indication of the correct choice. The intersection of roads did make for a spacious staging area, complete with stone benches built to one side.

And maybe there is *a clue.*

Something seemed to echo down from the path that climbed up in long steps, each like a landing, with old wagon ruts still visible.

"This is the fourth day," Zenia said as she stood before the climbing path, hands upon her hips. She glanced back at everyone else, in particular, Sir Eciven.

He nodded. "That it is."

"How do we solve this? Do we split the search?"

Sir Eciven turned to Kilek. "Anything?"

"I actually feel something from the northward…" he trailed off. Blood Wolves were approaching. And not just a few scouts. All of them. *How are they so fast?*

Alira took a step toward him. "Kilek, what's wrong?"

"The Blood Wolves are coming." He threw his cloak and hood back. "Scores of them. We don't have time to flee."

As if on cue, howls rose from the eastern path.

Sir Eciven strode to the fore, greatsword gripped in both hands. "Kilek, join me in the vanguard."

Kilek nodded as he strode to the knight's side. Hunger had returned; it churned within now – could the Blood Wolves be eaten when it was over? *Assuming we survive.* But the thought of such a meal gave his limbs extra energy.

Sir Eciven was still organising their defences. "Your Highness, in the centre. No complaints." He pointed to Tyar, who'd approached one of the trees as if to climb for vantage. "Stay close – we can't afford to have anyone isolated."

Zenia frowned, but followed his advice, drawing her own sword.

Blazing green feathers were already hovering above Alira's grip, and nearby, Mathi's eyes had begun to bleed blue. Even the smallest movements she made seemed tight with suppressed power and speed.

"Tell me when you are wounded," Paxoph said, raising his voice above the howls.

"How long, lad?" Sir Eciven asked.

Kilek closed his eyes a moment. *Closer and closer.* The slap of their pads upon rock-strewn earth. Thunderous heartbeats. Snarls. Whatever it was that remained unnatural about their blood… "On the count of forty."

"Stay together," Sir Eciven commanded, lifting his voice. "They'll spread to surround us. If anyone falls, pull them to the centre. Someone will take your place until Paxoph can get you back on your feet. And remember, we don't know exactly what these things can do."

And then the first Blood Wolf loped into view, slowing so the others could join it… and without his dragon form, Kilek make have taken a step back.

Each Blood Wolf stood closer to the size of a pony. Their fur was a mix of brown and a deep red, gleaming as though bloodied. Yet the name most likely came from the way blood flicked and splashed from both their feet and mouths, staining yellow fangs. Almost black, the blood hissed when it hit the ground.

Dozens of sets of golden eyes regarded them.

Toward the back, standing head and shoulders taller again, was the wolf most likely to be the pack's leader. Unlike the others, its eyes were purple – the colour streaking across the face and head, like a mask of webbing.

It snarled and the others attacked.

Tyar's bowstring snapped, felling the first wolf, his arrow driven deep into its skull. Alira's blazing green feathers followed. Where they struck, the animals collapsed into balls of flame, howling as they burned.

Other wolves leapt high, but Kilek stepped forward and swatted several from the air. His claws drew blood. Stinging droplets struck his scales, but he shrugged off the pain, a faint suggestion only. He fought on, crunching bones and slashing through their red fur to reveal pulsating organs. Silver streamed forth too, statues crashing to the ground, shattering when he struck with his clawed fists.

Shouted warnings and encouragement flew between his friends. At one point, he saw Mathi's limbs moving like a precise whirlwind that smashed skulls and bones alike.

He fought on until finally, finally, he had to pause to catch his breath.

Not that the wolves gave him time. Forced to draw a giant breath and exhale once more, he enveloped yet another tangle of fur and fang in silvery mist.

How many were left?

He swiped at a new wolf, more bones crunching beneath his blow – and then a deeper snarl reached him.

The leader.

It bore two arrows and a still-burning feather, the green flickering in its chest, but the creature had not fallen. Instead, it snarled, blood spraying from its jaws.

Kill the leader. The remainder will falter.

Kilek charged.

The Blood Wolf leapt to meet him. Kilek let more stone-breath burst from his chest. It covered the wolf's head. Even with purple webbing as protection, the leader wasn't strong enough to resist, its face hardening to stone.

Kilek followed with a double-fisted, overhand blow that shattered the wolf's head into dozens of pieces.

The body slumped against him but he shoved it aside with a growl.

A cry of frustration rose behind Kilek, but before he could check on whoever it was, the huge corpse started to twitch where it lay upon the earth.

He blinked as a wave of weariness hit.

Had the Blood Wolf's body really moved? *I imagined it...* Another wave of weakness crashed against his senses, and

Kilek had to drop to one knee. *Did it do something to me?* The fur was turning black.

Something twisted, wriggling from the severed neck, blood pumping forth – joined by sharp mandibles and the chattering of insects.

Cabeku!

Something bulged against the sides of the corpse…

Kilek strained to keep his eyes open. Cries were echoing all around now. Who was calling his name? *What's happening to me?*

But he could no longer hold his head up.

Chapter 20.

Kilek woke to darkness, his mouth dry and the edges of his eyes clogged with gunk. He rolled onto his back to rub at his eyes – then flinched.

But there was no pain.

"What?" He lifted his hands. Covered in skin, not scales! He'd obviously transformed after the Blood Wolf attack…

He sat bolt upright, head brushing the top of a tent.

Where am I?

Outside, calm voices. He rubbed at his eyes again then crawled forward, finding that he wore a dark-brown tunic and pants, someone's spare clothes. The fang and War Heart still hung from his neck. Had the Herisman relic helped him? Not with the hunger, since his stomach rumbled as he moved.

When he poked his head from the tent, he found his friends sitting around a campfire, the light almost too bright compared to the night.

"Good evening."

Yet it wasn't everyone, and though they smiled and

greeted him with relieved expressions – Zenia was nowhere to be seen, and Pax and Alira were mostly focused on the prone form of Sir Eciven.

"What happened?" he asked when he joined them. The golden glow from Pax's hands seemed to be removing a dark pallor to the knight captain's skin. Slowly.

"Too much blood from the wolves," Alira said.

"We're holding it at bay, but we don't know why it's worse for Sir Eciven," Paxoph said. "It seems that whatever Cabeku-poison infected the wolves is near as powerful as Avendria's healing."

"Did you –"

"Don't worry," Mathi said, placing a hand on his shoulder. "We destroyed it. How about you?"

"Well, I feel better." His stomach rumbled again, fainter now – a good reminder. "Something happened before. I don't know if it poisoned me too." But he shook his head. Wasn't the answer far more obvious? *You need food, you idiot.* "Maybe it didn't poison me. Is it too late for me to eat?"

Tyar ladled something from the fire-pot into a bowl. "Try this."

Kilek took a bite – meat and root vegetables with the broth, and the flavour widened his eyes. He ate another spoonful, and then another, barely noticing the heat except for the way it warmed his stomach.

And then he ate a second and third bowl without speaking another word, finally looking up at Tyar's expression… that of a raised eyebrow. "None left."

"Oh."

His friend chuckled. "Don't sound so disappointed. We'll do a little more hunting when it's time to eat in the morning."

"Sorry, I just… a hunger came over me." He glanced around the camp – they were near the stone benches, where dark shapes lay strewn about just beyond the firelight's reach. "Where is Zenia?"

"Relieving herself," Mathi replied.

"Is it safe?"

"A few of the Blood Wolves escaped, but we haven't been attacked in hours," she replied. "Can you tell us anything?"

Kilek paused. He couldn't sense them – couldn't sense much beyond his own hunger. "I might have to be transformed." He raised a hand, reaching for the fang, but hesitated.

Do I really want to hold it again, so soon? For one, it wouldn't do to become reliant upon the bone. He closed his eyes, listening to his heart, to the power deep within – and stopped. He didn't reach for it, more for another reason. *I want to stay me as long as I can.* "I might need more rest."

"No need to worry, Kilek." A new voice answered – Zenia appearing from the shadows. Her movements were a little slow as she sat beside him with a sigh. She glanced at Sir Eciven. "Any change?"

"A little," Pax said. "He's still breathing steadily but it's persistent."

"That's something," she said. "We'll take turns watching him, and then keep climbing in the morning. You might not get much sleep tonight, Pax."

"Avendria will aid me," he replied with a nod of acceptance.

"Thank you." She gave a small smile. "Why don't we all get some rest, then?"

"Let me watch," Kilek offered. "I've had plenty."

She stretched her legs closer to the flames. "That would

be welcome." But she didn't join the others as they rose and prepared to rest.

Pax stood. "I'll only be a short while."

Zenia nodded, still staring into the flames. Kilek glanced at Paxoph, but his friend was nearly beyond the firelight already, and so he turned back to the princess. "Zenia, I'm sorry."

"Why?"

"I should have been able to stop them. Maybe then, Sir Eciven wouldn't be like this." He spoke softly, so as not to disturb the others.

She smiled at him. "Taking responsibility for all our woes?"

"Well…"

"There's no need for that, Kilek. Without you, we wouldn't have survived. At all."

"Well… I guess I helped."

"Very modest, Kilek," she said, her gaze now back on Sir Eciven. "You know, I rely upon him as much, or even more than my brothers or my father... but seeing him like this reminds me of the last time. Of how dangerous this all is." She sighed again. "He actually taught me the sword when others refused. I was quite young, but I still remember him correcting my grip for the first time. The way the sword was lighter than it seemed."

He waited for her to continue.

"When I mentioned how light it felt, he told me that even if the blade seemed that way, that it *should* be a heavy burden. That I should only draw it to defend others." Now she smiled. "I don't know if I understood, but that didn't stop him repeating it more than once over the years."

"That seems to be how he lives."

"It is." She swallowed. "I'm sorry, Kilek. Some leader I'll turn out to be, right? But… it's not like the giant Cabeku. This is worse, if Paxoph cannot heal him right away."

Kilek hesitated but reached out to put a hand on her own. "Pax won't give up. None of us will."

She nodded, placing her free hand upon his own a moment. "Thank you."

"You could rest, if you want?" Kilek suggested. "Leave the watch to me. And Pax will be back soon." He nearly added something more, that she would be a great leader, that she probably already was. But it seemed too late, somehow.

"Right." Zenia turned away as she stood, perhaps wiping at her eyes? She headed for her tent, pausing before she slipped inside. "Thanks for listening, Kilek."

"Of course."

Chapter 21.

The next morning they created a stretcher for Sir Eciven as best they could, accompanied by Tyar's grumbling about 'having to do this all the time' then resumed their search – choosing the path Kilek felt was correct: the northern climb. "I can't explain, but even now, without being transformed, I can sense something."

It was faint but familiar. *Familiar to me or the other me?*

"That's a lot better than nothing," Paxoph said from where he carried one half of the stretcher with Alira. The Luminous Clarion lay with the knight, half-concealed.

"What about the wolves?" Zenia asked. She seemed less pensive now, more impatient to act. Somehow, a little more like herself.

He nodded. "I can sense the survivors. They're not close." He pointed to a ridge waiting beyond a rather deep gorge, just visible upon the eastern trail. "There's a series of caves, over that way."

"More welcome news," she said, before glancing up to the sky and its wall of grey clouds. "Let's see if we can beat that bad weather."

Yet no sooner had she spoken, drops of rain began to strike Kilek.

Tyar sighed.

On they trudged, seeking clues, such as the fading stone wall or ring of shadow, until the rain grew heavier and a mist rolled in, obscuring their view. Mathi found a blanket and placed it over Sir Eciven.

Kilek followed the vague sense that assured him they were on the right path, but he had nothing specific to show for it, which gave his doubts fertile ground. The Myth of the Silver Dragon and the map placed the hidden lake at High Rios squarely in the mountains north of Agenac, but the myth spoke as though its location was so obvious that it need not be described.

Or it was always meant to stay hidden…

Why not? No-one had been able to discover the ancient lake since the dragons left hundreds of years ago.

He lifted his gaze from little white flowers that littered the roadside, sagging beneath the weight of the rain. They were still bright against dark stone, but the occasional petal was lost, sliding away in tiny rivulets that ran downward. *Aimless, like us.* He frowned, as if in response to his doubts.

By time or by stone and for whatever reason, their destination had remained undiscovered for centuries. Would even Surrogates of Avendria be able to find it? *How many others had searched? Is this what she wants us to do? I should have followed Alira's advice and tried to speak to her, somehow.*

By noon, the rainfall had eased though it remained an annoyance. He glanced upward, as he had so many times, and still no sign of blue skies.

We could use some sunshine.

Especially Sir Eciven. Despite his condition not seeming to worsen, with Pax and Alira taking turns to help him fight the poison, their efforts to fully heal him were still to yield an overwhelming victory.

"There's someone up ahead," Zenia said, breaking through his musing.

Where the paved stones gave way to a less even stretch of road, there waited a barefoot young man wearing pale yellow robes, golden hair curled around his shoulders… and none of it wet or appearing the least bit troubled by the misty rain. He leant on a smooth staff, its handle curled into twin horns.

"Do not hesitate, travellers." His voice carried easily.

Kilek came to a halt.

"Another enemy?" Mathi asked, lowering her voice and directing her question to the group.

"I sense no great evil, at least," Alira added.

"Correct." The young man was smiling as he approached, walking with the aid of the stick. Still, the rain did not touch him nor the cold seem to bother him – even his steps were soundless. Probably of most concern was that he'd clearly heard them from a distance, despite Mathi and Alira having spoken softly. "But I will be observing your actions from this point onward."

He came to a stop before them.

"Who are you, if we might ask?" Zenia's eyes were a little wide.

The young man smiled, and it was so joyous it seemed to lessen the chill in the air. "Left behind, I suppose. More importantly, your search is not unknown to us but please be warned; you must not be found lacking. We will expect you to make the correct choice."

"What choice… My Lord?" Alira asked after a slight hesitation.

"I am lord of nothing, here," he replied, still smiling. "Climb to the Suffering Twins and you will see. Be wary of the tunnel – do not leave the bounds of your conveyance."

"You raise many questions," Pax said.

The golden-haired man nodded. "A fair warning is all I can offer. While most heed it, few have reached the lake itself. I hope to see you all again." He faced Kilek then. "And you'll have to make the choice, seeing as Avendria and Daciael chose you."

"Wait, does that mean –"

The stranger was fading swiftly, already nothing but a mere hint of cloth wavering where he'd once stood. Yet the strange man's voice echoed in Kilek's mind. *Don't let your doubts win, Kilek. You are pivotal to what must come.*

Me? There was no-one visible to answer, but a response to his silent question came anyway.

Of course. Consider everything. Chosen by the Goddess, anointed by Daciael, able to transform, able to use the Luminous Clarion.

Yes, but I'm not the only –

Dense boy! Very well, consider it this way. Do you think Nakir would be trying to capture you *specifically, if you were not actually quite important?*

And for some reason, he had not made that obvious connection. Nor should he have needed any reminder – of course he was a target. Nakir had said as much; that he'd serve some purpose to the other Gods. He was important enough for that. Obviously, they all wanted the dragons.

When did they know I was… whatever I am?

No answer echoed in his mind.

"Kilek, is something wrong?" Zenia asked. "It seems you were right, doesn't it?"

He nodded. "Just wondering about the young man, and how he knows all about us."

"Well, whoever he was," Tyar said, "I want to get out of this rain. It's obviously never going to stop."

"Let's find some shelter, then," Zenia said.

She led them on until finally, an overhang of stone appeared upon the mountain road. It was barely enough for everyone to huddle beneath, and Kilek's position on the outside still exposed him to some of the ill weather, but it was easier to converse, at least.

More importantly, their bodies provided Sir Eciven with shelter. Whenever Kilek had taken his turn carrying the stretcher, it was clear the captain's skin was still tinted with the dark of poison, even if Pax was sometimes able to drive it back. So, too, for the efforts Alira made to draw the darkness out via her magic, in a manner not so different to how she used to draw out impurities from puddles.

"What do we think of the stranger's warning?" Pax was glancing back toward the road.

"Was he mage or Surrogate?" Mathi asked.

Tyar ran a hand through his wet hair. "Or ghost?"

Alira suggested, "I think it likely he was something similar the dragon's spirit Kilek met in the valley."

"He certainly seemed to know about that," Kilek added.

Zenia sighed. "Above all, can we trust him?"

"What of his story, then? The Suffering Twins and a

choice?" Paxoph asked. "Does it align with the Myth of the Silver Dragon?"

"The myth does mention the Suffering Twins of High Rios," Kilek said. "They're a pair of trees. Saplings, supposedly. They can never grow beyond their infancy, but they were planted to commemorate all that the Silver Dragon did for humanity."

"And are they related to the choice that the spectre mentioned?"

"I don't know." Kilek closed his eyes a moment, doing his best to recite the rest of the myth in his mind. "There's nothing about a choice in the myth."

"At least we seem to be on the right path," Zenia said. "In the meantime, let's see if we can wait out the rain."

But the weather was growing worse, water running from the overhang in streams now. Thunder soon joined it, bringing white shards of hail. These quickly became small balls, bouncing and shattering where they hit the rocky earth.

There was little to do but wait.

Chapter 22.

A final few pieces of hail clattered down the mountain path behind them, as above, the setting sun cut through tattered clouds at long last. The awful weather had receded beyond the ranges and despite no-one being fully dry, the search for a new campsite – and the fire it would allow them to build – drove everyone on at renewed speed.

Kilek quickened his step from where he now led the group, as the mysterious young ghost appeared to be directing him without words; just an urge to turn from the main path, to take a certain fork, to look behind a jumbled landslide.

And finally, before darkness had fallen, to approach a smooth wall of stone, one that towered above.

The so-called fading stone wall?

Its surface was covered in faint carvings, their shapes suggestive of features only, hard to discern in the growing shadows. The ground, too, bore traces of the past, with uneven flagstones sitting at angles, their edges so thick they would have reached Kilek's knee if he stood alongside them.

"Another hidden passage or a dead end?" Mathi asked as

she examined the wall.

Howls rose from their back trail.

Kilek spun.

Blood Wolves. Half a dozen, prowling closer. Not within striking distance yet but the animals did have everyone cornered. *I didn't sense them at all!*

Tyar cursed as he reached for his bow, and even as Zenia called for everyone to take arms, a new voice cut through the shock.

"This way, if you please."

Again, Kilek wheeled. An enormous opening now stood in the wall without even a single scrape of stone to have signalled the change. But rather than a tunnel, a dark cavern met his gaze. Giant too. Easily able to accommodate a five-storey building from the capital!

Standing before the opening was the young man in his pale robe, welcoming smile upon his face. "Do hurry," he added.

Almost as one, Kilek and his friends rushed for the darkness. Fresh howls rose from behind, now seemingly tinged with frustration. But once inside, footfalls and breaths echoing, it seemed the darkness would offer protection.

Or it would entrap them.

"I can't find the stone wall. It should be behind us," Mathi said, her voice right on the heels of his doubt. "It's like it was never there."

"And where's our guide?" Tyar asked.

The young spectre was also gone. But the darkness was not complete in all directions.

"Look," Kilek said.

Mere paces away, a field of feathers was blooming. Pink

and white blanketed the ground, stretching forth like a river. A *wide* river. Kilek approached and it brightened further, as if the feathers grew from a bed of light. And it was no longer only white ones with pink stripes, but gold now joined the river, adding a beautiful tint to the glow.

Tension flowed from his limbs as he watched; relief and peace enveloping his body.

Soft murmurs rose around him – Alira and Paxoph – with the others silent, small smiles upon their faces. Even Zenia and Tyar stood as though Sir Eciven weighed little.

The feathers swirled.

Something large stirred from below...

He approached, slowly, and dark wood appeared, its surface gleaming as if coated in varnish. The higher it rose, the wider it became, until the enormous shape revealed itself to be a barge. Though it did not span a range from dark bank to dark bank, it was broad enough to accommodate everyone *many* times over. Many horses. Many wagons.

Simply enormous.

Without knowing how, but with little doubt anyway, Kilek was certain it would take them to the Suffering Twins. He climbed down, finding firm footing beneath his feet, not unlike standing on stone. His weight was obviously and utterly negligible to the surface. "This will take us to our guide."

The others joined him, and once they were settled, mostly leaning against the sides, the barge started to move. Sluggishly at first. But the speed soon grew steady, colours steaming by, shifting at their passage.

Here and there, tiny pieces of the feathers rose like dust, glittering where they hung in the air.

"I wonder what's below?" Zenia asked where she leant beside Kilek.

"We probably shouldn't try to find out," he replied with a smile. And then his smile faded. "That might be the warning we were given."

"True enough," she said. "Did the ghost say how far we have to travel?"

"Nothing, yet."

The tinkling of small bells echoed from the rear. The princess tilted her head. "Did you hear that?"

"Everyone, listen to this!" Alira was some ways down the barge's length, and she'd extended her arm over the side, letting her fingers brush against the feathers.

And where she did, music followed.

It was an ethereal, sweet sound – not unlike bells.

Alira glanced back to everyone as they gathered around, a wide smile on her face. "It's amazing!"

Once again, his friends moved as one as they reached out to touch the feathers.

Despite his doubt, it seemed safe enough, and so Kilek found himself grinning as each feather-top brushed against his hand, ringing quick to follow. And for every pink and white feather there came a similar sound, but when his fingertips grazed gold, the chiming was deeper.

A gentle riot followed as strange music rose from each hand.

It ought to have been cacophonous, but somehow, everything was complementary, as though the pieces Zenia touched were a little different to those he hit, even if one happened right after the other.

And on it went, with all in harmony.

"I see a red one," Alira exclaimed, and leant right across the rail. Paxoph caught her to be safe, and when she hit the red feather, it chimed even brighter – causing answering notes to come from all across the river of feathers, red popping up here and there.

At one point, Tyar even started tapping out a silly tune that had everyone laughing.

"You know, I wish Eciven could see this," Zenia said at one point. "And Dion would have loved every moment, too."

Kilek agreed.

Beautiful as it all was – especially to see everyone full of cheer – as the journey continued, they soon met in the centre of the barge, laying out some of their still-damp clothes and talking of what lay ahead.

Even so, little could be decided, not with such limited knowledge.

But finally something changed. A pair of wings appeared ahead. They hung above the river of feathers, somehow expectant.

The wings were just like the feathers below, white tipped in pink. But unlike the river, when something ruffled the wings from within, it was a pair of black eyes that stared down at the barge, which had now come to a halt. No sooner had the mighty raft stopped, than a deep, rasping voice echoed in Kilek's mind.

You are presented with a choice.

Kilek nodded.

"What are they, Kil?" Tyar asked.

"Our guide said I had to choose, remember? The wings are asking me, now."

Simply answer this. Save your own life or the lives of your friends?

"My friends," Kilek replied, the words coming without a moment's hesitation.

The eyes receded, wings covering them. The barge slid forward again, heading toward another bend in the river. Ahead, only darkness and more feathers, more light, without any sense of an end point.

"Was that all?" Zenia asked.

"I'm not sure." Either way, he'd not received any answer. No sense one way or another as to how his decision had been received.

Alira pointed. "There."

A second set of wings floated above, and this time the colours were opposite the first – pink feathers bearing white tips. Another pair of dark eyes appeared when the barge stopped.

You are presented with a choice.

Again, Kilek nodded.

Simply answer this. A mighty hero, free of doubts, will come to collect the Clarion at the Suffering Twins. Will you refuse? Will you keep the Clarion for yourself?

Now, Kilek hesitated.

On the surface, another question about selfishness. Or self-sacrifice. But a flicker of relief struck him – perhaps someone *could* come and take the burden. After all, would it be such a terrible thing for a truly competent hero to save everyone? Someone better-suited to the task?

It would give all lands the best possible chance of survival.

Yet…

"No. I will keep the Clarion." He'd spoken with more firmness than he'd expected. *Should I be surprised?* Perhaps not. Being tasked with something vital, having struggled and suffered for it, and finally finding himself in a position to make the difference which the Goddess and others expected of him – that wasn't something for someone else to simply wander in and take. "Tell your hero they are not needed."

The eyes closed without speaking again.

Chapter 23.

The river of feathers ended not in darkness, but light.

Once Kilek's eyes adjusted, he stepped from the barge and into a forest of black pine. The trees grew so densely that without the straight and narrow path, and without a blue sky above, he would not have been able to see very far ahead.

And they were not alone.

Standing with what seemed to be his usual smile was their guide, assuming that was his actual role. Still, he'd not been hostile.

"Welcome all, to High Rios." The young man gestured to the trees with their dark, uneven bark and mess of needles. "I am what remains of its steward. You may call me Fisathali. Please meet me below at the Suffering Twins. Be sure to tread carefully, and don't lose that lovely horn."

"Wait," Kilek said. "This means I chose correctly?"

"Of course, yes. Though it is more of a formality, to be honest." Then Fisathali faded away.

Kilek frowned. "We don't have a reason to distrust him, yet."

"I agree," Zenia replied. "Let's go."

And so they started through the trees. Not a long walk, but once beneath the canopy, the scent of sap filled the air – with an added sweetness, strong enough to actually make his mouth water. *If I was still a child, I'd probably try to find some and eat it.*

Once on the other side of the small wood, Kilek stood aside and paused. High Rios *did* conceal an ancient lake, precisely as promised.

But it was like no lake he'd ever seen. Waiting a notable distance below, like descriptions of volcanoes that he'd read… and based on where he stood, the lake was, in fact, resting beneath a ring of the black pine. *The second clue from the myth?* The trees lined a vast gorge, one that looked to have been cut in a perfect circle. Faint streams of water cascaded down its side in giant steps clad in – or made from – sheets of gold.

Mist rose from the bottom, where shallow water glistened around the base of a grassy hill. And that was where the ancient 'lake' waited: within the hill's peak. More of a large pool, it must have been fed by rainfall, since the cascading water did not reach it. And, more obviously, since the sky was open above them.

Still, High Rios was an unnatural place.

If nothing else, at least it was daylight now, instead of night as he'd half-expected, and only now come to appreciate.

"There's a dais in the centre," Zenia said, her voice hushed.

He accepted the Luminous Clarion from Tyar as he followed her gaze.

It was a white circle, perhaps of marble or maybe bone, with nothing else to suggest its importance save its size. That, and the pair of saplings in the centre, of course, but any other details were unclear from such a height.

"How do we reach it?"

The gorge did not seem to have steps… unless… There, on the far side. Was that a narrow, darker line? He pointed. "What about that?"

She nodded. "I think it is a stair."

"You can see from here?"

Zenia grinned. "You can't?"

Kilek squinted but it made little difference. "No. I'll just have to trust your eyes, Your Highness," he said with a smile.

"I don't know if we'll be able to carry Sir Eciven down there," Paxoph said from where he and Mathi held the stretcher.

Fisathali appeared – right beside Tyar, who flinched.

"Oh, I am sorry," he said, placing his hands together in what was presumably a gesture of apology. "Large groups of visitors that include the wounded are not at all common." He raised a hand. "Ready?"

Kilek took half a step forward. "For what –"

Between one blink and the next, they'd been transported below, to find themselves standing upon the spacious dais, the water so still that it did not even make gentle lapping sounds.

"Set him down for the moment." Fisathali lowered himself to cross his legs at the edge of the water. "Take a moment for respite, if you wish."

Kilek hesitated, and while resting his legs would have been welcome, he did not sit. "Thank you, Fisathali. Can you explain what's happening here?"

"Obviously, you've been chosen. You only need to play the Luminous Clarion."

"Then the dragons will come?" Paxoph asked.

"No. Then you will visit the Vanguard," the ghostly steward said. "There, you can plead your case."

"I see…"

Kilek frowned at the information. Not what he'd expected, and a little excitement did run through his body, but having to prove that their need was great? *Why should we? It's obvious.*

Paxoph was looking down at Sir Eciven. "Then I will stay here and watch over him."

Fisathali cleared his throat.

Tyar groaned. "Not more rules?"

"Alas, it is just so," he replied. "Only one may attend – that being Kilek, who was chosen."

Zenia folded her arms. "That's not acceptable. He shouldn't have to go alone."

"Well…" Fisathali paused a long moment before giving a shrug. "Perhaps a member of the Royal Deluargot family could be permitted, also. I'm not certain of the reception you will receive, but you are welcome to take the risk, Princess."

"Good."

Kilek faced her. "Wait, is that –"

"No arguments, Kilek."

He glanced at Sir Eciven. *What would the knight think if I let something happen to her?*

Now Zenia grinned. "And by the way, I can look after myself. So you'll not have to apologise to him. In fact, he'll be thanking us when we return with the dragons."

"I suppose so," Kilek said.

His friends exchanged a few glances, with Alira the first to smile. "Don't worry, we'll look after him, Your Highness."

Fisathali rubbed his hands together. "Wonderful! I may be able to help, though I must admit that this batch of filthy insects and their poisons are rather unknown to me."

"If you could, that would be most welcome," Zenia said.

"Of course." He rose. "Now, follow me and let's see how well young Kilek plays."

Chapter 24.

The Suffering Twins reached only his knees, their pale leaves spilling down to half-conceal wondrous bark. Somehow, it bore purple, blue, pink and yellow splashes, and even the tiny ants that climbed it were bright. *How much more beautiful would the Twins be if allowed to grow to full size?*

"I definitely don't recognise this tree," Kilek said.

"It exists nowhere else," Fisathali replied. "However, it may yet have a growth spurt, should you succeed."

"And how will we succeed?" Zenia asked.

"First, by standing before the Suffering Twins as you are. Then, Kilek must only play *Songs of Glory* upon the Luminous Clarion." Fisathali was already fading. "Worry not about your friends while you are gone."

And then silence, leaving Kilek to shake his head as he lifted the Clarion. "I hope I can play well enough. You know... I thought I'd be more excited."

"You're not?"

"Only a little. Only deep down, I suppose. I mean, I don't even know if this will work. Dionarc taught me enough to play the melody, but do I have to play it perfectly?" He sighed. "And where are we going?"

"And when we get there, how do we convince the dragons to return? According to Fisathali, it won't be as easy as we thought."

"Exactly." Kilek glanced back up toward the others where they watched from the edge of the gorge.

"At least he promised to watch over them."

"That does help," Kilek said, then arranged his fingers upon the keys. "Well, here we go."

He drew a breath, set the horn against his lips and blew. The first note squeaked. He stopped with a frown, starting again and getting only a few notes through this time, since his fingers weren't deft enough. "Sorry."

"There's plenty of daylight left," Zenia said.

He laughed. "I hope I won't have us stuck here until nightfall."

The princess slapped his shoulder with a grin. "Then try again."

Kilek lifted the Luminous Clarion once more, and this time when he played, the notes flowed – better, but hardly a wonderful performance.

It seemed enough. When he lowered the horn, the notes still echoed around the gorge. And somehow, the faint music was heavy. Heavy enough to make him close his eyes – yet he was still standing and Zenia was too, based on the sound of her uncertain question.

With some effort, he opened his eyes in time to witness a rainbow of feathers falling from above. They surrounded him, pirouetting in place. Without knowing how, he realised their purpose.

They would take him to the dragons.

Alone, if he didn't act.

He caught Zenia's hand, just as the feathers stopped spinning. A blinding light followed, and when it cleared, the plume had fallen away.

Kilek looked around.

The Suffering Twins were gone. The mountain and the pine trees too. Even the water around them. The lake had been replaced by stretching sand covered in feathers, and which led to a long stair of pale stone.

Kilek took a step and sand collapsed beneath him.

He lost his grip on Zenia with a cry, falling into shadow. He hit sand but tumbled down its slope, where his head thumped against something hard. He cursed but the blow wasn't too bad.

"Zenia?" He rose to his knees to rub at the back of his head, looking around. They'd fallen a short distance into a stone chamber. Golden sand sparkled as it trickled down from the hole above, where missing hunks of vaulted stone revealed the bright sky.

Another piece of the ceiling thudded down. More sand trailed as Kilek stumbled away from the opening. Zenia was already doing the same from nearby, and he joined her in the shadows of the large chamber. "That was lucky," he said. "If we're not trapped down here."

She nodded, moving to examine the walls. He followed, a slight limp slowing him. Up close, a line of quartz ran through the wall, like a horizon, only it was no more than a foot tall.

Inside, tiny creatures moved across waves of green and red moss.

Pale things, each with a dozen legs and a shell not dissimilar to that of a snail, patterns closer to pink. Antennae twitched as they moved, sometimes hopping, sometimes moving almost in some sort of… dance? There was a sense of exuberance to them, whatever they were doing.

"As curious as these things are," Zenia said, "I think we need to find a way out of here. Wherever 'here' is."

"Right. This isn't the welcome I was expecting."

Zenia laughed and together, they started toward the opposite wall.

An opening waited. Light from the hole in the ceiling did not stretch far, but they were able to see enough to discover a room similar to the last, and that it offered no exit.

He turned back toward the first chamber. "There's not enough debris for us to climb free, is there?"

"I don't think so."

Heading back confirmed her estimation, and he gestured at the rubble. "This can't be what Fisathali had in mind."

"Agreed. Let's look again. We must have missed something."

They resumed their search, and this time, Kilek paid attention to the floor – following a faint pattern. It had some resemblance to one of the carvings on the mountain wall, and led to a single piece of stone somewhat different in colour. It was difficult to be certain in the dim room, his own body blocking a certain amount of light, but he pressed it with his foot.

Stone ground against stone, echoing from the other chamber.

"Did you do that?" Zenia asked from her side of the room.

"I did. Let's see."

An opening now led to a third chamber, and here, the lines of creatures – or the moss – gave off a glow. It was enough to walk freely, enough to see narrow side passages that led to smaller rooms, or occasional flights of wide stairs and wider chambers that interrupted the main corridor.

All empty.

"No choice but to keep searching," Zenia said.

On they walked, accompanied by only the glow and faint taste of dust.

Until a rumbling reached them.

It grew swiftly. The source came from a nearby passage, this one larger than the others. They continued a cautious approach, since thin, gleaming strands criss-crossed the opening to form a barrier. The tendrils could have been soft as webs or strong as steel.

"This doesn't sound good," Kilek said.

"Can you transform, if you need to?"

"I think so." But he didn't try, not yet…

The rumbling became distinct; thundering footfalls as something approached from the dark – grunts soon joining glimpses of a large shape that filled the passage, a mess of scarred scales and twisted fangs.

A roar rang out, and Kilek fell against the opposite wall.

Dragon!

The creature hit the strands with a sharp crack. It thrashed against them, hissing saliva flying, eyes blazing, but the strands did not give. Did not even creak. Not even bulge as the mighty bulk of orange and white scales crashed against them.

Kilek could not drag his gaze away, despite a thundering within his chest.

It was a dragon… yet smaller than he imagined, and more lithe than paintings he'd seen. Its narrow head bore twisting horns, rows of fangs. Leathery wings half-concealed scales ranging from orange to brown and white.

All over its face, body, and wings were scars and old wounds, dents and even missing scales. One eye bore a milky film and the opposite nostril was half-closed by scarring.

What happened *to you?*

The dragon smashed itself against the strands a few more times before falling back, sides heaving. It thumped to its haunches with a growl, and then stared from the shadow, eyes blazing.

Obviously, not a dragon that would be able to help them…

Zenia grabbed his arm. "Quickly."

But he hesitated.

She was trembling. "Kilek, we don't know how long the strands will hold."

"Right. Sorry." He followed her down the main passage with a single backward glance, but of course, it told him nothing about the dragon or why it was imprisoned. Or why it was smaller than he'd expected… or the answer to dozens of other questions.

"I only hope it cannot somehow circle around," Zenia said.

"It looked like it had been trapped for a long time."

She nodded. "Probably. But you have to be ready, if there's a next time."

Even without touching the fang, he could transform. The sense of his other half – his hidden self, perhaps – was closer than before. Whether that had something to do with an extended period of time in his half-dragon form earlier, or to do with help from the fang, the closeness of the scarred dragon, or just the passing of time did not seem to matter.

And yet…"If I have to."

"What do you mean?" Her attention remained focused on the path ahead, where a long stair waited.

"I don't know."

Now she did give him a look, but quickly switched her attention to the stair. "Just be ready, Kilek." She drew her sword as she climbed, leading him up to another large chamber. This one was more than twice as large – be it measured from floor to shadowy ceiling or wall to wall – but unlike many others, Kilek blinked against the brightness of the moss and the creatures within.

"I think the light's been growing," Zenia said. "It wasn't like this before."

He nodded. "I hope that's a good sign."

Their footsteps echoed as they crossed the chamber. The far wall showed no entryway, no door, no clues upon the floor. Trapped again, with the only dragon's cell representing any kind of meaningful break in the stretch of walls and rooms with their quartz bands and little creatures.

"This is a surprise."

A new voice, soft, spoke from above.

Kilek glanced up and there, a pale head floated down from the shadows.

Chapter 25.

The pale head was… mostly human. It had long hair of gleaming white, elongated features and bright eyes. The face did smile down at them, but Kilek was not able to smile back, for somehow, it was drifting and sliding lower, as if upon strong threads…

Maybe it was? Just ones of incredible length that were hidden beneath the hair, where it curled around the throat? He stared. *No. It's the hair itself!*

"Oh, you should be above ground," the head told them, floating gently.

Kilek could not answer.

Something thin glimmered as the talking-head descended farther. It swung smoothly from the head, connecting to the floor with a soft click, as though it had always meant to do so. And then another two, and then more, all drifting down from the ceiling, coming from all sides, until the head rested before them at roughly eye-level, supported by its powerful strands of hair.

Again, it smiled. "You must be confused, but do not

worry. I will open a stair."

"Thank you," Zenia said after a moment of hesitation, her diplomatic training perhaps keeping her voice steady. "We would appreciate that, ah…"

The head chuckled. "Call me Rischan."

"I am Princess Zenia of Deluargot," she said. "And I travel with Kilek of Hasere, chosen by Avendria. We seek aid from the dragons."

"Welcome, yes. We are aware of you. In fact, Sparkena awaits you now."

"Then, they will help?" Kilek asked.

"That is not for a lowly servant such as myself to say," he replied. "Very few of the Vanguard have awoken as yet. They may wish to converse with the Elder, first. Nevertheless, I will say that since Avendria has sent you, your request will be heard."

"Suggesting that the Goddess would not compel the dragons to come to our aid?" Zenia asked.

"Not in my opinion."

"Then it's up to us, Kilek," she said.

"We won't leave without their help," he replied.

"Good." Rischan nodded, something of a bobbing motion. "Now, let me open a way, and off you go. There is a stair that will take you to Sparkena who is waiting in a Scale Nest; he will hear you."

It was not a familiar name if he thought back to what history of dragons remained. "Sparkena?"

Rischan was moving toward the far wall, glimmering threads leading the way, latching onto stone and pulling him forward – graceful movements still. "He will introduce himself, but I must reveal that the older dragons consider him somewhat rash."

"Oh."

"Rash, as though he might burn us to a crisp?" Zenia asked. "Or more like the dragon below?"

The floating head paused. "Neither, thankfully. And do not worry about her." His voice now bore a trace of sadness.

"Then, for whose protection is she kept caged? Yours?"

"All, but mostly her own, in the end," he replied. "Again, while hers is a sad tale, I am not in a position to share it. Sparkena may answer."

At the wall, his threads tapped upon the quartz. Inside, dozens and dozens of the creatures spread apart, creating an empty section of moss. "Thank you," Rischan said, then spoke unfamiliar words. Quartz and stone alike split, then slid upward to reveal more stairs, these lit by what seemed to be a bright sun, as if noon had lingered.

"Thank you, Rischan," Zenia said.

"A pleasure." He drifted aside so that they could access the steps. "While advice is not for me to offer, I do wish to grant you a small gift. Something that may be useful in the future."

"You do?"

"Yes. Take a strand of my hair, if you will. I am sure you will find it far, far stronger than it seems."

Zenia hesitated.

Rischan smiled once more. "It will coil easily, if that is your concern."

"Thank you, but I had wondered how I would take it? It doesn't seem very polite to simply pluck it free."

Yet, she had barely finished speaking when an ivory strand drifted down, hovering in the air before her. She reached out and took the hair, winding it around her wrist only loosely, then adding the coil to her pack. "Thank you, again."

"Of course. Now, tarry no longer, the both of you."

Kilek thanked Rischan as he started up the stair, and had barely taken half a dozen steps before the stone behind them closed. They walked on, surrounded by high walls of stone, a row of trees half-visible at the top.

"What happened down there?" Zenia asked after a time.

He slowed. "I can transform now, if you need me to."

She stopped to take him by the arm. "No, Kilek. I'm just a little worried. Your gift is important to us, but I need you to tell me if something is wrong. I'll help you."

He hesitated. How to explain it all? Would she be disgusted? *Sometimes, I am.* "When I transform… something happens. It's a hunger that starts to take control. I don't want anything bad to happen, Zenia."

Her eyes widened a little, but the princess only took his other hand. "I know you'll protect us, no matter what."

Kilek swallowed before he answered, a little thrill at her touch lingering. "Thank you."

"Just don't keep things to yourself," she added, then pulled him up a few steps. "Let's go. We've got a dragon to meet."

Some of his doubts were eased – enough to have him climb faster until they reached the top, where trees blocked any view of the land below. It was not unlike the path leading to High Rios, the pine just as dark from needle to branch. Here, too, the woods also grew in a ring that surrounded a gorge.

But the differences were more striking: a stone dais extended some of the way over a nest below, which had been built from wave-shaped wood pale enough to seem frozen. While it was not so far beneath Kilek and Zenia where they stood on the dais, it was vast.

And, more importantly, full of scales. All colours and sizes, like a shifting rainbow beneath the sun!

Each sparkled where light hit the surface. There were green and purple scales large enough to be doors – and one like half a wall! Gold and crimson ones too, mighty as shields, each joined by white and black, along with blue and pink scattered throughout. It was a veritable ocean of scales, glittering with hints of pearlescence wherever he looked. A few, such as the ones that could have been lavender or the softest blue sky, were not reflective. Yet more appeared translucent, jewel-like where they reflected other colours and created actual tiny rainbows!

Once more, he found himself unable to speak.

Nor could Zenia, and together they simply stared at the scale nest.

Chapter 26.

The nest shifted and Kilek flinched, as if woken from a powerful dream. How much time had passed? *And we've just been starting in awed silence the whole time.*

The scales were clattering, rising to a mound as something climbed up from below.

Gleaming wings broke free first, plates of deep red becoming silver near the bottom. The body featured the same pattern – a colour that only changed with the dragon's head, which bore no silver at all.

All red, save for white fangs and a pair of green eyes.

The dragon was far larger than the one in Rischan's chambers. When it lifted its head to align with Kilek and Zenia, they stumbled back; clearly, the dragon could have swallowed them both whole.

Kilek could hardly speak.

Even his limbs were suddenly useless. The sounds of scales clashing together grew muted as his senses receded – dominated by a powerful scent. It hit hard, like the sun against stone, and only eased when the dragon tilted its head.

"You are the chosen one, and your friend is the princess, isn't she?" The dragon's voice boomed but was not unbearable.

Kilek nodded, finally able to move. "Sparkena?"

"That I am."

"Then, you know why we've come?"

"Assuredly. Avendria sent you. But let me set your mind at ease, perhaps. It is not entirely true that you must convince either the Vanguard or the rest of us to help you."

Kilek straightened. "Then, do you mean everyone has agreed? Rischan mentioned an Elder."

"The Elder will plan and prepare with the others once all are awake – well-meaning but a little slow," Sparkena said with a wink. "What you have been sent here for is not to convince, but to *offer*."

"What does that mean, My Lord?" Zenia asked.

"That the Elder and others will expect help with our own problems, I am certain."

"But not you?"

His eyes seemed to brighten. "I *want* to burn those insects."

While that was good news, Kilek found himself unable to smile, just yet. "What problems?"

"Restoring the Sky Islands to their former glory, I imagine, but the others will have to answer your questions. I have one of my own."

Sky Islands? Hadn't Daciael mentioned the dragons being several oceans away? "Yes?"

"Can you control yourself when you change?"

Kilek opened his mouth to answer… and had no words. "So far. I don't know."

The dragon nodded. "Well, remind me to offer some

advice before we encounter trouble below."

"Below?" Kilek asked. "And ah, thank you, My Lord."

Sparkena nodded. "Yes, below. You are on Harbour Island, high above the lands beneath us. Did you not realise?"

"No, we didn't..." He glanced around, though of course he saw nothing that suggested they hung in the sky. *How powerful are the dragons to have made this?* "Daciael mentioned oceans separating us."

He nodded. "That is true, of course. Most of my kin are quite distant. But the Vanguard remained behind, here upon the Sky Islands."

"Do we need everyone?" Kilek asked.

"Not yet, so there is no need to fret. Feel free to ask other questions, since I'm sure you have many."

"We do," Zenia said. She gave Kilek a questioning look – it might have been about what they might eventually have to offer the dragons. "Can you fly us to our friends, and can you take us all to the west?"

"Of course."

"Will the Cabeku interfere?"

"Likely. But they are as gnats to me," Sparkena replied. "The bigger ones can be a problem, but there aren't many of them hatched yet. Javoteth is rushing."

"You can tell all that, from here?" Kilek asked.

"It is not difficult. Remember, if you are Avendria's chosen humans, we are her chosen birds," Sparkena said. "Well, 'birds' isn't grand enough, but we were first. She endowed us with many gifts."

"Gifts matched by the Cabeku?"

"In some ways. Yet their greatest gift – and threat – are their numbers. If you want to strike a decisive first blow, you're going to have to do something about that."

"Then, there are enough dragons to meet the hordes?"

Sparkena exhaled in what could have been a sigh and a little flame crackled. "Not yet. But humans will be helping us, of course."

"We will," Zenia said. "My father will want to meet you, to seek your counsel in how best to –"

The dragon chuckled. "Slow down, Your Highness."

"My Lord?"

"King or man, I have not decided whether I will bother to spend my time in talk. The Elder or others will probably handle that much. I am built for action."

"Oh." Zenia seemed at a loss for words, at first. "Then… can we be introduced to the Elder, in due course?"

"He will certainly wish to speak with someone, at least," he replied. "Tell me, what's worrying you right now, Your Highness, for I wish to spread my wings and… remind my teeth of their purpose. Kilek, what of you?"

He glanced at Zenia, who nodded. "How long would it take to reach the western lands of Minjao?"

"Not long at all, if I take you."

"I don't know what we'll face," Kilek said. "The Minjao army, mages, maybe Cabeku too, but my friends need to find their families. It's been too long."

"None that wander the land are able to best me," he said.

The dragon was right. *We can do this.* Kilek made a fist. "Thank you."

"Kilek." Zenia wore a slight frown. "I have another idea. What if we split up?"

"Oh?" He hesitated. Forming groups might make it easier to deal with all the problems that faced them… but simply, he didn't really want her to go somewhere else. "Even with only Sparkena to help?"

"He can drop me and Eciven off at the palace. That way I can check on Dion and Phantom. They may need help with Gianh. Anything could be happening, by now." She hesitated. "And maybe the healers there can help Eciven."

"That makes sense," he said. Of course, she'd be worried about her city.

Sparkena shifted. "No need for that. Let me call my sister. She can take you, Princess."

"Then you're not the only one awake?" Kilek asked as Zenia gave her thanks.

"There are a few of us, the younger ones – and don't worry, we'll be sure to remind our Elders who heard your Song first," he said, baring more fangs in what could have been a grin. Then he paused. "You're no bard, are you?"

Kilek had to laugh, the comment catching him off-guard. "No, I'm not."

"Feel no shame. It was enough," Sparkena replied. "Now, let me take you both below and I'll call Lilira."

"How?" Kilek asked. "There's no… saddle?"

"For now, my magic will be enough." He lowered his head and wings, presenting his back – a raft of red scales. "Just hold my horns while you're there."

Kilek stepped down, and it seemed his weight was as nothing, in a reminder of the barge on the river of feathers.

Zenia joined him, and he settled as best he could – cross-legged, since there was so much space – and gripped one of the dragon's many horns. They were of varying sizes, but all had the same impenetrable feel; textured enough that he took a firm hold.

The princess joined him and then Sparkena lifted his head, moving slowly.

"Hold on, the both of you."

Chapter 27.

Kilek grinned as they soared through the air.

A breeze stirred his hair – a breeze that should have been far stronger but was not, thanks to Sparkena. Thanks to his magic. Another undeniable reminder they were finally able to fight back.

It was enough to rekindle the excitement he'd thought lost.

Zenia was smiling too, and together they pointed at each wondrous vision, or gave little shouts when Sparkena roared into exhilarating dips and turns, a chuckle barely audible from the dragon.

From their vantage, the surrounding Sky Islands seemed to sparkle where each one hung in the sky – an astounding display of magic. Trees, flowers, and pools of water covered most, while other islands boasted watchtowers or small collections of buildings. And even though no people moved among them, Kilek still saw plenty of birds and once, what he thought was a hare, racing across one of the larger islands.

Time and again as they flew, his gaze was drawn to

something beyond the harbour, where a truly giant ridge of white stone waited. Or perhaps it was bone, he could not be sure.

But something about it sung to him. *Like a joyous homecoming?*

Sparkena was soon curving away, tilting his wings so that they sailed over an enormous grassland, one that ended quite abruptly – and then there was nothing below them but clouds of white!

The dragon roared as he plunged into the cloudbank. Kilek's stomach flipped.

Zenia's too, by her gasp of surprise.

White and grey whipped across his face, and then the clouds were gone, and far below – *very* far below – green and blue, and shadows of mountains, all rushing closer as Sparkena beat his wings to twist around. He dove once more, narrowing in on a single mountain this time. And soon enough, on a single patch of forest… and then, the sparkling water of High Rios' lake.

Below, everyone was shouting and pointing, enormous smiles upon their faces – including Sir Eciven, who was now upright. Even though his face still bore a dark pallor, he, too, grinned.

Sparkena beat his wings to hover in place. "You can just step off, Princess," he said. "You'll float down."

"Are you certain?" Zenia asked.

"Very."

"Good luck at home," Kilek told her, and she gripped his hand a moment before stepping from Sparkena's wing – where she floated gently toward the others, her limbs flailing a little at first. The dragon lifted his voice then, speaking in a language unfathomable to Kilek.

Fisathali appeared below. He nodded up at the dragon before snapping his fingers. Suddenly, everyone but Zenia and Sir Eciven had joined Kilek upon Sparkena's back. Yet, as one, his friends fell into crouches, or even to their knees, most holding their heads in their hands.

While it did not seem to be a gesture of pain precisely… they did not answer him when he spoke.

"What's happening?" he asked as Sparkena rose once more. *We can't be leaving already?* Kilek glanced around, and from above, another dragon was nearing. It seemed their scales were pink and silver. Sparkena's sister?

Zenia and Sir Eciven were waving from below, and Kilek waved back as their figures grew smaller, before turning his attention to his friends once more. Still, no-one lifted their heads, moving only slightly, and all breathing deeply. *They don't seem to be suffering.* "Sparkena? What's wrong with them?"

"They're not hurt. I just explained a few things to save time."

"Which had this effect?"

"It was a lot, admittedly. The best way their minds can arrange everything is to dampen their other senses for a short while. Don't worry, I warned them. And it won't last."

"Thank you…?" *Rash indeed.*

The dragon beat his wings harder, climbing more swiftly. "Before I fly a little faster, I must advise you of something. You'll all be safe, but don't move around too much. We won't be able to talk either, when I really get going."

"I understand," he replied. *Hopefully, everyone else does too.* "How long will it take?"

"Before nightfall."

"Amazing."

"I'm actually swifter still when flying unburdened, if you will excuse that description of you and your friends."

Kilek smiled, but before he could answer, the others began to recover. Tyar first, looking around with wide eyes. "You know, as amazing as this is, I don't think I'd like to do it too many times."

"You're doing better than back at that bridge near Jecomar," Alira told him as she rubbed at her temples.

"Well…" He sighed. "I don't think it's all me. Sparkena's helping."

Mathi put a hand on his shoulder. "Good." In contrast, when she looked around, seeming to focus on the rush of colours below, it was with a clenched jaw, her determination clear.

"I'd still like to know how we're staying safe," Tyar said.

Sparkena chuckled. "I wouldn't be much of a dragon if I couldn't control the air, now, would I?"

"A good answer, I guess," Tyar said.

"What about landfall?" Sparkena asked. "Where do you all wish to begin?"

Kilek looked to Paxoph and the man shook his head. "Even I haven't travelled far beyond the Wickerlands, remember, Kil?"

"Well," Mathi started, lifting her voice a little, "there's no point trying to pick up the trail from the western edge, but I'm torn between two better ideas."

"The eggs Sparkena mentioned?" Alira suggested.

She nodded. "We'd be saving a lot of lives if we can prevent them from hatching. We don't even know where our families have been taken. Or if they're alive," she said, lowering her voice on the final line.

Tyar put a hand on her shoulder. "It would be hard to find them, but it's too early to give up."

"He's right, Mathi," Kilek said as he met everyone's gaze. "We *can* find them. We're not the same scared villagers anymore. Somehow, even with my doubts, I'm beginning to think that Avendria was right to choose us. Because we actually did it – we found the dragons. No-one can stop us reaching Minjao, now. I don't even know if anyone can stop us when we get there, since we've finally got all the advantages!" Nods followed his words and Paxoph smiled as Kilek continued. "Not even Prince Yan will be difficult to find, if you think about it. Because his passing would have spread and probably lingered in each place. Especially with prisoners in tow. The only thing we really need now is a guide, since we'll stick out as foreigners while we search."

A sigh echoed from the dragon. "I have your answer, but first, I'm going to set you down somewhere. I need to eat. Cattle, before anyone asks."

"I'm not sure they want to be eaten either, Lord Sparkena," Alira said.

"True enough. But I'd make even more of a fuss if I swallowed half a Minjao village."

Sparkena dove, veering away from what seemed to be a large town below, and finding an empty field of grass instead. The colour verged on blue, long shadows visible where the field rested within a deep depression.

When the dragon beat his wings to slow his landing, dust stirred and the grass was flattened. They dismounted and started on a makeshift camp, gathering beneath a lone tree.

Large, fur-covered berries hung from spreading branches, but Kilek was not willing to try them, in case they were poisonous.

Sparkena left with a promise to return soon, and Kilek set off to gather as much firewood as he could find. Which wasn't a lot. Aside from the blue tint to the grass, still moving in the breeze, and the berries, the land of Minjao did not seem so different to western Luargot. *But the Wickerlands were a little more unique before their destruction, weren't they?*

When Kilek rejoined his friends, Pax had already started preparing a meal, having rummaged through their supplies, noting that food was running low. And while everyone certainly devoted plenty of time to discussing the problem, they were no closer to solving it when a voice called from across the field some time later.

Kilek stood, a hand on his blade, his actions mirrored by the others.

The stranger was a tall man wearing dark pants and red silks that fluttered in the wind. As he drew nearer, long black hair and fine, almost angular features became clear – a striking figure. Perhaps a local noble? When the man raised his hand to wave, however, brass knuckles were visible. "What do you think?" he asked when he stopped at the campsite's edge. "I've mostly chosen beauty over brawn."

Kilek stared at the stranger, his mind rather slow to pick up on the words – they'd been spoken in Luargot. Another detail that should have stood out was that fact that one of the man's eyes was actually a dark red. "Sparkena?"

"Of course," the Minjao stranger replied.

Around the camp, relief filled his friends' postures. Paxoph chuckled to himself. "You will be our guide, I take it?"

"Not precisely. I have no knowledge of modern Minuyjao." He toyed with the brass knuckles. "But I *will* be able to provide cover and ask questions easily enough. None of you speak Minjao, I assume?"

"No," Kilek said, but he was nodding. "This might work."

"Might?" Sparkena roared with laughter. "Might? Have some faith, Kilek. I'm a man of many talents, even if I'm not a man."

"What about the eggs?" Mathi asked.

"If you're close to running out of time, I will warn you," he replied. "Depending on where your families are, there's no reason you can't solve both problems. I can fly you where you choose, remember."

"Perfect."

"Then it's settled." Sparkena motioned them closer. "Gather round and I will show you what I know of our surroundings."

"Are we flying again?" Tyar asked. "I should probably just take a moment behind the tree first, if no-one minds."

"No need," the dragon replied. "I can show you from here."

Chapter 28.

Sparkena waved a hand over the grass between their feet, and a pale glow appeared, resolving into a map that bore shapes and contours: the dark mountains rose, the twisting rivers sparkled and the colourful cities shimmered. There was even an oversized tree with a red dragon beneath its shade to represent their own position.

"Amazing," Alira said, her eyes alight. "How do you make the horses run across the plain?"

The dragon smiled. "I've just replicated what I can see when I fly above the land. If you practise more with illusions, you'll be able to do something similar. Most likely, once you're about as good as you seem to be with those feathers of yours."

"You can also create illusions?" Tyar asked her. "I didn't realise. That could really come in handy."

She sighed. "Well, I'm almost always practising, but it's difficult."

"For now, let me draw everyone's attention to the following places that you will have to consider," Sparkena said. A walled town rose from near the tree. "First, a settlement of several thousand. A place for supplies, perhaps. Mere hours away, if you walk. Next, beyond these mountains to the north wait a large series of caves, resting near the ocean." Jagged coral reefs rose from the water. "This is where the Cabeku have their hatching groves. With horses, you would need to travel several weeks to reach it."

Mathi pointed to the largest city, a place filled with monuments and canals. "And this is the capital?"

"I assume it is still such."

"Fenkao-Hin," Paxoph added with a nod. "Probably only two weeks from the edge of the Wickerlands. Prince Yan may be there, I suppose. If not, someone who knows where he is *will* be. Or where our families have been taken."

"Yan mentioned protecting his people," Mathi said. "We assume it meant a war. Can you see where that is, Sparkena?"

The dragon pointed to a mighty forest that covered nearly a third of the map's west, where the nation of Jasoria had often struggled against Minjao. "Both here and to the north."

Tyar nodded slowly. "So, it's the Jasorians that we were conscripted to fight. I suppose it make sense."

"Still not our fight," Mathi added.

"Right."

Sparkena raised his hand. "I must note, it is not the forest-dwellers that the Minuyjao are fighting to repel. Did you not realise?"

"It's someone else?" Kilek asked.

"Yes. The Cabeku. I sense them attacking humans in great numbers to the west and north."

A hush fell over the group. Kilek stared down at the map.

"How?" And why would Javoteth unleash the Cabeku *upon his own people*? Did it mean Yan was fighting against the Cabeku in defiance of his own God… and, more alarmingly, that the prince was using the people of Luargot and possibly Jasoria as fodder?

Tyar kicked the tree. "He's using us so his own soldiers don't have to die."

Mathi's eyes flashed blue, but she did not speak.

"Possibly," Sparkena said. "It would be safest for me to search at night, if you wish. However, I cannot guarantee anything. Even with your scents as starting points, it is difficult to find specific people, especially if they bear no magic. I'd have to be *far* closer than half a nation."

Alira asked, "Would it be faster for us to search the towns and cities for information?"

Paxoph shrugged. "I don't think we'll know for sure until we try. Yan *was* training everyone to be a soldier, but what if something changed and we search in the wrong place?"

"That's where they are," Mathi said. "I'm certain."

"Don't be," Sparkena said. "You cannot rush this, human. Nor do you need to. I can take you to the front line *very* swiftly, once you have everything you need to make your decision."

She nodded, though it was a little short.

"If we do go west, what will we face?" Pax asked.

The dragon closed his eyes, as if remembering – or perhaps seeing what he described. "Death at every turn, I fear. The Minjao, and whoever they fight with, are facing hordes of Cabeku. They number in tens of thousands, and they continue to hatch from other groves there. It is a siege. The Minjao have given a lot of ground, loosing several cities and towns but for now, they seem to hold."

"Tens of thousands?" Kilek frowned. Whatever number of the insects Luargot had suffered so far was absolutely nothing in comparison. His friends appeared similarly concerned.

Sparkena opened his eyes, and his red eye seemed aflame. "Nothing that could stand against our fire."

Alira posed the question on Kilek's mind. "But how long until everyone else wakes and the Elder decides?"

"It could be days or a season."

"Do we have that long?"

The dragon shrugged. "I'd need to see the eggs to guess. You do have a difficult decision before you, but remember, Lilira and I will fight tooth-and-nail for Avendria's chosen, for these lands."

"And for that you will have our gratitude forever," Pax said. "We could not stand against the Cabeku without your aid."

Sparkena smiled. "I'm ready to burn whatever must be burned."

"Everyone," Alira started. "I'm finding it difficult to see how we can make the right choice. We actually have two hatcheries to destroy *and* we have to find our families at the same time. Avendria gave us these powers to stop the Cabeku, so that should be our path. We could start with the ocean hatchery since it's closer, then head west to wipe out the Cabeku there, and hopefully find everyone on the battle grounds, or find Yan wherever he is and get the answers we seek…"

"But?" Kilek asked, after she paused.

"I don't want to." Her expression was somewhat crestfallen.

"I'm sorry, everyone. But I want to find my father first."

Mathi strode across the group and took Alira into her arms. "We understand. Don't apologise."

Alira gripped Mathi tighter.

Sparkena was shaking his head, though he did not seem angry. "I keep telling you all, I am like the wind. No-one is faster than I. Well, perhaps my sister," he added with a grin. "But Avendria will not begrudge you a little time to yourselves. Especially with the giant eggs in the ocean being dormant still. Whatever your first step, I will take you there and then to the next step with barely a day between, if it need be coast to coast. So please, do as you must."

"Truly?" Tyar asked.

"You've flown with me already. You should know how fast I am. Have a little faith."

Chapter 29.

And so they had come to swift agreement indeed.

One trip into the large town nearby to test their story, though it seemed destined to succeed. After all, a Minjao mage with fresh conscripts would not be an unusual sight. Once they'd gathered whatever information they could, Sparkena would then fly everyone to the battle lines. There, at last, the search to rescue the people of Hasere could begin. Not just Alira's father, Paxoph's uncle or Innkeeper Ganoit, but everyone else that had been taken.

But as Kilek followed Sparkena toward the walls of Fadoi, set off from a highway paved in uneven stone, he came to unpleasant realisation – it was the first time in a long while that he'd even spared a thought for the others. *Can I even recall their faces properly?*

"Sparkena, can you speak modern Minjao?" Paxoph was asking as they neared Fadoi's open gate, which did not seem to have any guards. People in pale vests with dark, flower-like patterns had gathered together, but they did not appear to be armed. *What's their role in the town?*

"No," the dragon replied. "But I'll use what they'd consider an ancient tongue, and leave the rest up to my magic."

"To… make them understand the old words?"

"Approximately."

Tyar whistled. "Must be nice to be a dragon."

Sparkena laughed. "It's quite wonderful. Aside from the hibernation cycle – you'd probably find that little tedious. I know I do."

Beyond the open gate, they soon began to draw stares while striding down a wide street. They passed inns and taverns decorated by dried leaves, workers in their spotless aprons calling for customers. Sparkena greeted the locals, the sound of language familiar from Kilek's time in captivity, and while some people responded to him, few seemed willing to engage in much conversation.

Most frowned or looked away.

In spite of their poor welcome, Sparkena still received several recommendations for an inn. He chose one close to the centre of town with polished wooden windowsills and a painted door of deep green, which was in turn adorned by a gleaming knocker.

"Can we afford to stay here?" Alira asked.

"Just the one night," Sparkena replied. "And I have some jewels. Enough to pay."

Inside, the richness of the furnishings extended to the large rooms. Each included table and chairs enough for several to eat. In fact, the place bore no common room at all, as per the innkeeper's rather short answer, when Kilek asked via Sparkena.

After the dragon paid for their three rooms, they ate in small groups. Kilek found himself with Sparkena, who explained the food – most of which had been delivered on steaming plates by a cheerful young woman. "The smaller dish is full of spice," he said. "The meat is obviously savoury, and the little bowls are sweet."

Kilek's first bite was a burst of flavour, and he found himself gobbling up the rest. It wasn't until the sweet dishes that he had to stop, finding the flavour too intense. He slid the bowls across to the dragon. "Please finish mine, if you wish."

"Gladly."

Sparkena had barely finished swallowing the sweets when a knock came upon the door. Minjao words followed. Calm words spoken by a man. Kilek couldn't say why, but it didn't seem to be someone working at the inn.

"And your name?" Sparkena answered with equal calm.

Did I understand because of his magic?

"My name is Yenu." The man spoke with only lightly accented Luargot. "I am one of Lord Inacien's Knives. I must share news with your party."

Kilek half-rose. Potentially, it meant the man could be trusted. Unless he was not actually working for Lord Inacien at all.

The dragon looked to Kilek. "I do not know exactly what he claims to be, but I can tell you he is not lying."

"Then we should hear him out. Inacien is King Hadeon's spymaster."

"I'll call everyone," Sparkena said. "You let him in."

Kilek did so, admitting a local man with broad shoulders and hulking arms. It gave him the look of a blacksmith, and maybe he was. He nodded in greeting, but did not speak, seemingly content to wait for everyone else to crowd into the room.

Once Kilek explained the man's claims to his friends, he addressed Yenu. "We're all here."

"Thank you. I have news you must hear."

"Then you know where Yan took the people of our village?" Alira asked.

He nodded. "They were sent to the old mines."

A moment of quiet fell across them before she continued. "Not to the battle?"

"Lord Inacien is meticulous. He expects the same from us, Alira of Hasere. Most people from your village were sent north, that we know. Other conscripts went to the battle. Still more were taken to the capital for other menial tasks – usually to replace Minjao who have left or been killed in the war already."

"Is that what Yan planned all along? You're certain he didn't do something else with our friends and families?"

The man shook his head. "While his position within the court grows tenuous, he followed his uncle's orders. Reluctantly, some would say."

"Reluctantly?"

"At first, he spoke against conscripting from your lands, understanding that it could lead to a war on two fronts. He was overruled and eventually complied."

"Overruled by what? A madman?" Tyar asked.

"Some would say," the fellow replied, his gaze darkening.

"Meaning what?"

"Among other concerning stories, we have been encountering assassins that have been changed by magic – some have traded their ability to speak for strange powers that prevent them from being detected, for one. Some are less human than before," the man said. "Whatever the truth with the emperor, we believe Yan was more interested in locating the Night Thorn, and using *it* to protect Minjao lands."

"He still stole our families," Alira said.

"He did," the spy agreed.

Mathi folded her arms. "Where are these mines?"

"North, in the mountains by the Coral Coast of Arjei."

She exchanged a glance with Sparkena before looking back to the spy. "You're certain?"

"I am. But I must warn you all. *Something* is being hidden there. We have sent several Knives to follow, and none have returned," he said, before his voice grew heavier still. "Lord Inacien himself included."

Chapter 30.

In the pre-dawn light, they flew north toward Arjei's Coral Coast, dim landscape flowing below. Once again, Sparkena protected everyone from a howling wind that should have ripped them from his scales all-too-easily.

"Do you think we shouldn't have told him?" Paxoph was asking, now able to be heard during flight, thanks to Sparkena adjusting his magic as needed – another reminder of just how far-ranging a dragon's abilities really were.

Kilek glanced back toward the tiny spot of light that was the slowly-waking town of Fadoi. It probably *was* better for the spy to be aware that a Cabeku hatchery waited by the mine, as confirmed by Sparkena. But no matter where the spy's loyalties truly lay, Minjao soldiers would probably soon be on the march.

"You all worry too much," Sparkena said. "No-one is going to beat me to the reefs – and once more, I'd appreciate some positivity, children. Take heart! Things are going to change now that you've called us, remember?"

"So it seems."

He chuckled. "If you absolutely must worry, then let it be about Prince Yan's uncle."

"Yenu didn't argue with me about the emperor sounding like a madman," Tyar said with a frown. "And if he really has taken to twisting people into mute assassins with silent footsteps, then we cannot let our guard down."

"So he may be, based on his actions. But I suspect it is worse. I spoke with Yenu again, after you'd all sought your rest and he shared one more thing."

"Because of your magic?"

"That may have helped, but I believe it likely because he took me for one of his countrymen – and I must add that I heard similar things in the streets when I sought confirmation."

"It's worse?" Kilek asked.

"Yes. Emperor Xiadan does not only seek dominion over his old enemy but has plans to invade both Jasoria and the lands beyond the northern ranges, at first."

"While fighting the Cabeku?"

"Perhaps not. For I suspect this means Javoteth has chosen one Anesca in the emperor, and set madness loose upon this land. The God cares not for his own people, because he wishes to devour all, just as Avendria warned." Sparkena tilted his wings to avoid a notably slower flock of birds. "We dragons have fought other iterations of the Cabeku in generations past, and there is something you may not yet know."

"Bad news, right?" Tyar asked.

"Yes. Cabeku learn and change quickly. A hive-mind, is the phrase we once had. What one creature learns before and even *in* death, all have learnt. New insects are born with better knowledge. Better bodies."

Kilek was nodding slowly despite the horrifying news. They'd certainly encountered more than one size or type of insect already, including two seemingly distinct humanoid creatures.

"We've seen them change, even in a short time," Paxoph said, his own expression troubled.

"And it will only go faster," the dragon said. "Especially if, as I suspect, Emperor Xiadan has been forcing his people to fight the insects in order to train them."

"With the blood of his own people," Alira said, her voice lowered.

"So it was in the past, yes," Sparkena said.

Tyar's frown only grew deeper. "That's definitely the kind of secret I can imagine Lord Inacien being able to ferret out."

"Do you think he's still alive?" Alira asked.

"I'd be surprised if he *wasn't*," Mathi replied. "It's just as likely that he's chasing Nakir again, which is good for us."

Kilek nodded, and silence fell across them.

"You know," Tyar started, after a long moment had passed. "I actually *was* feeling more hopeful. Especially once we found out that no-one had been sent to the battle, but now you're telling us we're going to be facing stronger, smarter Cabeku? Because that's obviously what's been stopping Lord Inacien's Knives from reaching the mine."

"Are you not stronger and smarter compared to whenever you set out?" Sparkena asked.

"We all are," Tyar said. "But is it enough?"

"You can find out shortly," the dragon replied as he banked, heading for a partial clearing below. Shadowy trees protected the clearing where it sat on a ridge. It overlooked the coast, sheltered by a mountainous region with a barren valley within. There, a large camp had been established.

But it wasn't until Sparkena drew closer to the treetops that Kilek got a better sense of the scale; rows and rows and rows of tents, enough for close to two hundred soldiers, surely. Campfires suggested a first meal being prepared in the growing light of morning, but he could also see something nearby, which led off toward an opening at the mountain's base – a series of pens and cages.

"How many dozen Cabeku would fit in each one?" Alira asked from beside him.

Kilek nodded, but did not have an answer.

Once the dragon had let everyone dismount, they gathered at the ridge, crouching to look down on the camp. "Wherever the hatcheries lie exactly, we can't ignore that many soldiers," Paxoph said, his arms folded.

"And how do we find everyone?" Alira asked.

Mathi turned to Sparkena, who had already transformed into his human form. "You said before that you'd have to be closer to sense our families. Is this close enough?"

He nodded. "Although, it's also close enough for any mages down there to sense us, if they're looking."

"Do you think they saw us land?" Alira asked.

"I cannot say for certain. But they'll be looking with more than their eyes," he said, before closing his own.

In the hush that followed, Kilek found himself holding his breath.

"They are not in the camp," the dragon soon said. "None even from Deluargot can be found below. They're being kept inside the mine itself, I believe. There are humans quite similar to you beneath the mountain."

Mathi slammed a fist into her palm. "Perfect – you can burn them all."

"Wait, Mathi…" Alira seemed about to say more, but trailed off.

Sparkena merely observed them.

And while Paxoph and Tyar murmured something, Kilek found his gaze drawn to the camp. Even if only Minjao soldiers were down there, even if it was to save the people of Hasere, did that make it right? Even in war? Even in a war where enemy soldiers worked with ravenous insects?

To simply burn them all to the ground?

"I have no qualms about this, if that is why you hesitate," the dragon said. "As soldiers, death is a risk they all accept."

Alira was shaking her head. "But we don't know if they're all down there by choice."

Mathi's hands remained fisted at her sides. "Anyone who wanted to desert rather than work with the Cabeku could have done so by now."

"Ali. They've got our family underground," Tyar added, then pointed. "But they're keeping the *insects* above ground. In the air. They're treating Ganoit and your father worse than those monsters."

She blinked through tears. "I know. But it's wrong. We're not like them."

"We might have to be," Mathi said.

Pax cleared his throat. "We can't afford to change *that* much."

Mathi flung her hands into the air. "Then what? How do we pass through? How do we make sure we aren't followed into the mine? How do we get through and then get everyone home *after*? We don't have a choice."

"We always have a choice," Alira said, her tone sharp.

"Do you have a better idea?" Mathi glared back at Alira, and almost as one, Tyar moved to Mathi as Pax took a step closer to Alira.

Yet no-one spoke, and Alira only shrugged.

Mathila spun to face Kilek. "Well? What do you think, Kil?"

He turned back from the camp below to find all eyes focused on him. Expectant. *As though I'm suddenly our leader.* But he didn't know what to say. They were both right. *Everyone* was right. Anything he said, someone would be unhappy.

Disappointed.

And no matter what was decided, a lot of people would die. People who were committing evil acts… and… people he would not have to face. Not have to actually kill by his own hand.

Or claw.

Why doesn't that make this any easier?

Inaction was its own curse, too. The people of Hasere deserved to return home.

Finally, he exhaled – yet it was tinged with relief, since he had an answer. A painful one, if he could take it. If he could swallow past the lump in his throat and speak. And no-one else seemed able… "Before I tell you what I think, will you each promise me something?"

"What?" Mathi asked, and the others were expectant.

"That you'll accept what I say. That you promise not to argue or blame each other. I'll make the decision and you can all feel better knowing you didn't have to do it." He raised a hand before Pax could speak, noting the way Tyar and Alira both glanced toward their feet. "But if I do this, I really am going to lead," he said, and though he stumbled over the last words, he meant them.

Silence followed his declaration. It seemed that maybe Mathila tried not to smile. Or was it something else? Not amusement... It could have been pride? "Tell us, Kil," she said, then glanced around. "I don't think we're going to object."

And when no-one did, he nodded. "Then I have a question for Sparkena."

"Please."

"Can you drive the soldiers away without killing every single person in the camp?"

"Of course," he said with a nod. "But survivors present a risk for your escape. I present just one possibility. What will you do if I drive at least half of them away, and they return just as we bring your friends and family out from the mine? Can you hold them all off while the people of Hasere climb aboard? If the Minjao bring reinforcements?" He paused to tilt his head. "And sadly, there's a mage who's found us, now. You don't have much time left to decide."

Kilek exhaled and turned back to the slowly-lightening camp. *Forgive me... I think.* "It's not only our families we have to protect, by doing this," he said. "It's everyone. It's every nation. We know that."

Alira put a hand on his shoulder. "Kilek?"

He swallowed as he turned. "Don't blame anyone else, Ali."

Her gaze widened.

Kilek looked to Sparkena and nodded. "Clear a path for us."

Chapter 31.

Soot and ash dragged at his feet.

Kilek avoided glimmering red embers where he trudged through the camp. The distant sound of Sparkena's roar as the dragon chased down survivors was faint, especially compared to the hard breathing from his friends.

Or maybe it's mine?

The terrible, blooming orange that crashed down from the sky earlier had not truly left his mind. It clung to him somehow, interfering with his vision of the smouldering death that surrounded them. Most shapes were hard to recognise be they tent, wagon or weapon. But the few bodies that hung together in black… those were more than he'd bargained for.

Not the corpses that might have been insects – the bodies of people.

People who'd fled, perhaps caught at the edge of powerful flames.

I made this happen.

Blackened claws stretched up from the ashes. Shrivelled

bodies with nub-like heads that had been pummelled into the very earth by fire. The lone limbs. Pieces that were only vaguely recognisable… and the scents that struck as they passed by – sweet, nauseating scents that grew acrid near the pens. So strong that his eyes watered.

He turned away, leading everyone to an ash-strewn road bound for the mine's dark maw.

What horrors are we going to face inside?

Kilek stopped and Paxoph joined him. "Pax. Will you hold this a moment?" He extended his pack before starting on his borrowed clothes. "We don't know what we'll find down there, so I'm changing now," he explained, then glanced to his other friends too. "I don't know if you want to look away… it's probably not pretty, when I change."

"With what I've witnessed here, I don't think I will be too disturbed," Pax replied as he collected more garments, and the others turned their backs. "But give me a moment and I'll turn around, too."

"Right." Kilek removed the last of his clothing and let his dragon side come to the fore – glad not only for the moment of privacy, but for the ability to hide his face from the others.

To hide doubts about the choice he'd made.

"It's a good idea, Kil," Mathi said, her back still turned. "We don't know how long Sparkena will need. And even if word doesn't spread from the… firestorm, we're still in hostile territory."

Go, Kilek. I will find the last of the survivors and guard the rear. Mathila is more right than she knows – additional Cabeku are already coming. They know the threat you pose.

"Can you deal with them all?" Kilek asked, speaking

aloud, assuming the dragon would still hear, somehow. Mathi and the others turned, expressions of confusion plain, but seemed to understand when he gestured to Sparkena's general direction.

Of course, and yes, I can hear you. It's also far easier when you've transformed. And I know that this is late for advice, but eat before you change. It will delay the cravings.

"I've missed that chance this time."

There's something you can drink, if desperate. I'll arrange for it to be made for the future, the dragon said. *Move swiftly down there. I sense something in the ocean.*

"In the ocean? What do you mean?"

Those hatcheries rest underneath the mine, deeper – in caves beneath the waves. And something old is moving down there.

He nodded. "I might know what that is."

Then be careful. Bring your families out of there and I will fly them home.

"Thank you, Sparkena." Kilek accepted his pack from Pax, both he and Tyar helping arrange it, remarking upon the way his lack of wings helped with the task. Kilek glanced at the group, and though Alira did not meet his eyes, he found it easy enough to continue – now that he'd made the change, even being essentially naked in half dragon-form. "He said that the hatcheries are actually below the ocean, in the caves, so we'll have to work quickly."

"But we'll free everyone else, first, right?" Tyar asked.

"We will," Kilek said as he led them past a shattered mine cart. Debris from what was once a crate and another item was less clear, these smothered in soot or melted into new, awful shapes.

Yet, being in his dragon form, it was all a little easier to face.

The destruction had lessened by the time they entered the mine, where more carts and neat stacks of equipment waited – save for a conspicuous pick-axe lying abandoned upon the steel track.

A large space off to the side seemed to contain sleeping quarters. It was a rather modest, thin construction for a guardroom. Empty, too – confirmed when he approached to peer through the windows. There, an overturned table and spilled food was drawing flies, lanterns still burning strong.

"Look at the stone," Tyar said. He took a lantern then pointed. "There's more on the ceiling."

Kilek looked up but saw only shadows. Even his presumably superior-to-human dragon's gaze wasn't better than Tyar's eyes, but the walls were clearer. There, light penetrated enough to reveal uneven stripes of blue and grey, some peeling away. Only, when he neared they did not have the look of bark, moss or some other plant-life, but brittle-seeming rock.

"It might be dangerous," Tyar said. "I don't see it being used for anything here. And since this place is a mine, wouldn't that make this stuff worth harvesting, if it was safe?"

"Agreed," Paxoph said.

"It continues down each tunnel." Kilek approached the first and strained his admittedly still-new senses... but found what seemed to be familiar scents. No-one specific, but most recently, plenty of people from Hasere had passed down, along with several Minjao. Their scents were understandably different, yet he could not put a finger on exactly how.

No matter. "This one," he said as he pointed.

"Guards too?" Mathi asked. "Some would have fled Sparkena by heading down there, I'd wager."

"I can't tell their number, but I can sense them."

"What of Lord Inacien?"

He shook his head. "I don't think so."

"And the Cabeku?"

"Nothing yet," Kilek said as he led them down. "Stay alert, everyone."

The mine shaft had been lined by wooden supports, spaced evenly between walls and smaller passages, all bearing their share of tool marks. So, too, the strange patterns followed the main passage. Here, they had been cut back so only tiny strips in certain places protruded from the walls. Sometimes, the passage grew quite steep, which would make the climb back up arduous. Just how often was everyone forced to make the trip? And were the Minjao mining the strips, after all? There didn't seem to be precious stones or minerals – or anything else of value within.

And the camp above could tell no tales about it, either.

Whatever the case, without sign of guard or villager, they had to travel deeper.

Kilek led the way until a chill filled every breath he took, an oppressive damp that weighed heavily. He pressed on, claws scratching as he quickened his stride. The others kept pace without complaint, and only slowed when he finally raised a hand.

An open chamber, at last.

Here, pens of steel and wood revealed the people of Hasere dressed in filthy smocks and chained to the stone. Crates of food were stacked beside water-barrels, basically in reach – so long as the prisoners passed provisions around the camp.

A wave of relief slowed his steps. Yet his approach seemed to draw nothing but wide-eyed fear, and even whimpers from some. He moved to the back of the group, urging someone else to speak.

Yet even that did not go well when Paxoph attempted to calm everyone.

"You aren't Orasef's nephew. That much is obvious." One man spoke up, chains sliding as he moved closer to the torchlight to fold his arms. And though they hung thin within his sleeves, and though his face was just as gaunt, the man *was* familiar... Ganoit.

Silvery touches to the hair at his temples were gone now – instead, barely a glimpse of *black* left behind. Once reddened cheeks were pale and lined. His eyes bore a deep distrust – and why not?

Tyar stepped forward. "Gan, it's me. Tyar. Look closely." He addressed everyone, as the innkeeper frowned. "You know me. You know us all. Please. Avendria changed us so that we could save you."

An older woman gripped Ganoit's arm – it was Delielle, Blacksmith Oran's wife. "It's another trick," she said, her own expression hard. And while she appeared strong as ever, her hands bore coloured stripes not unlike those found on the walls... "They travel with a monster, after all."

Kilek did not reply, though for a moment, he considered transforming back. But doing so would leave him vulnerable to attack from guards or whatever new and troubling type of Cabeku waited further below.

Mathi raised her voice. "Stop wasting time, everyone! We can free you – we even have a dragon to fly you home, but you have to trust us. I *am* Mathila. The Minjao killed Amain and Gabriette and I buried them before following you here – me, Kilek, Tyar, Pax and Alira beside me. Be afraid if you must, but don't spoil this chance at freedom."

Silence. Ganoit was still studying Tyar, as more and more people came closer. Murmurs rose, a few eyes twinkled with hope too, smiles following as people whispered to each other, cautious as they crept toward belief.

"Answer me this, then." The innkeeper had moved on to studying each face – save for Kilek. "Who found the Summer Star old El wove back when you were younglings."

"I did," Alira replied. "It had gotten stuck to a merchant's wagon, somehow. I found it on the southern road at dusk, because the fabric caught just enough of the fading light for me to spot it."

Murmurs of joy rose, and the innkeeper grinned – now pulling Tyar close. "My lad. We'd almost given up all hope."

Still others came forward, the limits of their chains preventing them from reaching out, but his friends moved among them. Kilek held back while the happy reunions took place, with much smiling and laughter.

But it soon faded when the people described how splinters and fragments of the coloured strips latched onto them when they worked, blending with their skin. For some, it made them ill, weakened them – sometimes to death. Others, it strengthened somehow. Those, the Minjao were pleased with, since it allowed for longer working hours.

"I don't see my uncle," Pax asked. "Is that what happened to him? He's working elsewhere in the mine?"

No-one answered at first. A nervous determination grew as the villagers gathered, freed by Mathi and Alira while they spoke. Some, those who needed help to stand, leant on those with striped skin – colours sometimes escaping from their sleeves, or climbing up from their throats.

"Lad, they sent him away to help fight insects," Ganoit eventually replied with a shake of his head. "I don't understand it, but they claim that the insects *here* aren't so bad. It never made sense."

Pax stiffened. "They what?"

"One of the westerners thought he'd be able to help them build and repair whatever it is they use to fight back."

"Then… he might not have had to fight himself?"

"By Avendria, I hope it so," Ganoit replied. "And before now, I might not have made that prayer but it seems the Goddess isn't the one who turned away from us."

"Perhaps," Mathi said. "What of the guards?"

Ganoit nodded, seeming to have missed the trace of pain in her voice. "Headed deeper. Only three left, but down there is where we sometimes see the bigger insects. Some walk like men."

Delielle waved her hand. "But they die like men too. The accident with the overloaded cart proved that."

Pax moved closer. "Delielle, can I examine your hand now? I may be able to help."

She frowned. "Can't be helped."

He turned to Alira. "We must try."

She nodded but did not speak from where she sat, holding her father's hand. He had not said much either, and now that Kilek took a closer look, the man bore more stripes upon his face, sliding down from within his receding hairline. Even his gaze was listless; nothing like the sharp gaze of a man who'd been quick to make a joke or surprise the children with his sleight of hand, doing his best to keep them entertained during classes.

Kilek, you must strike now. Keep going.

He stepped away as the others worked together to help Pax and Alira, gasps and more murmurs rising from the villagers at the golden, healing light. "Sparkena?"

There is nothing down there that can match you as you are – leave your friends to finish the rescue. I will meet them outside as soon as I can.

"Are they hatching already?"

Only one. It's being encouraged by the guards. I doubt they will succeed in full, but even a failure will be a problem. Go, now.

Kilek removed his pack, then charged for the only exit that led deeper.

Shouted questions followed him but he didn't stop. "Look after everyone," he called back. "I have to stop one of the eggs."

"Wait, don't you need help?"

"Sparkena didn't think so." Kilek barely slowed, lifting his arm in a wave.

And neither do I.

Chapter 32.

The deeper he went, the more his eyes adjusted to the darkness, and with the strange stripes offering a very faint glow, he had no trouble finding a way. The urgency of Sparkena's words had driven him on, claws scraping the stone once more, but he eventually had to stop for a cave-in.

Or perhaps a deliberate blockage, since some light peeked through gaps at the top of the slide. Kilek sucked in a mighty breath and sprayed the rubble with silver mist. It creaked into a different stillness, something that would be perfectly brittle beneath his fists.

He hurled his first strike. Shards of rock flew.

From behind the wall, a shout of warning in the Minjao tongue. *Good, I'm closer than I thought.* Kilek exhaled again, followed by another series of blows – breaking free with a roar.

Nearby, two armed figures fell back.

Watery, shifting light flooded a vast chamber with tiled walls and floor. The two men who were scrambling away obscured his view of evenly-spaced alcoves resting at floor-level. Green uniforms without heron markings suggested both were regular soldiers – no threat.

It was what lay beyond that he had to worry about.

A black egg, several storeys tall, rested beneath a clear ceiling of glass. Or something far stronger, surely. The ceiling revealed floating lights within dark water, the distant surface too far above to see daylight.

And flickering at the edges of the light, the faintest touches of red. Sentient veins?

Or something else?

The soldiers pushed themselves to their feet, spears in hand. Kilek unleased his stone-breath again, encasing both almost instantly. He glanced at the little openings near the floor as he approached the egg; all empty. Cabeku hideaways? If not, what were they for?

Nothing important, until he learnt otherwise.

Kilek circled the dark shell, discovering two more chambers. Both contained eggs, but no sign that either were close to hatching. At least, not the first two, being the ones he could see clearly. *Hurry up, fool.* He spat forth more stone-breath and a large section of the shell grew grey.

He drew back his arm and punched through. Large pieces of shell clattered to the floor, revealing green, pulsating mucus.

"You too." Kilek tore into it with his claws, only pausing to rip more of the shell free – creating a bigger opening. He slashed deeper, slicing and tearing, mucus splashing around his legs and soon covering his scales. Yet it did not burn, for it was not acidic. Instead, it gave him strength, as though his arms would never tire, as though he could crack the entire egg in half with a single blow.

Now able to climb inside, he finally found the softer, more translucent shell of the Cabeku itself. It towered over him, the tips of dozens of legs only half-visible, most of it lost within the rest of the egg. He sucked air into his lungs and let the stony mist burst free, tearing up through the Cabeku like a whirlwind.

The legs twitched and then fell still as the creature began to sink toward the egg's base.

Kilek freed himself with a grunt, then strode to the second shell. More mucus dripped to the tiles as he strode forward, but it continued to energise him too. At the second egg, he took half a running swing.

A sharp crack split the shell clean in half.

Both sides crashed against the walls and tiles clattered to the floor. A clear shape was revealed this time. Even half-buried in gunk, dozens of legs were visible, folded wings and over-sized mandibles all towering over him. Not so large as the thing everyone fought with Florique, but presumably, it would grow.

"Not that I'm giving it a chance," he muttered as he stepped forward with another roar.

A wall of silvery mist sprayed from his lungs, entombing more than half the creature.

One left.

Kilek strode into the final chamber, met by the scent of steel, faint beneath the sharpness of mucus. A third soldier hid somewhere in the room. Kilek circled the egg and there, another Minjao. This one stood before a funnel that had been inserted into the shell, and was pouring what looked like blood into the egg. Feeding it?

"No!" Kilek exhaled and the man was frozen in stone.

He stomped forward and smashed the funnel free before swinging again – shattering the shell to pieces.

Flashing limbs of white shot forth.

Pain erupted in his abdomen and shoulder as he hit the tiles, a grunt of shock following. Worse, he'd been pinned to the wall. A third limb flashed toward his face. He twisted his head. Tiles shattered by his ear. He spluttered more mist, almost a reflex. Stone cracked then broke – dumping him to the floor.

But it wasn't enough. Pain swam across his body in dark waves now, as if pressing him down.

The Cabeku had found its way free, hulking within the chamber, rows of eyes regarding him from above – and *around* – pairs of darkening mandibles that dwarfed him where he lay. Kilek sucked in another breath, only for fresh agony to interrupt.

My ribs…

The Cabeku would devour him.

A torrent of black water crashed down from the ceiling. The ocean filled the space, bubbling like a storm. The churn tossed him this way and that, spinning Kilek until he slammed into another wall.

He cried out again, water rushing into his lungs.

No! I can't drown here!

Somehow, he forced the water back out thanks to his power but it wasn't enough. His strength was already flagging… And then calm. Quiet. He blinked at the stillness. At the wall of bubbles packed tightly around him, at their little fins.

Saved by the Creeping Death! Even the pain was fading where mucus still clung to his wounds… *Is that safe?*

He coughed up more water, retching upon his hands and knees.

Something stung his neck – strong enough to find a way between scales, and then he was floating up, out of the chamber into the ink of the deep ocean. He twisted, catching a glimpse of something red dragging the enormous form of the Cabeku deeper.

We have saved you, of course. You have a task yet to complete. The wall of veins, speaking again in his mind. *And yes, you will survive your wounds. In part due to your transformation, in part due to healing properties found within the egg-womb of those creatures.*

"Are you certain?"

Verily.

"And that Cabeku?"

Is already dead.

Kilek didn't ask for any more details. "I have to make sure my friends are safe."

We will return you. Continue your transformation and come to us once more.

"Thank you," he replied, but could not hold back a frown. What more could he become?

Chapter 33.

Kilek splashed through the shallows, avoiding the sharpest parts of a colourful reef. Most of his pain and difficulty moving was gone by the time the mine's entrance came into view, where Sparkena and a second dragon waited – Lilira, by her pink and silver scales. And while she was smaller, it was not by much.

Was she younger, perhaps?

He glanced up at the noon sun. It hadn't taken so long to escape the depths, surely? But then, maybe it had. *I'm already tired of dragging myself from the ocean.* Twice was enough. *Not to mention this blasted coral.*

But he still found himself able to smile as he came to a halt, letting his shoulders slump a little. The people of Hasere were already being loaded onto small, makeshift platforms upon the backs of the dragons, ready to be flown home.

Despite his relief, there was no rush to rejoin everyone. The villagers would only ask about his transformation, or ask if he wanted to give a message to his sister. And there was nothing to say and much to do – another hatchery had to be destroyed and Paxoph's uncle needed rescuing.

The longer he watched, the more it became clear that the village of Hasere, while never truly large, would not be welcoming scores of its members home.

Only dozens.

Kilek turned his gaze on Sparkena specifically, trying to somehow drive his question across the space between them without shouting, just by adding the desire to his words. "How long will it take to get them home and return here?"

You're dragging your feet, aren't you?

"A little. You knew I survived?"

Sensed it once you escaped that… deep presence.

"It expects something of me – when I'm ready, whatever that means. It seemed to think I'd transform again. Is that possible? And do you know what *it* is?"

No. I don't believe it revealed itself last time I was up and about. Maybe the Elder will know. You can ask him yourself, if you like.

"Do you mean that he's awake?"

He's already sent someone to collect you. So be ready, whoever it is will arrive soon. Before the Minjao or more Cabeku, thankfully. And to answer your question, it depends.

"On what?"

Your choices. For now, you've got enough to worry about growing accustomed to the existing changes. As an example, you shouldn't transform until you're fully healed.

"You mean that my human body would be –"

In some pain and not in any condition to fight. It is best you wait until tomorrow morning. Something about the Cabeku egg's mucus seems to be helping, but don't rush.

"Understood," Kilek said. "Will you meet us on the Sky Islands?"

Most likely. Across the way, Sparkena was already rising, his wings stirring dust. *Rejoin them, put their minds at ease.*

"I will." Kilek picked up his pace, drawing nearer, waving to both dragons as they flew overhead, wheeling toward the distant lands of Luargot. Toward home. *Why don't I feel any urge to go back?*

He called to the others as he neared, and while relief was clear on everyone's faces, Alira didn't actually speak to him. Before he could even consider it properly, he found himself answering questions. By the time he'd explained what had happened, another dragon approached.

This dragon bore scales of a dark blue, and when it landed, again stirring dust and ash, it regarded them from quite an elaborately horned head. "Well met, Anesca. I am Ketaket. I understand Sparkena has already explained that Elder Usvedal wishes to speak to you."

"Thank you for taking us," Kilek said.

"Wonderful." The dragon extended a mighty wing. "Please, climb on and we will be off."

Kilek and his friends did so and swiftly took to the skies, once more protected by magic far, far beyond what seemed possible.

They spoke little, perhaps mostly just relieved to have seen their loved ones heading for home, where surely the king would have by now restored the village. *But that's not quite true, is it?* Pax still had plenty to worry about, and Mathi would never see her parents again, thanks to Prince Yan…

As they neared the same expansive Sky Island that

contained the enormous bone ridge, Ketaket seemed to be growling. When the dragon dipped down to land with something of a thud, the ridge was near, visible in glimpses above the treetops resting below. Was it the Elder's seat?

More importantly, why was Ketaket growling?

"My apologies, all. But I must leave you here," the blue dragon said. "A giant Cabeku is attacking the nests, and Usvedal requests my assistance."

Before Kilek or anyone else could speak from their new position on the soil, the dragon's wings were already thrusting it back into the air, stirring their hair and clothes, even driving him back a step. "Wait," he called. "Where is the Elder?"

Regenerating on a nearby island. You can reach it via the White Wing below, if you do not wish to wait. I imagine you ought to be able to restore it. Otherwise, I will return when I have vanquished the Cabeku. The dragon's final words were faint, and his blue scales were already blending into the bright sky.

"Did everyone hear that?" Kilek asked.

"We did," Tyar said, nods following from everyone else. "Should we take his advice, and head for this White Wing, wherever it is?"

Paxoph gestured toward the bottom of the hill. "It probably lies near that white stone down there. Little else seems of note."

Mathi started forward, pointing to an overgrown trail. "This way, I suppose." The trail circled the hillside, leading down toward a forest that concealed most of their view of the white ridge... maybe it was bone, after all?

Kilek took rear guard, his clawed feet making steeper

parts of their trip easy enough but before they reached the woods themselves, he stumbled to one knee.

It had not been his grip that failed him.

Pain seared the insides of his stomach. So strong that he could not at first recognise the cause – hunger. Hunger once again. The price of his transformations? Of his recovery? *Just like when I pushed myself fighting off the Blood Wolves.*

Ahead, his friends walked on, but the scent of their flesh lingered.

He opened his mouth and drool hit the earth.

No!

Kilek slammed a fist into the golden grass. "Pax, I need my clothes," he called, keeping his voice even as best he could, and more, keeping his eyes fixed on the ground so as not to be tempted by the sight of flesh...

Footsteps approached. "Is something wrong?" his friend asked.

"Only if I don't change back," Kilek said. He ground his teeth – his fangs, really – and closed his eyes too, reaching down for what was human to close off his dragon side, to forget about cold scales and searing hunger.

And it worked.

Somehow, it worked! Whether desperation or something else, he'd succeeded – the hunger hadn't been enough to stop him. It even faded swiftly, replaced by a normal, human appetite with no desire to eat his friends. Throbbing pain in his torso returned too, but he was able to rise. He accepted his clothing from Paxoph, along with his pack, which was a little too light now.

"Thank you," he said as he began to dress, moving swiftly enough to fumble – being dragon-naked was one thing, but human-naked was another thing entirely.

Even – or especially – in front of his friends.

"You're wounded, Kil."

He tied his belt, glancing at the fresh scars upon his torso. "It was the Cabeku." He ran his fingers across the scars, not tender beneath a light touch, at least. "It could be worse."

"Let me help anyway." Paxoph reached out and gold glowed. The pain vanished, along with redness from the wounds; more, a tenseness to his entire body was now simply floating away. His mind cleared of doubts, especially about the Cabeku mucus, and even his hunger faded. He smiled. It was as if Avendria herself had expressed approval for all that he'd done so far.

"I didn't know that your healing could do this, too," Kilek said, speaking softly.

He grinned. "It's a little different for everyone, if you're talking about how you feel in your mind."

"Well, I'm really glad," he said as he finished dressing.

"Hurry up, you two," Tyar called.

"On our way," Paxoph replied, and together they continued toward the forest, where leaves of green and red were fluttering to the earth, slowed by a rising breeze.

Kilek checked on his friend as they walked. "What about you, Pax?"

"How am I feeling?"

"Yes. I thought it might have been a little difficult to see Sparkena and his sister taking everyone home."

He nodded. "In a way. But I am happy for everyone, Kil. And there's no need for me to give up hope. If he really was taken for his skill at fixing things, then there's a fair chance he's still alive."

"Right. We'll find him. After all, we found everyone else," he said, and then he sighed. "Those who'd survived, at least. Were you able to save them from those stripes?"

He frowned. "To be honest, I don't really know what they were, so I can't be sure. But I was able to help everyone, at least a little. Some quite a lot. Whatever it was, it resisted my healing."

"You must be tired, then."

Pax's smile split his beard. "I don't think I can remember a time when I wasn't weary down to my bones. Isn't it the same for you?"

"Not right now, actually. I feel more alert, more focused. Stronger."

"Well, I can ask Avendria for strength too, if I decide things are that dire. And if I'm lucky enough that she deems me worthy."

He hesitated. "That sounds like you think she might refuse."

"Her gift is for others. If I give in to selfishness and use it on myself, she may not grant my request when I next need to help another person."

Now Kilek stopped. "That's not fair."

Pax looked to the trees ahead. "I'm not sure I disagree, but I have to work within the limits of my gift if I want to heal people. And I do, Kil. It's a beautiful gift I've been given."

"Well…" There was a kind of Goddess-logic to what his friend described. And everyone had limits imposed on their gifts – yet, it was too cruel. Even if Pax seemed happy enough. "Then make me a promise, will you? Ask *us* for help if you need it. We're going to worry about you, since you're

worrying about us."
He smiled. "You have my promise."

Chapter 34.

Two large Cabeku corpses lay within the shade of the forest, a single red leaf caught within broken wings.

"These are certainly different," Mathi said from where she knelt.

Ichor had pooled, leaking from between the usual segmented bodies of a darkened purple, but this pair were closer to the size of dogs rather than cats. More, their wings were smaller – too small for them to fly? Their many legs bore red, mottled hooks and were obviously responsible for the churned loam leading deeper into the forest.

When Kilek joined her, it became clear something had sliced both creatures clean in half. *Not so different from when Tyar and I found the first ones.*

"Look at what they did to the ground," Alira said. "And the trees."

Not just torn earth and crushed shrubs but trunks, too, looked to have been mauled. A series of blossoms peeked from where they'd been trampled into the loam.

"What are they doing up here?" Tyar asked. "They can't

really pose a threat to the dragons, not at this size. Or number."

"That would be the giant one," Mathi said with a nod. "These are more like scouts."

"Scouting what? Our destination?"

"Or *us*, perhaps," Pax said.

"Why not?" Tyar nodded. "So, based on their wings, I suppose they rode up on whatever is attacking the dragons' nest?"

"That could be the case," Pax replied.

"We also need to know what sliced them in half." Kilek gestured to the bodies as he rose, heading deeper into the forest. "Watch for threats."

Tyar chuckled. "Aren't we always doing that?"

"It definitely seems that way."

His friends readied their weapons – or appeared a little more watchful in the case of Paxoph – as they headed deeper into the forest. The high sun overhead promised a hot day, but shade from the canopy offered protection upon the still-overgrown path.

Once, Kilek caught a hint of movement, but it was only a deer bounding away.

Near what he hoped was the far side of the woods, he stopped before a patch of plum trees, their dark fruit ripe enough to eat where it hung, with several already lying on the grass below.

Considering how empty his pack was, and how the grumbling in his stomach had only grown as they walked, surely a minor risk was worth taking. And right after being healed by the Goddess? He reached up and snapped a few plums free, then took a bite. The juice and flesh hit his tongue in a mix of sweet and sour. "They're amazing," he said, and pulled a few more plums free, tossing them to his friends, who approached with smiles.

Save for Alira.

While she did eat the plums, it seemed she was still making some effort to avoid him; instead choosing to speak softly with Mathi upon the trail while Kilek and the others gathered more fruit. "Some meat wouldn't go astray, either," Tyar was saying.

"You didn't shoot that deer from earlier," Paxoph observed.

Tyar shrugged. "It seemed wrong. I don't know why. It's this place… I don't want to disturb it any more than the Cabeku already have."

Kilek swallowed another mouthful of the delicious plum. "I understand."

Mathi raised her voice from where she and Alira stood a short distance away. "I can see a path out of the wood."

After taking their fill of fruit, Kilek led the others out into the sunshine, only to come to a halt immediately.

Their destination stood before them. Not a building or a pale ridge of stone, but bone in the form of a gargantuan dragon's skull. It reared over another wood that lay upon a hillside, its jaws closed, eyes like caverns and its horns extending back almost as modest mountain peaks in their own right.

No dragon had ever been so large, surely?

Though plenty of myths and legends about the dragons came to mind, none spoke of something so enormous.

What was waiting inside? *We'll be the first to visit in centuries.*

With murmurs of awe, his friends strode on, Tyar and

Alira leading. Kilek didn't follow at first, still staring up at the colossal skull. Who had the dragon been? Onakor the Golden was supposedly the largest dragon, but even he had not been measured like a mountain...

It wasn't until Pax and Mathi turned to urge him on that he moved, and there was enough excitement in their expressions that he had to smile back. "I'm not far behind."

The trail soon became more of a dirt road, even bearing uneven stretches of wooden fences as it wound its way up the hillside. Once, it must have been a busy road, but little other evidence remained of that. No buildings or even ruins nearby, just stands of trees and gold and green grasses.

When they reached the next wood – a wall of white towering over them now – the first hints that any human had once used this particular Sky Island revealed itself. Three bone chairs sat connected to a rail. It stretched up to dip out of sight at the crest of a rise, before climbing farther into the trees. Nor were the first three the only set of chairs, since the rail featured more at evenly spaced distances.

Tyar rested his hand upon the nearest chair with a grin. "Now, if this does what I think it does, I'm going to be very happy."

Mathi gave him a shove. "Lazy fool."

He chuckled. "It's not just that. What if this is the only way into the skull?"

Pax knelt to examine the rail's track, where weeds poked free. "And somewhere inside Ketaket's White Wing is waiting for us?"

"I hope so."

"Will it move, even if we can discover how?" Kilek asked.

Pax shrugged. "I don't think I could say. The weeds aren't

that bad. Someone might even be maintaining it, especially if it's in this condition after such a long time."

"Dragon-bone *is* said to be the strongest material known in all the lands," Kilek said. "Let's search the area. There must be a way to make it move again. And if there isn't, let's just follow it up."

A new voice reached them. "If you wait a moment, I can help you."

A pale head floated down from the trees above – only it wasn't floating, but lowering itself from steely strands of silver hair, tiny thuds echoing when it found a new trunk or branch to use. Its face was similar enough to the last floating head he'd encountered, only broader with a rather welcoming smile.

Tyar had an arrow set to his string, but Kilek raised a hand. "Wait. Zenia and I met one of these servants before. They help the dragons."

"Truly?"

The head bobbed in an approximation of a nod. "That is one of our responsibilities. This place, a specific one of my own." A single gleaming strand of hair flashed downward, scraping against the insides of the track. "Forgive me while I perform some overdue upkeep, after which I will restore motion to the chair-rail."

"Which will take us to into the skull above?" Kilek asked. At the same time, Mathi asked whether the head had killed the Cabeku.

"The answer to both your questions is yes."

"How did they get up here?" Mathi continued. "Their wings didn't look strong enough."

"By clinging to the back of the larger one that Ketaket is

battling. Others may yet lurk beyond the reach of my senses. Come, join me above where you are welcome to either rest while waiting for Ketaket or prepare the White Wing for flight."

Chapter 35.

The servant-head was already moving back along the rail, almost bouncing as it picked up speed. Dirt and weeds flew in the wake of its scraping, unable to resist the considerable force from the hair.

"Wait," Kilek called. But it did not slow, and his question trailed off. "What is the White Wing…?"

With little to do but await its return, Kilek took a seat and explained the few details he'd learnt when he and Zenia met Rischan on the other island. Mathi sat beside him, tapping her foot while they waited. Tyar and Pax had settled on the next set of seats, while Alira was not too far away, bending often to gather herbs or leaves, it seemed.

He glanced at Mathi, whose curls obscured her expression.

"I know what you're going to ask me, Kil."

"Oh."

"Of course, I do. But I'm going to let Alira speak for herself."

"I know she's upset. About the camp."

"Just let her speak when she's ready."

He sighed. No point continuing. *I tried to take the burden from them.* And it weighed a little less now, thanks to the rescue. He'd *had* to walk the graveyard of ash, for if he could not face the horror he'd caused – even facing it one step removed via the aftermath – then he should never have made the choice to begin with.

Hopefully, Alira would find a way to forgive him soon. It felt wrong, not having her to talk to. Wrong that she no longer seemed to trust him.

He took a drink from his pack and leant back in the bone chair to wait. It was comfortable enough. Smooth beneath his palms when he searched for a seam or join, as if carved from a single piece.

Alira soon returned, walking a short distance to take a seat on her own. He tried to catch a glimpse of her expression but failed.

The seats jerked into motion.

Kilek gripped the bone, his action mirrored by Mathi beside him. The chair slid smoothly on the rail, with only infrequent sounds of grinding from the track below. The ride was steady where it rose and fell with the land. Even so, there were plenty of instances when he needed to dodge low branches, but the chairs of bone eventually reached the dragon skull.

The floating servant welcomed them from an expansive platform when the ride came to an end. Open doors that stood at least two-storeys tall waited to admit them into the skull itself. Visible from their position, stairs and curving handrails led down to a floor of paved stone, patterned like flame.

"Thank you." Kilek paused. "Ah, what should we call you?"

"Please call me Nischar," he said, as several of his strands appeared to gesture toward the doors. "This is the human entrance, where once they could visit to pay their respects to Marengivaro, Avendria's first child."

"Truly?" Kilek couldn't hold back a little rush of excitement. The first dragon? For some reason, it was almost like discovering buried treasure.

"His skull is a shrine?" Tyar asked.

"And more," Nischar replied as his strands of hair drew him smoothly inside.

Kilek followed to find an enormous interior; the hollowed skull still retained its jaws, where tiny beams of light slipped between fangs, but it was from eye sockets that mighty beams dove through.

Above and to the rear waited smaller openings and rooms of varying sizes, their purpose unclear. More stairs led up toward the ceiling but his gaze was drawn to the base of stone, to yet more bone that had been arranged in a sleek triangle.

The White Wing?

Nischar was already floating up over the rail, his hair spreading out to spear into various surfaces as he lowered himself. "Join me below and I will explain how the White Wing can be restored."

High-pitched cries rose from outside. Each screech was faint at first, but they swiftly grew near.

Kilek dashed back to the landing.

Below, dark shapes swarmed between the trees – like a roiling carpet. The creatures tore earth and shrub alike as they neared, yet were difficult to see clearly. Still, they had to be Cabeku. *What else?*

Tyar joined him, arrow nocked to string. Alira was right behind, glowing leaves already hovering near her grip – but neither attacked.

Why bother? Nothing they could do would make a difference to the horde below. The longer he stared, the more it seemed to be a mix of the new Cabeku and familiar ones, those smaller insects already rising on chattering wings.

Below, the moving wall of Cabeku hit bone.

White light pulsed.

Cabeku shot into the air with shrieks, crashing through the branches. The next wave hit on the heels of the first, blasted back just the same. More high-pitched cries filled the wood, and then the Cabeku retreated.

"Inside, quickly," Nischar called.

Before Kilek could turn, a figure stepped from the trees – parting the Cabeku as he approached to examine the bone. A chill ran across Kilek's limbs. "There's someone down there."

Mathi and then Pax reached the rail, eyes wide. "Who?"

"I can't see the details. Tyar?"

Tyar rejoined them, staring down with a furrowed brow. "It's a Minjao officer by the crane-in-flight on his armour. He doesn't seem worried at all."

Buzzing wings neared, and a pair of green feathers shot down. They tore through the Cabeku that had come too close, leaving only blackened ash drifting on the breeze.

"They're not attacking him?" Mathi asked.

Tyar shook his head.

"They made room as he walked," Kilek said.

"I entreat you all once more," Nischar said. "Take shelter, they cannot breach the bone."

Kilek finally left the ledge, helping Pax close the doors behind him before turning to Nischar. "What about the eye-sockets and the little openings?"

"Leave that to me," the servant said. This time deadly strands of hair shot to the ceiling of bone, to the rail, to the stone floor below, to any surface that would allow him to hang in the centre of the space.

There, yet more hair flew to every small opening and began to weave steely barriers. It turned the light silvery as it covered even the enormous eyes. If the threads were as strong as Rischan's work, work that could hold back a dragon, no mere Cabeku would pass.

"Head below," Nischar said. "Restore the White Wing before the creatures find a way inside."

Chapter 36.

The White Wing was an enormous bird of bone, unfolding from the sleek shape below, a combination of both sturdy and intricate pieces, but a bird that also bore *seats*. And reins connected to its pointed beak.

Kilek approached with a faint sense of awe, strong enough to outweigh the threat from outside. Contrary to the rest of Marengivaro's skull, the reins and seats were made from grey and pink feathers, not so different from those found on the magical river Fisathali sent them down.

And hopefully just as durable as the dragon-bone.

"Eight seats, plenty of room," Tyar said from where he tested one with his hands, pushing on the back. "Strong, too."

"Nischar. What's wrong with the bird?" Kilek asked.

"As you can see, the White Wing was built for humans. But since it has lain dormant for centuries, there is nothing to drive it forth once launched."

"What does it need?"

"Nectar from the Hives. You can find them within the caves to your rear. I cannot harvest it, but you will be able.

Do not hesitate, for the Cabeku are now attempting to tunnel beneath us."

Mathi glanced to her feet. "Stone." She looked back up to the floating head. "Can they break through?"

"In time. But once you are safely away, they will find nothing here."

Kilek had already reached the rear of the skull – no door, just an opening that led to a dim corridor and a short flight of steps. Daylight beckoned from above. He took the stairs two at a time and found himself in a wide chamber lit by high windows. It was hard to discern whether the openings had already been sealed by Nischar's hair, since they waited at the end of narrow tunnels, high in the ceiling of stone.

But it offered more than enough light to see rows of blocky hives, each with glimmering slits. Inside, he found more of the pale creatures that lived within the quartz back in Rischan's chambers. Only these ones were drawing gleaming nectar from dark blooms growing within the stone itself, pushing it up and into small pools that were touched with a faint blue.

When he reached in with a flask taken from his pack, it seemed he stirred an unexpected scent – one powerful enough to cause a wave of dizziness. But he gripped the hive until the room grew still, then turned to run down the stairs.

In the main chamber, everyone was already seated on the White Wing. Mathi held the reins, others gripped their seats as the ground rumbled. Paxoph was waving. "It's here, Kilek. An opening for the nectar."

Grinding rose from the floor between them. *Am I already too late?*

He sprinted.

Stone burst upward. Insects poured forth like an awful fountain. They blocked his path, an endless stream of dark bodies, chattering sounds echoing throughout the skull.

Kilek fell back, gripping the flask with a growl.

Do something!

"Pax! Catch!" He hurled the flask.

Precious nectar sailed smoothly through the air. Pax stretched an arm, and the flask slapped into his palm.

A new grinding echoed throughout the dragon skull, this time coming from above.

The jaws were opening, light pouring in.

Cabeku surged toward him. "Go," Kilek called as he transformed, clothes suddenly no more than shreds of cloth, claws ready, twitching for a chance to strike.

A whirlwind of silver threads flashed around the White Wing. They eviscerated Cabeku, not only sending halves flying through the air, but turning those that came too close into a purple mist.

Good.

The first row of Cabeku neared Kilek, their beady eyes bright, sharp legs flashing as they charged. He exhaled, turning all to stone. Without pause, the next wave clambered over their frozen fellows.

He slashed them to pieces with barely a grunt.

Clacking sounds followed, drowning out the voices of his friends as they called to him, but he only had a moment to glance up. The White Wing was already flying from the mouth – it seemed to have been hurled forth from some manner of hidden sling. No matter the specifics, they were away.

Safe flight, everyone.

He spat forth another cloud of mist and tore yet more Cabeku into pieces. Specks of their acidic blood occasionally struck him, and while it could not penetrate his scales, the press of their bodies was becoming so great that swinging his arms was difficult. Even if he turned them all to stone, impossible as that was, he'd only manage to seal himself beneath their corpses.

"Climb free," Nischar called. "I will entrap them."

Kilek roared, kicking and clawing his way free – his escape only possible thanks to more lashing threads from above – until he reached the sling's support at last, breathing hard where he glanced up.

The nearest ledge was not close. But he summoned his strength and charged for the top of the sling, bending his knees to thrust himself into the air.

His claws caught bone.

Kilek hauled himself up, taking a moment to glance over his shoulder at the mass of Cabeku below, then back to the jaw where he now stood. An impressive leap. Clearly impossible as a human. *But I'm more than that, now.*

Below, several Cabeku were clambering atop one another in a futile attempt to reach him. Yet the clamour of their bodies, their useless wings and voices created a sound of pure chaos. So much so, that he winced at a particularly sharp moment of cacophony. "Nischar. Where have the others gone?"

The floating head turned from where he still hovered above the Cabeku, silver lines of hair slicing through the insects. "Travel south from here. You'll find an old harbour and a shrine. If your companions haven't circled back to collect you, I suggest asking Avendria for guidance."

"Thank you," Kilek said with a nod, then paused. "Will you be able to deal with the rest? They have that human working with them. Probably a mage."

"Not a worry. Go, and fare well."

Kilek ran along the jaw into daylight, where he smashed a few more flying Cabeku and leapt free. He crashed through the trees, landing hard enough to cause a rumble. And more, he'd left a dent in the very earth behind him, caught in a glance as he strode through dust. Angry chattering rose again, but the longer he ran, dodging tree trunks and hunks of stone alike, the further the sound of insects fell behind.

There was no path, even once he broke from the woods, but he crossed the grassy hills, drawing farther and farther from the giant dragon-skull and the Cabeku. *I hope they're all dead by now.*

Finally, he found a road, slowing when his claws hit old paving. Though much of the way was overgrown, becoming covered in moss as he jogged through a long depression, it was one of the few signs of human construction he'd found. After all, what need did dragons have for roads?

When the harbour came into view, it was similar enough to what might have waited for him at the ocean – a dozen long piers with mooring posts stretched out across the very sky, only without supports beneath the stone.

More unfathomable dragon's magic.

Unfathomable, but impressive. *Is such power in my future?*

The mooring posts stood in bone, but most of the pier was sandstone – like the buildings nearby. They bore an ornate look, with arches connected to round openings and doorways. Here, too, bone only seemed to be used in certain instances, as crossbars in smaller windows or for handles.

He also saw bones placed above the main entryway, attached to the outside of the largest building, where something large and round had been carved from perhaps a single segment. It bore five different-length pieces, arranged like uneven spokes.

Inside, there waited more unusual sights. Within a room that stretched quite wide but not far, he found a long bench, almost like a bar at an inn. Yet, it featured evenly spaced arches on its top and when he moved around, and then to the rooms beyond, he found nothing to confirm its purpose. It *seemed* vaguely like a harbour master's room in some ways, even empty of much furniture.

He searched the halls, coming across benches and podiums for… something. They were shaped like dragon's claws and offered little else, obviously missing some focal point or clue that might have revealed their purpose.

It wasn't until he turned a corner and found himself at the rear of the building that Kilek located the entrance to a shrine, an opening carved with feathers, all frozen in stone.

"Wait," a voice called.

Kilek spun.

The Minjao mage from Marengivaro's skull stood behind him, hands raised in a gesture of peace.

Chapter 37.

For a change, Kilek didn't rush to a violent response. Somewhere within, the awareness that he'd so often been choosing violence first was troubling. But he could not give the realisation much attention. Instead, he regarded the Minjao mage before him. Little differed from other western officers he'd seen; same colours, same heron design – but something *had* to be different, considering the man's ability to control Cabeku.

And now, was the calm approach just another ploy? What exactly were western magic-users capable of? Yan had summoned blades of light...

"How are you controlling them?" Kilek asked. Hunger stirred as he spoke. *How much meat could I rend from his bones?* Kilek clenched his jaw, fighting the desire.

"I cannot control the Cabeku," the man replied, his voice soft. "Not consistently. My magic can only direct, and only some of the time – it is the same for all animals."

More bad news, if the man wasn't exaggerating. Kilek folded his arms, kept a breath of silver mist deep in his lungs, ready to shoot free. If nothing else, turning the mage to stone would prevent him from being eaten. "What do you want?"

"To offer you a temporary alliance."

Kilek narrowed his gaze. "Between whom? And why?"

"Between you and your companions, and Prince Yan."

Now Kilek laughed, a hard sound in his dragon-like form. "Madness. You have sided with the most vile creatures and you think that I would trust whatever you or Yan have to say?"

"We have not sided with them." The man's voice rose a little. "What we do, we only do in order to appease the madman upon the Throne of Fans."

"A likely answer."

"But the truth. I am willing to make any attempt to convince you."

"Begin by answering my questions."

"So be it."

"Why did you come here?"

"In search of the Sky Thorn – the sixth blade taken after King Isidon's folly."

Kilek frowned. He knew most of the Thorns from the legend – seven in all – but Prince Yan obviously had long sought more than the Night Thorn alone. "Not to follow us?"

"We had considered it possible, once we learnt of the Sky Islands, but stumbling across you and the dragons is most fortunate."

Not for us. "And who told you of this place?"

"I learnt of the Islands through the Cabeku, but please know that Prince Yan wishes an end to them by any means. Finding you here, in addition to the Sky Thorn, is an opportunity I cannot ignore."

The answers brought more questions to mind. Especially about the Sky Thorn, but he would not ask them yet. "Including conscripting innocent people from another land."

"Including that, yes," the man replied, and his voice wavered.

"As per your emperor's orders."

"Yes."

"That does not absolve Prince Yan of his crimes."

"I would have him speak his own words, Kilek of Hasere."

"He may not live to speak them, if we meet."

The Minjao mage nodded. "So be it, if it means his people will be spared."

Was the alliance offer a sincere one, after all? The mage had not hesitated in his answer. Not for any question, so far. "If you truly do travel with Cabeku in order to work against them, you must have learnt something of their weaknesses."

"I would share those things, if you agree to join the prince in his struggle."

We have our own struggle. "Should you convince me, I am not the only one."

"But, you are the leader..."

He sighed. "What is your name?"

"Zhavin. *Banro* to the prince."

"Very well, Zhavin. You are not doing a terrible job of convincing me that you are genuine, but if you cannot fathom that I would offer my friends a say in their future, or that I value their words, then your attempts are doomed. I may as well shred you to pieces now."

The man went to one knee. "I swore an oath that I would not fail. I must convince you."

Kilek frowned down at the mage. One fist was clenched, a glimpse of chain-links visible, as though he held some manner of locket. Was the display all part of a plot? Or actual desperation? If Zhavin could actually guarantee Prince Yan's help, what would that be? *We'd become greater targets of the emperor by aligning with Yan.*

Kilek almost laughed at himself – flying a dragon or two over Minjao lands to burn the Cabeku to a crisp would be enough to draw attention from the emperor, with or without Prince Yan.

"What else can you offer?"

"For one, some knowledge of the Sky Thorn."

That would be of value. *Most of all for the sixth blade.* Not that he knew all there was to know regarding any particular blade, but myths about the Sky Thorn were especially scarce. "It is here?"

"Yes. Further to which, let me say that I will not seek to take the sword. I believe that you will be better able to use it against the Cabeku."

"I don't know enough about your magic to decide whether that's an actual offer. Could you even stop me from taking the sword?"

"My honest answer is that I do not know."

"And secondly?"

"I offer myself as hostage for however long you require such assurance."

Now Kilek exhaled. *If I can trust him, I'll finally have a good excuse not to eat him.* Even so, food was still a problem. And one that he did not know how to solve. Yet. Exactly how much would the gnawing hunger impact his abilities? If the mage *did* end up attacking… "Send the Cabeku away from the islands."

"Most of those I have some influence over are either dead or will soon be so. I can turn back the remainders, but not those Cabeku that will be sent by others."

For now, that would have to be enough. "Do so."

The mage produced three tiny branches from a pocket, each one bearing smooth bark. "A moment, please." He selected one then bent the branch until it cracked, but not so far as a clean break. A scent that was somehow *cold* filled the air. The man dropped the branch to wave his hands slowly. Threads of light appeared, and he wove them into small circles where Kilek imagined the scent still hung, and then the mage flung them back toward Marengivaro's skull.

The scent lifted, and the light soon vanished.

"That is enough?" Kilek asked.

"For most insects, most of the time. Repelling is far easier than compelling."

Better than nothing, assuming Nischar had already dealt with the bulk of them. "And the giant Cabeku you rode up here on?"

The man stiffened a moment before bending to retrieve the damaged branch. "Near to death, as best I can tell. The blue dragon will soon be victorious."

"Is that a problem?"

"Not for me," he said as he straightened. "Now, I have offered all I have. Made every argument I can, granted all concessions. Will you at the very least hear what Prince Yan has to say?"

"If no-one else does, *I* will – after you direct me to the Sky Thorn, Zhavin."

A little relief seemed to flow into his bearing. "Thank you,

Kilek of Hasere. Based on our research, you are quite near already." He gestured to the shrine as he strode forward.

Kilek followed into a stone chamber with generous skylights, the room built to appear as a pair of wings – walls curving down to narrow points, with fewer and fewer stone chairs closer to the wingtips.

And all of them facing a central statue.

Avendria.

Here, her feathered collar had been arranged around a scaled head, though the same golden eyes gleamed where light struck some manner of jewel. That the jewels remained in place further confirmed no humans had reached the Sky Islands for centuries.

In her hands waited a thin sword of blue. The hilt was plain silver, but the blade so mirror-like that clouds seemed to move across its surface. Only, the sky was clear when he glanced to the skylights – meaning the clouds drifted across the blade itself…

Alone, he might have asked her for help but not with Zhavin beside him.

"It is said the youngest dragon flew the Sky Thorn here before they all disappeared, working at the bequest of a suitor," the mage explained. "He sent the sword away from where he lay upon his deathbed, in order to keep it from his squabbling children. He needed it to wait for someone worthy of its power."

"And that power is what? I know something of Night Thorn… and the Ashen Thorn said to lie in Jasoria, or the Rose Thorn beneath the ocean, but how is the Sky Thorn different?"

"We have some stories in Minjao, where the sixth thorn

has also been called 'Storm-Singer'. It's unclear whether the tempest pours from the blade or whether it acts more as a focal point. Other writings suggest the sword will reflect the temperament of the one who carries it."

"Preventing its use?"

"No. Supposedly, it would be a useful mirror and an indicator of what the wielder could unleash upon their surroundings."

"Very well." Kilek reached up and lifted the blade free.

Storm clouds gathered.

Chapter 38.

Overhead, no thunder split the sky with its restless lightning. Instead, the sun was beginning to descend, blending into a cloud bank, still warming Kilek where he and the Minjao mage waited on the pier.

"How long do you estimate?" Zhavin asked as he paced.

"Soon." Kilek glanced once more at the Sky Thorn, its surface now returned to a welcome calm. No heavier in his hand than any other sword, yet the weight of its power was a lurking suggestion that unnerved him, even in his dragon form.

Hopefully, the cause of unrest within the Thorn had been his hunger, and not some darker, more hidden facet of his self. Two things held back his craving. Two things only.

For one, Mathi deserved her chance at revenge and Zhavin could deliver Prince Yan.

And secondly, Yan could be a useful ally.

Temporarily.

I am near, Kilek. Sparkena's voice rang clear in his mind.

"Perfect," he replied. "How fares Ketaket?"

Hmmm. No questions about home?

"None so urgent."

Allow me an observation, but you do seem colder when transformed, you know.

"I do." It was a problem, similar but connected to the hunger, no doubt. Equally, too much was at stake to deal with it all right away. "If you have any more advice, I'll take it – once I've seen the Elder."

Gladly. And Ketaket is recovering nicely.

"Just how giant was the Cabeku?"

Very. But it was more that; so soon after awakening, none of us are as strong as we ought to be. It always takes time, after such a long hibernation.

"Then, are you too exhausted to fly us to the Elder?"

Not at all. Here I come, warn the Minjao you have there.

"Time to leave," Kilek said, and Zhavin stopped. A frown was fading from the man's face, replaced by realisation. He had obviously been curious about Kilek's conversation.

Air swirled and then Sparkena's red scales rushed up from below the island. The mage took half a step back as the dragon swung around, mighty claws gripping the opposite pier. Then, Sparkena extended a wing. And though it easily reached to the next pier behind them in turn, the angle was not impossible to climb.

"The next island is not so far. Hold on," Sparkena said, once they were settled.

He leapt into the air, beating his wings to gain enough height to turn, dip and swing around. Zhavin did not seem too concerned. He kept a firm grip on Sparkena and from his small smile, almost seemed to be enjoying the flight.

Kilek kept an ungracious thought about the man's

deservedness to himself.

It quickly became clear which island was their destination. This, too, bore a sky harbour and paved road, and a sprawling wood with a large basin above, set within the mountain walls. From his vantage, it was easy to see another enormous pit of scales, though when Sparkena took them closer, it became clear that all were black.

Nearer and nearer they flew, more details revealed.

The White Wing and his friends, standing upon a ledge before an enormous dragon's head – easily twice the size of Ketaket – peering out from the enormous pit. Even from a distance, a little thrill ran through Kilek's body at the sight of the Elder. Some of the scales seemed a deep, dark purple or even a possible crimson, not unlike the Elder himself.

Pale eyes of white observed their landing, and as if by some agreement that Kilek missed, Sparkena reminded Zhavin not to approach. Orders from the Elder?

"Hear what he has to say, Kilek," Sparkena said. "Daunting though it may sound."

"I will." He joined his friends on the ledge, coming face-to-face with the Elder. Or face-to-fang, since the dragon's head was so imposing. So too, his aura. Even dampened by Kilek's transformation; the sense of ancient knowledge, of careful patience and fathomless power – and an equal restraint to go with it – still weighed against Kilek and dwarfed the Sky Thorn's own presence.

But he had not lost his voice, by any stretch. "Elder. Thank you for your help in the fight against the Cabeku."

"It is our own fight." The dragon's voice was a grinding whisper, but the words were certainly audible. As though Kilek's mind heard them as much as his ears did, not dissimilar to when Sparkena or Ketaket spoke in his head.

It was also clear, up close now, that many of the Elder's scales were greying, and around the eyes and mouth, thin lines suggested fractures. Runes were visible within his fangs, like those borne by Daciael, and they pulsed faintly. *Close to death or slow to re-awaken fully?*

Kilek nodded. "You wished for us to offer what help we can, My Lord."

"Yes. Break the cycle."

Kilek waited.

When no more words followed, the Elder merely breathing and waiting, he glanced to his friends. Paxoph shook his head, and no-one else looked any more pleased. In fact, all were tense. Cowed, even. And why not? It was not unlike facing Avendria.

"Elder?"

"Destroy Javoteth and break the cycle of death. Free all living creatures from the threat."

Kilek could not speak, and someone gasped. Even being in dragon-form, where his confidence was higher, his doubts fewer... he found no words to respond. How could a God even be destroyed? It wasn't possible. If not for a dragon, then certainly not for a human. Anesca or otherwise.

"Why do you hesitate?" the Elder asked.

"Do you ask me in jest, My Lord?"

"No." The whisper became a growl. "All things are possible."

"Then... you would help us, once we defeat the Cabeku? And suppose we accomplish such a stupendous task as to kill a God, would that be an end to the Cabeku ever returning?"

"Of course, of course."

Again, Kilek glanced at his friends. All wore expressions of doubt. "Would not another rise to take Javoteth's place?"

"In time. However, there is no certainty they would bear the same foul fault lines within their heart."

"My companions and I will discuss your request, My Lord," he said. "In the meantime, can we still count on the dragons?"

"Whelp!" The Elder's eyes widened, his voice ringing out. "I have said as much."

Kilek went to one knee, heart thumping within his chest. "Forgive me."

"Sparkena, take them to the ruin."

Kilek glanced up. Steam exhaled from the Elder's mouth, slipping between the fangs. Fangs that would barely taste him if he were to be eaten as a result of the dragon's displeasure.

The Elder's pale *gaze* could probably end his life, for that matter.

But the enormous head was sinking back into the nest of scales instead, apparently having said all he intended to say.

Sparkena, in his Minjao form, approached, shaking his head with a grin. "Kilek, I understand that his request must have been quite the surprise, but I didn't realise you and I were quite so alike."

"Well…"

"Well, believe it or not, the Elder understands what he is asking of you all – but for the moment, you have other concerns."

"What ruin did he mention?"

"I'll show you. It's a disused temple, but habitable enough," he replied. "I imagine that's where you'll want to have a conversation with your hostage, since it will be more private."

"What do you mean by hostage?" Tyar asked.

"Come closer and I'll show you all. I've already placed him there," Sparkena added. Kilek joined his friends as they gathered around the dragon. "Good, good. Now, this isn't something I can manage over long distances, but we should be fine."

"Should be?"

Kilek heard Tyar's question just as their surroundings were lost to a swirling blur of colours. When it eased, they stood within a circular entryway, white stone beneath their feet, a faint breeze stirring old leaves.

The ruined temple.

It bore no ceiling, and the statue of Avendria here was crumbling. Most walls looked sturdy enough, and the temple also included a few connected corridors leading to other buildings, but it was the campfire burning nearby that caught his attention – that and the Minjao mage waiting patiently.

Tyar reached for his bow.

"Wait," Kilek said, quickly. "He's our hostage."

"The one who brought those Cabeku to the skull?"

"Yes. He gave himself up, and revealed the Sky Thorn," Kilek said, gesturing to the blade he held and going on to explain. When he finished, he turned to Mathila. "I want everyone's option, but first Mathi. What do you think?"

Mathila was already nodding. "I'm more than happy to work closely with him."

Tyar raised an eyebrow. "Mathi?"

"What?"

"Nothing. It's just… surprising."

She shrugged. "It shouldn't be, Ty. We have a task to complete, and if Prince Yan can help us, I see no need to turn down his offer of a temporary alliance."

Alira stepped closer. "After which?"

"Yan answers to me."

Chapter 39.

They posted no watch at assurances from Sparkena, but Kilek still found himself pacing the night. He walked in a vague circle just beyond the temple walls, moving in and out of moonlight where it fell across the island and cast long, deep shadows. Cries of a night bird came from the nearby wood, a sweeter sound than that which suited his mood.

It shouldn't have been such a dark one. After all, he'd transformed and eaten – very well – and his hunger was gone. The occasional tendency to see his friends as possible meals vanished, too. He even carried a mythical blade. The dragons had returned and most of the village was safe!

All in all, a stunning series of victories. *I should definitely be happier.*

Or weary, if nothing else.

But sleep had been impossible, leaving him to walk alone, back and forth, back and forth…

Footsteps approached. He paused, waiting for the figure to exit one of the shadows. Alira come to speak with him, now that their conversation had a better chance of being private?

But it was Tyar, his friend's hair in some disarray.

"Oh. Hello, Ty."

"Expecting someone else?" he asked with a grin.

"Maybe."

"Alira, right?"

"Right," Kilek said with a sigh. "I don't want to upset her, but…"

Tyar nodded.

"You too?"

"Me too, what?"

"You're not going to give me your opinion."

"I suppose I just did," Tyar replied with a chuckle. "But I will say that I think she understands why you took the decision away from us."

"Clearly no-one else wanted the burden," Kilek said. Reliving the moment in his memory once more, no longer dampened by the colder side that dominated whenever he was half-dragon, the guilt returned, stifling his next words.

He'd been spared the screams of horror, the faces of the dead.

But was having to imagine them just as bad?

"We didn't," Tyar said, then folded his arms. "I actually thought the Elder's request was keeping you up."

"Well, we hardly settled it over our meal."

"It *is* the kind of thing we'd usually ask Florique about."

"He'd have an opinion." Kilek frowned. *And we'd probably listen, if we felt he could be trusted.* "Sparkena seems to think that it's possible."

"But he won't say how."

"I'm actually glad of that."

"You are?"

"Absolutely," Kilek said. "The Cabeku is enough for now, right? And we need to get Pax's uncle home first, anyway."

"We do." Tyar hesitated. "Actually, Kil. I wanted to ask you something."

"You did?"

"It's about Mathi. I need your help when she goes after Yan."

"Of course. But what makes you think she'll even need either of us?"

He smiled, though it fell away quickly. "No. I mean we have to stop her."

"Why?" Kilek asked with a frown. "Even if Yan works with us to stop the Cabeku, he has to pay for what he did."

"Oh, I agree." All of Tyar's cheer was gone now, the moonlight revealing worry in his eyes. "But Alira told me something. She's seen their fight. If Mathi attacks him, she won't survive because something goes wrong."

His stomach flipped. "What?"

"She doesn't know exactly, but she's certain. And I *know* that I haven't always taken Alira's feelings seriously… but I can't stop worrying about this." He slammed a fist into his thigh. "It's pathetic of me, if this is what it takes to make me believe. Especially since we've all seen her magic grow and grow, right?"

"We have," Kilek replied. When Tyar didn't continue, he asked the first question that came to mind. "She hasn't told Mathi, has she?"

"No. Neither of us want to risk that, if we can avoid it."

"Then do you have some sort of plan?"

"Not really. We just kill Yan before she can," he said with a shrug. "I know she won't like it, but I can't think of anything better."

Kilek put a hand on his friend's shoulder. "Let's keep thinking. If that ends up being the best idea, I'll help you, of course."

"Thank you."

"The only problem will be beating her to it," Kilek said, then smiled. "Actually, maybe not. Mathi's not as furious as I was expecting. She held her temper while we questioned Zhavin."

Tyar spread his hands. "I'm sure she'll have more questions tomorrow. But you know, we're not young hotheads, anymore."

He grinned. "No?"

"I'm serious, Kil. We've all changed. Been forced to change," he added.

And that was the truth. *Some of us even more than others.* "Do you still regret it?"

"Sometimes. What about you?"

Kilek sighed. "I… don't know."

"Why don't you get some sleep, then," he said. "There are lines beneath your eyes so dark that they look like ink."

"Truly?"

"No. They're closer to grey in the moonlight," he said with another chuckle. "But you should take my advice, anyway."

Kilek raised a hand. "Fine, fine. Don't worry, I will."

And this time, when he returned to his bedroll and lay back, closing his eyes, it was with weary limbs at last. Even the soft sounds of Tyar settling down across the camp were soon lost…

When morning came, chatter over a meal being prepared woke him – and for the first time in a while, he rose without a heavy head. His body seemed lighter, his mind clear. When he belted on the Sky Thorn, the blade was equally unclouded. *Which one of us is influencing the other?*

Over a breakfast of fruit and nuts, Zhavin continued to explain details of Yan's request. "The prince will meet you within the city of Shanhu, his home. Shanhu rests near the border and is the final stronghold against the insects. However, the meeting must be secret, for reasons discussed last night."

Kilek nodded. "How is he deceiving the emperor?"

"By outward obedience, firstly. The quest for the Night Thorn is, on the surface, meant to be for the glory of the Empire. As a favoured prince, he was long afforded leeway that others do not always enjoy, even if that seems to be changing."

Paxoph frowned. "And how did he discover the truth to begin with? Can we be certain he actually *is* deceiving the emperor? Or worse, that this isn't an elaborate ruse to draw us in?"

Zhavin frowned. "Suggesting that his highness is an unwilling pawn?"

"Willing or unwilling."

The mage frowned. "I believe that Kilek explained his belief in my word."

"I did," Kilek replied. "But I also told you that I trust my friends. If you have to convince them further, so be it, Zhavin. We don't need Prince Yan to burn the Cabeku."

Sparkena nodded. "At my call, there will be three other awakened dragons to join me."

The mage put his head in his hands a moment. "I do not know what else I can offer."

"Think of something, for I will listen," Paxoph said. "Though I do not speak for everyone."

Kilek's friends nodded along, then waited.

Finally, Zhavin lifted his face. His jaw was clenched. "I will ask you a question, instead. What did you do in order to save your village?"

"Much," Alira said in the quiet that followed.

"Then know that I do the same for my city. Prince Yan is no different."

Tyar sighed. "You make a fine point, but we can't just trust you immediately. That must be obvious."

"Then demand what you will of me."

Sparkena gestured to the mage. "If it helps you all, I assure you this man is sincere. You humans are not impossible to read, after all. I cannot say the same for Yan. Nor be certain that Zhavin himself isn't being deceived, in some way."

Zhavin stiffened but spoke no more.

Kilek sighed. "I think we know that in the end, we need Yan to find Pax's uncle. Or at the very least, to make it easier to do so while Sparkena is fighting."

"Likely," Pax said.

"Then let's hear what else he has to say," Kilek suggested. "Where does Prince Yan want to meet? How will we sneak into the city?"

"It's an old estate, some distance from the keep. It is secure and includes expansive grounds for Lord Sparkena to launch himself into the air."

Mathi snorted. "That would place us in a state of constant threat from the city's population *and* those loyal to the emperor. How do we launch an attack on the Cabeku from within the city?"

"It is offered as an option only," the mage said. "The battlelines stretch far and wide. You could attack from any point inside or outside the city."

"Very well," Paxoph said. "And entry?"

"The guards will let any I travel with into Shanhu, but it must still be in darkness."

"I can help, if needed," Sparkena added.

That was of more comfort than Zhavin's claim. "Then before we set off, I have one more question," Kilek said.

"Please."

"What is Prince Yan offering when it comes to destroying the Cabeku themselves?"

The mage nodded. "Aside from our forces, his magic and his own blade, he offers a guaranteed escort to the hatcheries. He will destroy them by your side."

"Are these tasks we could not complete alone?"

"Possibly. But you will face less threat from the emperor's men, if you accept," Zhavin added. "His Highness can still shield you. If you wish, he will explain when you meet."

Chapter 40.

Once more, Kilek found himself benefitting from a wide-ranging view afforded from the back of a dragon.

Though night had fallen earlier, they'd travelled quite the distance before dark, often flying so high that Sparkena informed everyone that he was also protecting them from deadly cold. But now, at last, they looked down upon two sets of lights that stood bright against the darkness.

One, the city of Shanhu, which blazed from within a mountain pass. Its walls and keep protected buildings arranged in deepening circles – as if the inner rings had been dug deeper into the earth than others.

Beyond the walls, a long, long line of campfires rested upon the plain: the second set of lights.

The line holding back the tide.

How close were the forests of Jasoria? Invisible in the shadows below, just like the Cabeku themselves. Of course, he'd see plenty before long, if Zhavin was to be believed, and there was no reason to doubt him about the number of insects.

Sparkena soon landed upon the plain beyond the city walls, transforming and joining the mage at the lead of their party.

Kilek found himself walking to the rear, the fake chains Zhavin had created being light as air – yet there was a heaviness he'd not expected, for Alira strode beside him. She did not speak, and only seemed to glance his way once or twice. He wasn't certain due to the darkness.

Yet warnings from Mathi and Tyar rang in his mind, and so he did not speak.

By the time they stood before towering gates of closed steel and timber, blazing lights above, he thought it best to give up on reading her expression. *I'm probably bothering her. I should let her talk when she's ready.*

He just needed to be patient. Somehow.

Though I'm obviously failing.

At the front of their group, Zhavin and Sparkena spoke with the gate guards. Like most soldiers from the west, they wore black and green, but here the men and women also bore leather bracers upon their wrists, which Pax thought he'd heard was due to their affinity with hawks and falcons.

They were admitted entry, after which Zhavin lowered his voice a little. "Word will still reach the emperor's men, routine as the sight of conscripts may be. We will hurry to the estate, heading off any further questions that might be asked of us."

Shanhu's dark stone bore an almost golden glimmer, and when they passed gardens or parks, the trees grew in spiral shapes, their leaves tight against the branches… almost like scales. Many had been cut, or perhaps encouraged to grow, into graceful shapes that sometimes appeared vaguely-human.

Despite the late hour, there were still plenty of people in the streets, moving from market to tavern or just as often, to large halls where men and women were training with spears, and hammers or axes. The military feel to the city extended to the clothing even of those not training, since most wore a minimum of leather jerkins and boots. All were armed, even if it was a dagger. He missed a step.

Even the children.

A little one was running a whetstone across his blade under the careful gaze of his father where they sat within a tiny garden.

Gazes from other citizens that fell upon them were not suspicious, like in Fadoi near the Wickerlands. Instead, many smiled or spoke a few words. Several citizens even approached with small gifts – thin wooden emblems, triangular-shaped with circles cut from the bottom.

"They are old symbols for strength," Zhavin explained when Kilek asked. "The people of Shanhu are expressing their gratitude. Some will be survivors from outlying towns."

"To conscripts?"

"Yes. Some people believe the emperor's lies that Luargot has agreed to help us."

That's news to me. What else had the emperor lied about? "Is that what he claims?"

"Yes. Officially, conscripts fight as part of reparations agreed to by your king, after the war. But some of the people here simply appreciate that the conscripts risk their lives to protect the city."

Kilek exchanged a glance with his friends, who seemed equally surprised.

"I don't know how I feel about that," Mathi said.

"It's better than arrows or blades cast our way," Tyar replied with a shrug.

Mathi nodded as they walked on, detouring a market square. It appeared as any other market; bright lights and plenty of food on offer – only with plenty of guards too.

"Is the city expecting a Cabeku attack inside the walls? Everyone is armed," Kilek said as Zhavin led them down a side street. It offered fewer lamps, longer stretches of shadow between.

"Sometimes the flying ones land within the walls, yes."

A voice called from the next lamp, where an overturned cart blocked most of the street. While Kilek didn't understand the Minjao words, the tone seemed to suggest someone sought help.

"This is an obvious trap," Zhavin said with a frown. "Be ready."

Footsteps clattered up from behind, as ahead, figures rose from the wagon holding drawn bows. But Zhavin was already spinning his arms. Light streaked forth to knock each down, landing with heavy thuds.

"I caught the three behind us," Sparkena announced as Kilek turned.

"Would you bring them along, Lord Sparkena?" Zhavin asked he motioned for them to follow, detouring the cart.

Inside, Kilek noted the absence of any goods for trade. And the fallen men. Their clothing was little more than black tunics and pants, their faces wrapped in cloth too. The emperor's spies or thieves? Zhavin was steadily increasing his pace, moving at almost a jog by the time they had crossed the next few streets. He soon cut through a shadowy park and then he was waving everyone through an uneven hole at the base of a high stone wall.

"I will seal the way," he said.

Kilek found grass beneath his feet on the other side, trees blocking most of the sky above. Empty grounds stretched ahead, dotted by deeper, darker shadows in the earth. Some were quite large too, but once Zhavin set off again, there was no chance to examine any.

"Who were they?" Paxoph asked as they followed.

"Emperor Xiadan's spies, working on orders from his generals, no doubt."

"And not the only ones?"

"The prisoners may reveal what we need to know. The prince has the estate under watch, so we'll have time to question them without being interrupted."

Light flickered, speeding from his hand to cross the grounds and strike a door nestled within a stone alcove. The light clung to the wood, a glowing guide that lasted only so long as it took to reach and open the door. From what little illumination the night sky offered beyond, they seemed to now stand within a large courtyard of empty stalls...

A brighter glow blossomed from Zhavin's hands once more. It stayed with his skin this time but was not at all close to blinding. "Bring them near," he said, glaring at the three spies.

None spoke.

Sparkena remained close by, along with Tyar and Mathi.

The mage sighed. "If they can no longer speak, this will not be a long interrogation."

"Is something wrong with them?" Paxoph asked.

"Possibly," he replied. "Some give up certain aspects of

their awareness in exchange for more clandestine abilities. They're usually difficult to notice, or follow let alone capture, for that matter."

"No match for me," Sparkena said. "Not to mention the stench of the Cabeku all over them. Sensed it before their footsteps reached me."

Kilek frowned. *If I'd been transformed, I would have been able to sense them.*

"I will commence," Zhavin said, before switching to Minjao.

Chapter 41.

The prisoners revealed nothing. *Could* reveal nothing, for as Zhavin had feared, none were able to speak. He'd explained more regarding what the former criminals had given up in order to become the emperor's servants. "Most sacrifice their pasts or specific memories, though their crimes are often preserved."

A chilling fate. But Kilek had to stay focused on the emperor. "How much does the emperor already know, then?"

"For now, he will be no more informed than before. All that the gate guards would have shared was word of me escorting additional conscripts into the city. Hardly anything unusual. No, they would have been fishing without knowing who you are," the mage said as he used both his magic *and* ropes taken from the nearby stables to bind the spies. His power made them slow-moving, eyes heavy where they seemingly teetered on the edge of sleep, but it wasn't clear exactly when or how Zhavin had acted upon them. "These men will be sent back to report on a routine inspection of fresh conscripts, followed by a deadly scuffle with thieves that cost them half their men."

"How does that work?"

"Their master will read their memories – or in this case, memories that we create, so you need not worry."

Memory manipulation. Something Kilek was all-too familiar with. He frowned. It was worth worrying about, and for more than one reason.

Mathi spoke next, voicing Kilek's concern. "You mentioned Prince Yan's position in the court being tenuous before – what impact does our entry to Shanhu have if we are discovered? Will rescuing Pax's uncle be more difficult either way?"

"Not if we move swiftly, as planned. If the emperor's generals learn the truth of what transpired here, it will be too late for the Cabeku."

"And the emperor?"

The mage paused. "I will let His Highness answer that question, if he chooses to do so."

And thus, in the absence of any answers the spies could have given, and the end of Zhavin's willingness to share details, all that remained was to wait for the prince and his men. Which meant a meal of hard travel rations and water to accompany conversations filled with guesses and predictions about the Cabeku or Pax's uncle, and where nothing was solved. And though Sparkena urged patience, Kilek soon found himself pacing the perimeter – a new habit, it seemed.

There, he located three other exits. One was a set of stairs and the other two were locked doors, but Zhavin's modest glow permitted little detail about the paths.

"He will be here momentarily," Zhavin announced, mere

moments after Kilek rejoined the group.

Footsteps echoed from the staircase, a shadowy figure descending at a brisk pace, and who strode into the light's range without slowing.

Prince Yan had changed from their last meeting.

The same black tunic with its green heron symbol rested over his armour, same faintly glowing tattoos on the backs of his hands when he raised them to acknowledge Zhavin's prostration. Same deep voice when he spoke to the mage, the words seeming quite formal.

The same intensity to his gaze when he examined Kilek and his friends.

Yet while Kilek could not recall the length of the man's hair from their meeting in his tent so long ago, there was a marked difference now. A long scar ran across Prince Yan's head. It interrupted short hair, and stretched from just above his ear and ran around to the back of his head.

Kilek checked on Mathi. Tyar had one hand upon her arm – even in the dim light, the tension in her body was unmistakable. For his own part, old resentment returned swiftly enough. Not heated, like in their first meeting, but colder. More patient. *My dragon side is helping.*

There would be time to strike. *Wait a little longer.*

The prince met the gaze of all those gathered. "People of Hasere, I appreciate that you have set aside your doubts to hear my words. My thanks go to you all, including you, Lord Sparkena."

The dragon inclined his head but did not speak.

Kilek did not wait for the prince to continue. "If you want to convince us that you're sincere then help us find Orasef."

The prince turned his gaze on Kilek. Instead of any

expected outrage, there was only determination within. "I pledge as much." He gestured to Zhavin. "Confirm his location with the quartermaster."

The mage hesitated. "Now, Your Highness?"

"Now."

Zhavin took the stairs without a backward glance, leaving the prince alone – assuming any troops he'd travelled with were busy watching for spies, and not watching over the meeting.

"My uncle really is alive?" Paxoph asked.

"He is. And well-protected."

"Then what is preventing you from bringing him here now?"

Prince Yan nodded. "A fair question. Allow me to explain more about Shanhu and our struggle, along with the emperor's role in events. After which, I will share my request and reveal the full detail of what I offer."

"We will listen, as agreed," Kilek said.

"Thank you." The prince's expression grew dark. "Emperor Xiadan has succumbed to madness. He is now little more than Javoteth's pawn, a husk sitting upon the Throne of Fans. His reach is long, and those loyal to him possess eyes and ears in every town, city and hamlet. Even here, in my place, not all can be trusted."

Kilek nodded. "Zhavin mentioned the spies. We have captured some."

Yan gritted his teeth. "Sometimes, such spies can barely be *noticed*. These days, those who may speak against the emperor on any matter risk simply vanishing, while others have suffered gaudy, public executions. High-ranking members of society are usually kept alive so that they can witness the deaths of loved ones. Or their subjects."

"Such as the people here," Kilek said. Which certainly helped further explain Yan's actions.

"Yes. They are under threat if I fail in both my allegiance to the emperor or my duties as protector of this city and its surrounds."

"That doesn't justify what you did to our village," Alira said. "To others."

"No."

She frowned at him. "No?"

The man gave a faint sigh. "Any apology I give would surely ring hollow. Instead, I offer everything I have in the hope that together, such a thing can be prevented from happening to other families."

Kilek spoke before anyone else could continue, though a bad taste lingered in his own mouth at the prince's words. Not only because Yan refused to offer even an apology, but because again, it was not impossible to actually understand his actions. Accepting them was another matter – but above all, Prince Yan was useful.

If he survived long enough.

And the man *was* taking significant risks with not just his own life, considering what had been said about Emperor Xiadan. On the other hand, he wasn't the only one taking risks. *There's a chance he wants us as scapegoats, isn't there?*

"Accepting our help puts you and your people in danger, as you've admitted," Kilek said. "If we destroy the hatcheries and your hand is revealed to the emperor, you will at least have convenient sacrifices to make, since you would have 'enemies from Luargot' ready to be blamed."

His friends were murmuring before Kilek finished

speaking, but Sparkena intervened. "He's not planning that, Kilek."

"Are you certain?"

The dragon nodded, once more falling silent. In light of both Sparkena's considerable power and wisdom, he might have led the negotiation. Instead, the dragon seemed happy enough to observe for the most part.

Prince Yan's expression had not changed, as if he'd been expecting such an accusation. "All efforts support our war against the Cabeku. While few know the truth, that does not mean that *no-one* is aware. Or that I won't risk everything to expose the lies being forced upon my people."

Pax raised an eyebrow. "Then you know that Javoteth is using all this death and destruction to breed stronger and more cunning insects?"

"That is exactly why I oppose it."

"How did you find out?"

"I saw the emperor's madness firsthand – all princes did. To my great disgust, most were only too happy to one day be able to turn such creatures upon those they consider enemies, or in pursuit of an even greater Empire."

Kilek frowned. "Then you battle alone?"

"There is one other prince I trust, but it is not your responsibility to fix the malignance within this Empire, and it is my own shame to need your assistance now."

Kilek exchanged a glance with his friends. Was it worth trying to push Yan? Or could it wait until an agreement was reached? That likely was the best approach. "Then tell us exactly what you expect from us and exactly what you are offering, Yan."

Chapter 42.

"You have grown since we last met, Kilek of Hasere," the prince replied.

"I have." He waited.

Yan replied with a nod only. "I will not risk having you join me on the keep's walls, but Lord Sparkena can show you exactly where the Cabeku lurk. While the emperor's generals lead the battle, I command the city itself."

"You aren't permitted to command your own soldiers?" Tyar asked.

"Disagreements over how best to stamp out the insects are rare."

"But, don't you doubt the emperor's men? They could sabotage your defence."

"Not until I am given a reason to doubt them," Yan replied. "While all generals are loyal to the emperor, few people are aware of the true purpose of the insect-attack. Like most in Minjao, it is believed that the Cabeku are a plague emanating from Jasoria, having been connected to old legends."

Alira shook her head. Kilek understood the reaction. So many people dying without knowing *why* they were dying. Dying because they thought they were protecting the very Empire that would use their deaths for its own foul ends.

Sparkena stepped forward. "I assume your men will not attack us when it is time to burn the hordes."

"You will not be mistaken for insects, certainly if you are magnificent as the legends say."

"We are magnificent, but I'll expect your soldiers to recognise our role in this battle very swiftly."

"I will ensure that, as best I can."

"How far are the hatcheries from the camps we saw?" Kilek asked.

"Some distance across the plains, but a short ride on horseback. They are not hidden, though we haven't been able to reach them in order to attack, and thus the creatures take no counter-measures to hide themselves."

"And how will you help?"

"Protection from the emperor while you are here. The return of Orasef. My own blade and life, if need be, when destroying the hatcheries. There are half a dozen at least, and we will need to work in several small groups to destroy them all before the Beiha becomes aware."

"The Beiha?"

"Beiha Lienyu. Spymaster would be an approximate translation of the word. Lienyu herself is new to the role, and zealous enough to be of concern."

"Does she know the truth, then?"

"I am not certain. At minimum, she is highly suspicious of me, for she believes that I am involved in a plot to depose the emperor."

"Aren't you?"

"That is not your burden," he said, without answering the question. "Once the Cabeku are destroyed, your people will be freed."

Pax folded his arms across his chest. "And what specific barriers stand between us and my uncle?"

"Zhavin will return with the correct camp before dawn, but your uncle could be working across several at any given time."

"Repairing weapons?"

"Yes. He is working as something of a smith. Or, perhaps more than a smith. Specifically, he repairs and teaches others to repair the Steel Jaw used against the Cabeku. His skills are much in demand."

"I see." Pax turned to Kilek, and it seemed a touch of pride was clear in his bearing. "Should we discuss the offer?"

"We should."

Prince Yan gave a nod and started for the stairs. "I will arrange for a proper meal and supplies and return for your answer at dawn. In the meantime, I will send men to collect the spies."

Tyar stepped after the prince. "Assuming we agree, wouldn't a night raid be better?"

"Of a night, the Cabeku burrow beneath the earth to sleep. Dragon's fire will be far more effective when they wake."

Tyar shrugged. "So be it."

Once Prince Yan's footsteps faded, Kilek addressed everyone, though he did focus a little extra on Mathi. She didn't seem overwhelmed by fury, but her jaw was still clenched. "We can simply vote on working with him, if you want. Or we could discuss it – I know we don't need him to destroy the Cabeku, at least. Pax?"

"At least until Orasef is safe, I would work with the prince."

Mathi sighed, the first sound she'd made in a long time. "Don't hold back on account of me, everyone. We use him and then I take my revenge, that's no problem."

Tyar and Alira exchanged a look, but only added their assent.

"Then we'd better get some rest, somewhere around this place," Kilek said. "And hope that whatever Yan sends along doesn't need to be cooked."

"Kilek, a moment?" Sparkena drew him away from his friends, who'd already started to search for a suitable room to use.

Kilek kept his voice lowered. "Do you have any more advice about the hunger?"

"Yes. And an apology, perhaps – I should have been more forceful in making time to speak with you. Especially in the absence of Avendria."

"Absence?"

"As chosen. She warned you about the rules surrounding the Anesca?"

"Oh, yes. But I don't imagine slaying a God is permitted."

He smiled. "No, but that can certainly wait. Let me offer one more piece of advice – and keep in mind, I do not know all you may need. Your circumstances are unusual, even in my experience."

"Oh… Then, only Avendria would?"

"I imagine so. But where you are different to both man and dragon, the hunger is clearly the same. You already understand that it is indiscriminate."

"I do." He fought off a shudder.

"And you already know the consequences for denying it too long."

"My strength."

"At first. While switching between your sides will help delay the effects, you must eat."

He nodded.

"Good. And keep these things in mind. Eating as a dragon is not that different to eating as a human, if you are hesitating. Someone killed the things you eat as a man, even if you did not."

The liquid eyes of the rabbits haunted him. "I suppose. I don't know if I should… I mean, it never feels like a choice. It feels like I'd eat anything, if I let go."

"So you might," he said. "That is the risk of denying yourself too long. You would eat anything, Kilek. Even your friends, as I know you worry."

He nodded again.

"This may be of little comfort, but once sated, you would naturally stop. No-one will have to band together and destroy you."

Kilek exhaled. "No. That isn't of much comfort."

"However, I do know that you can control yourself."

Kilek looked to the shadows where everyone worked to move their meagre supplies indoors. "Sometimes, I don't know."

The dragon put a hand on his shoulder. "Consider the fact that you have done precisely that so far. Where you can, simply transform and eat as a man. You don't have to feed while in dragon form. Just keep a full stomach."

Kilek sighed. It was better than nothing. "Then I should

ask, if I fail – is there something I *shouldn't* eat?"
"Of course," Sparkena replied. "Cabeku."

Chapter 43.

Everyone was awake and waiting when Yan returned, his own expression one of barely contained fury. Somehow, even his scar appeared angry in the dim light. The dawn sky still offered enough to see that he carried extra weapons today – not only twin swords of a shadowy blue, but a short bow and a mace, too.

"By your readiness, I assume you have agreed," he said, by way of greeting.

"We have," Kilek replied.

"Lord Sparkena has already taken to the skies?"

"He's joining the others, so that they can attack at the same time," he replied.

"Wonderful." The prince gestured to the stair. "Zhavin and my personal retinue will accompany us across the plain, where we will meet additional troops who are waiting with our mounts. After which, we break into groups to deal with the hatcheries – there are at least half a dozen to destroy."

"After we rescue my uncle," Paxoph said.

"Of course," the prince replied. "His camp has been

located. We will travel there first."

"And the city itself?" Alira asked. "Are we going to be exposed on our path to the battle?"

"During certain stretches only," Yan replied. "We will take underground passages for the bulk of the trip. If we encounter Emperor Xiadan's men, simply let me speak. If we are separated for some reason and you are stopped, use whatever means are necessary to free yourself and rejoin the fight. If my citizens stop you, you need not raise your hand against them."

"Assuming we can always tell them apart," Tyar said.

"If they are not clothed in their customary black with white belts, you will know the emperor's men not only by the questions they ask but the proficiency of their Luargot."

Tyar shrugged. "Such as yours?"

"Not quite so skilled," he replied. "In any event, I do not mean for us to be separated. Are you ready, then, people of Hasere?"

"Lead on," Kilek replied, following the man up the stairs. There, Zhavin and at least a score of soldiers waited with lamps. They, too, were heavily armed.

No-one spoke as they moved through bare corridors, soon descending once more to a damp basement, and then deeper still through a hatch. Below, in a cramped space, the prince unlocked a steel door and took everyone into a winding passage. It stretched on, but Kilek did not find his legs growing weary, nor his attention beginning to flag. If anything, he was tense with readiness. Finally, finally, it was time to *really* strike back – just as soon as Orasef was safe.

Even prudent doubts about Prince Yan were not stronger.

At another set of stairs, the prince led them up into the

city streets by way of a merchant's storeroom full of hessian bags and small, stacked crates. A boy writing in a ledger had offered a bow as Yan passed, but did not speak. The streets of Shanhu were quiet. Buildings cast dark shadows, and though lights gleamed within plenty of windows, few people were out and about. Once, they passed a pair of soldiers but the women merely nodded.

Otherwise, the only other noteworthy thing Kilek saw was when cutting through a square that stood lined by darkened taverns. It was a massive flight of broad steps that descended toward a row of homes and other buildings. Stepping down where the city centre had been built deep into the earth?

He did not have a chance to ask the prince or Zhavin about it, as they were once again being ushered underground by their guides.

This time, the hidden passage was broader and lined with old lamps. Some still burned, flickering as they clung to light, suggesting this passage saw more use than the first. And when it ended at another steel door, Prince Yan led them up and into a dim cavern.

Soldiers hurried to roll a boulder back, letting some light inside. Kilek squinted against it as he stepped outside, where a plain of pale earth stretched. More long shadows flew from rock formations and the occasional shrub – and insect corpses.

The corpses were scattered as far as he could see, twisted things of varying sizes and types. Many had been heaped near a highway, which stretched back to the towering city walls in one direction, and across the plain in the other. There, the camps waited but they were not so near that much detail became apparent.

Much closer were the various Cabeku corpses. Most seemed drained in death – an echo of Gianh's magic; but here, it was more likely that colour had been leeched by the elements. Save for a type of insect he hadn't encountered before, where turquoise bands had survived the leeching.

Their bodies appeared just as close to centipede as Cabeku – only tall as a horse, had they been able to stand.

"Bring the mounts," the prince ordered from nearby. He pointed to the centipede-Cabeku. "If you have not encountered those, they are faster than they seem. But they die, just like the others."

"Acidic ichor?" Kilek asked, glancing at Yan's soldiers, who were leading the animals from where they'd been concealed behind the cavern's entrance. *Well-prepared, as promised.*

"Yes," Yan replied. "And they have stronger jaws than the others too. I have seen them cleave a horse easily."

Kilek folded his arms. "We'll see how they handle dragon's fire."

Yan nodded, waving the horses closer. "Mount up and follow me."

Once they were thundering across the still-lightening plain, Kilek looked to the sky... and there, shimmering wings on the horizon.

At last.

He grinned as he pointed out the dragons to his friends – only for his joy to fade, as another set of hooves echoed across the plain. New riders approached, black-clad figures at the fore.

Chapter 44.

"It is Spymaster Lienyu." Prince Yan frowned as he pulled on the reins to slow his horse, and when the two groups came to a halt in order to meet, dust was slow to settle.

While Lienyu's group was smaller in number – counting but a few other black-clad figures – Kilek still noted extra tension the way Yan addressed her. Or perhaps it was impatience. "Is something amiss, Beiha?" he asked.

Lienyu shook her head. Her clothing was similar to others, dark, close-fitting clothes with a white belt, though she appeared unarmed. And her face was not concealed. The spymaster possessed fine features, with short dark hair that shone beneath the rising sun. Her gaze penetrated all it roved across, a cool curiosity that could not be brushed off.

Yet Kilek returned her gaze without flinching, something of his dragon-self stirring deep within.

She raised a feathery eyebrow before turning back to Yan, speaking in Luargot without trace of an accent. "Interesting new conscripts today. No time to give them their uniforms?"

"We both know the emperor is impatient for an end to

this threat."

"Oh, he is." She looked to the sky, where the dragons were approaching. "More friends, Yan?"

"Instrumental allies," he replied. "I trust you will share today's triumph with me when I report to the emperor himself."

"That I would find very pleasant," she replied, then signalled to her men. "Spread the word that the dragons are not to be fired upon." They wheeled their mounts, heading for one end of the not-too-distant camps where soldiers were already scrambling into action.

Prince Yan nodded to a pair of his own soldiers, who set off in the opposite direction, presumably to cover those camps.

Lienyu's mount began to snort, stamping a foreleg. The woman frowned. "Another one of the hives is hatching." She spoke softly to her mare but was not able to calm the horse fully.

Prince Yan muttered something that was probably a curse, before asking Lienyu a question – again in Minjao. Her answer was equally incomprehensible, but the worry on both faces suggested a troubling change.

"What's happened?" Mathi demanded.

"The Cabeku are waking – sooner than expected," Prince Yan replied. "And from an additional location, of which I was unaware."

"They'll *all* wake, if you don't hurry," Beiha said, then snapped her reins, heading for the camp. "Good luck with your triumphant victory, Your Highness."

Prince Yan glared after the spy. "The number of insects we've estimated is great, but with yet another nest, I wonder if even the dragons may not be enough to prevent a tide of Cabeku reaching the city."

"They won't stop until all are destroyed," Kilek said, certain that was what Sparkena would have said.

"Good. We must still fight, in any event." He snapped an order to Zhavin and his remaining men, who began handing out heavy flasks. Kilek accepted his, and even with the lid sealed, an earthy scent was strong. *Something for use... on Cabeku eggs?*

"I have none," Paxoph announced with a slight frown.

"Free your uncle," the prince said, and this time he motioned for one of his men to join Pax.

"I'll help." Alira nudged her horse across.

"Very well. Return here once you have succeeded."

"Stay safe," Kilek told his friends. And this time, Pax *and* Alira thanked him before setting off. Had there been a little extra worry to her gaze? *We have to talk. Once all this is done.*

The prince then divided the rest of his men and sent them toward the dark line of Cabeku just visible beyond the camps.

And large though the line of insects was – thousands upon thousands of them – an even greater cloud was forming above those that scurried across the ground. These insects seemed similar to the usual Cabeku, but from a distance, they were more varied in size. Some were larger, but a faint, haze-like smudge that lingered around the main flight suggested a dense concentration of even smaller insects...

"We'll take the final two hatcheries – one for each pair," Prince Yan said, gesturing to Tyar and Mathi, and then Kilek.

"Very well," Kilek replied. "Once Sparkena is finished."

"We must reach the camp first," Yan said. "It will be a race against time."

They rode on, hooves pounding against the dry earth until they reached the edge of the camp. There, soldiers admitted everyone without pause, allowing them to move between tan-coloured tents, stacks of spears and other weapons and supplies. Sitting atop one crate, Kilek saw a fletcher, fingers moving deftly, re-feathering a salvaged arrow.

While few people shouted or called to the prince, they all straightened when he passed. Others also began to work harder at whatever task was before them, be it checking a fellow's armour or readying their weapons.

At the edge of the camp, a group of four soldiers snapped into action – lifting a long, wooden platform and setting off at a jog.

"What's that for?" Kilek asked.

"A bridge," Yan replied, as he pointed ahead.

There, still some distance from the camp itself, was the actual battle line. Rows of soldiers stood before a palisade, the spikes angled toward the incoming Cabeku. Though in this case, Yan's forces had also created deep trenches as part of their defensive measures.

It seemed also that some of the westerners were moving along the trenches, pouring something within… was it meant to feed flames yet to be lit? Or was it poison, like that which Kilek himself probably carried?

"Here they come," Mathi called.

Above, the dragons swooped down from the sun.

Scales of red, pink and yellow flashed, blue right behind them. Roars echoed, as a somewhat muted rainbow of fire sprayed down. Not only orange flames, but green and white seared the rumbling Cabeku too, where the insects charged across land and air alike.

None were spared as the dragons wheeled.

Cheers from the soldiers and conscripts rose but were quickly drowned out by insects screeching. New roars from each dragon drowned that sound in turn, including from the yellow-scaled dragon Kilek did not recognise. Smaller and faster, the new dragon darted around the edges of the massacre, obliterating smaller groups of insects that tried to flee.

Sparkena and his sister sent their flames into the cloud of newly awakened Cabeku, incinerating them in an instant. Blinking flames and blackened ash drifted down after each breath. Not only that, but once the Cabeku numbers dwindled enough, Sparkena hit the earth with a crash, sucking in a breath and sending a torrent of flame down into whatever hive or burrow he'd found.

Lilira was still roaring across the sky, her fire slashing down to devastate rows and rows of the Cabeku.

And between her and the other dragons, now spread along the battlefront, there was more than enough room to pass.

"Go!" Yan cried.

Ahead, the soldiers had already set the bridge in place.

Kilek kicked his mount into action, charging his way between the soldiers, Minjao and conscripts alike. But he could not spare them much of a glance. Instead, he was soon guiding his horse around the large, sometimes still-burning clumps of Cabeku, doing his best to avoid pools of steaming acid.

Even so, hooves were still crunching through blackened shells.

"Kilek!" Tyar called from where he and Mathi were branching off from the same path. Their own mounts sent Cabeku corpses flying as they rode. "Don't waste this chance!"

"I won't!" he called back, and then he and Yan had crossed the blackened earth.

Ahead, an opening in the landscape stood ringed by surviving centipede-like Cabeku. As many as a dozen, their black and blue segments bright, heavy claws barring the way.

Kilek gripped the Sky Thorn. *Not for long.*

Chapter 45.

Cabeku rose upon their scores of legs, claws snapping as they shrieked.

Kilek swung the Sky Thorn from his saddle.

A gale roared forth. He flinched, but the attack still tossed most of the creatures across the plain. It whipped up dust and stone too, and even his clothing snapped against him where he clung to the saddle, his horse rearing before coming to a halt.

Beside him, Prince Yan lowered his bow.

It seemed the man had fired several arrows, considering that the remaining pair of Cabeku both lay twitching upon the ground.

Neither was quite dead and so Kilek lifted his blade – the surface a roiling cloudbank now – but Prince Yan had already leapt from his saddle. The man strode to the Cabeku and gave two short, sharp swings of his mace.

Ichor splashed out from each crushed skull.

The prince flicked the acidic blood from his weapon before returning with a sigh, reaching out one hand to pat his horse's neck.

Kilek dismounted as Yan spoke. "I admit that I did not think one detail through to completion."

"Our horses."

He nodded. "Rose will not be safe picketed here, nor accompanying us. *Nor* would I have her risk returning through the battlefield."

Kilek checked their surroundings. The plain was still a mixture of barren or blackened earth, and not too far away, Sparkena and the others still faced plenty of insects, while Minjao soldiers and conscripts alike were hacking through the rest.

Other small groups made up of Yan's men were heading for similar burrows to the one that waited before Kilek. The next nearest opening revealed two riderless horses nearby – Tyar and Mathi, already below, then. *Good luck, both of you.*

Further west waited a green expanse; the forests of Jasoria. Had the Cabeku infiltrated it, also?

He pointed. "Why not send them toward the forest?"

Yan was already nodding. He switched to Minjao then, and spoke to his mount before giving her a slap on the rump. Rose set off at an easy gallop. The prince led Kilek's mount a little way north before repeating the process and then returning. "We must discover what else the Sky Thorn can do." He prepared a lantern then raised his flask. "We may not need this at all."

"Lead the way," Kilek said.

The burrow revealed a shadowy tunnel with uneven footing, stone and earth alike bearing cracks. Not enough to present a deadly hazard, but rushing back up and out could present a problem. Thankfully at least, the larger of the Cabeku obviously needed spacious tunnels, preventing any need to crawl within.

Occasionally, they passed a brittle-looking shell but a chill came from something else – rows and rows of empty hollows. Just like the Cabeku themselves, each recess was of varying size and shape, scattered across the walls and ceiling. Sometimes, such openings were found at the end of smaller side-passages, these rounded rooms bearing even more hollows.

So many.

Roars from the dragons above had grown muted, and finally inaudible as they walked deeper, weapons held ready. The surface of the Sky Thorn remained stormy, faint flickers of lightning silent within.

"There," Prince Yan said.

Ahead, the tunnel widened into a stretching chamber, the far end lost to shadow, changing little when Yan lifted the lantern.

It was enough to reveal the eggs.

Thousands upon thousands of them covered the ground, so dark and densely packed together that there was no room to take a single step down between them. How far did they stretch? *It could take hours to destroy this many.*

"Let's not waste any time," the prince said, his voice echoing in the cavern. He unstoppered the flask and upended it over the nearest patch of Cabeku eggs. Pale orange oozed free, dollops hitting the shells. The moment they struck the eggs, what was most likely poison spread, as if having a mind of its own. It coated more and more eggs as Kilek watched, the earthy scent rising as it moved.

"It acts like it has a mind of its own," he said.

Yan continued to shake the drops free. "The magic gives it purpose."

Kilek lifted his own flask, adding to the pool of poison. It spread quickly, seeking more and more surfaces of the shells where it would, according to Yan's explanation, spread far beyond the limits of its own substance, infecting one egg after another.

Even now, some of the eggs nearest the sludge were twitching, colour draining…

Yet, obviously without having a chance to test the poison on a truly large group of insects prior to this very moment, it seemed that Prince Yan was not satisfied – he was already trying to speed things along; stomping through the eggs and swinging his mace. The shells cracked open, ichor splashing free, revealing broken shapes of yet-to-darken Cabeku.

These too, he crushed.

"It'd take days to finish," Kilek told the man.

"You are free to help. Use that sword, Kilek of Hasere."

Kilek moved away so that the coming path of destruction would not be wasted on already dead insects, and lifted the Sky Thorn. Swinging it would cause another gale, but was there a way to release the lightning instead? Or better yet – both? He took another few steps across and raised the blade over his head. Power seemed to crackle where it spiked against his palms, as if the sword could read his intent. *Good.*

"Look away, Yan."

Kilek swung.

Searing light burst free. He closed his own eyes, but it was so sharp that afterimages of jagged bolts had been etched into the backs of his eyelids. Even his mind was slow to fathom what he'd seen: a line of lightning, yes, but hadn't each bolt thrust up from the ground?

It had charged through the Cabeku so quickly that he couldn't be sure.

Thankfully, a row of carnage spread wide and far.

He glanced at Prince Yan, blinking away more ghostly afterimages, and the man only nodded and returned to his own work.

Completely focused.

Now was the best chance to strike. Two birds with one stone… *Tyar and Alira are relying on me.*

The prince was working steadily, smashing his way through egg after egg, showing no signs of slowing as he fought to protect his people from the unborn plague of insects. Kilek gripped the blade, and the lightning within grew wilder – but at the same time, sunlight began to poke through the dark clouds.

What? He clenched his jaw. Hesitating was a grave mistake. Yan was responsible for the deaths of so many people! *Do it. Strike now.*

Something struck his knee.

A grey and orange, slime-coated tongue had wrapped his leg. Poison! He flinched but could not free himself. Nearby, one of the larger Cabeku had hatched into a misshapen form. It was mostly folds around a gaping maw – from where the tongue strained.

Despite its condition, the insect obviously had enough presence of mind to lash out blindly.

Kilek lifted his blade… and the sword fell from his grip. It clattered to a patch of stone. He fell to his knees. Warmth spread from his leg, a warmth that caused his heartbeat to double. *How fast is the poison?* He tore at the tongue – only to find his movements no stronger than that of a newborn.

A splattering filled the cavern.

Kilek lifted his head with some effort. Yan knelt before him, a deep frown on his face. "Hold on."

The man reached for the Sky Thorn. Light flashed and Yan cried out in shock. The blade rejecting him?

Kilek's vision dimmed.

Yan's jaw was clenched as he drew a belt knife and hacked into the tongue. The blade did not cut deep. Yan switched to a sawing motion, gripping the surface with his free hand for leverage. His movements soon slowed but he managed to cut through with gasp, slumping back to catch his breath.

Kilek's sight brightened and his heart slowed.

Yan was wiping at his hand, but it was also clear that he could not move with any vigour, that he was still breathing quite hard.

"I am pleasantly surprised to find you here together, gentlemen."

Lienyu stood before the exit alone. Smiling.

Chapter 46.

No change to her clothing or her expression – still sheathed in black, no weapon on her white belt, gaze still quite piercing. Only now, there was a hunger on the lips to go with it. *For what? What does she think she's found?*

"Have you come to assist me?" Prince Yan asked. He straightened, but had not attempted to stand.

Kilek's own strength was returning. Somehow, he was fighting off the poison, but he could not yet rise either. Couldn't even reach for the Sky Thorn.

"No. I am collecting gifts. You yourself, Your Highness – and that magnificent relic there beside your ally. What was his name? Yes, Kilek. The popular young man with the secret."

Prince Yan muttered a curse.

Kilek frowned. "Popular?"

"Your modesty is not welcome, young man. After all, Anesca far and wide know of you and your powers. And all seem to want you just as much as I." She paused. "However, prime amongst my goals is still the prince, here."

"I need no escort."

"You are getting one," she said. "The emperor was most insistent about you being alive – in chains, of course."

The tattoos on the back of Yan's hands were glowing. He raised his voice a little. "Kilek, I do not know all she is capable of. Be wary."

While it was heartening to see the prince able to summon his magic, it didn't mean Kilek was strong enough to fight. "Sparkena, I hope you can hear this. We might need your magic."

"Oh, none of that," Lienyu said, as she placed her hands together.

She was smiling again.

A soft hand wrapped around his throat from behind – and *something* cut off his voice, and his ability to move. "Try to have pleasant dreams."

Lienyu's voice spoke from beside his ear.

Yet, Lienyu still stood in the entryway. He could not turn to see who had captured him, but whatever the magic, it was also enough to prevent him from even *attempting* to transform.

And then the strange woman was behind Yan as well!

The Minjao Spymaster had seemingly locked Yan's arms in place, the glow of magic fading. A *third* Lienyu?

Kilek thrashed against her soft grip – or tried to.

Instead, he remained absolutely frozen in place. His vision began to dim again, the sound of her voice now hard to follow. "When you wake, you'll be in the capital. But do not worry, young man. Fenkao-Hin is a lovely city."

A Note from Ashley

Hello! I hope you enjoyed *Scales of Fire* and thanks for reading.

To keep an eye out for the next adventure for Kilek and co, please consider joining my newsletter for updates via the link below!

I'd also like to ask if you could help me out by leaving an honest review of *Scales of Fire* at your place of purchase? Long or short, bad or good, it all helps!

Visit https://ashleycapes.com/newsletter/ where you'll be the first to know when the sequel to *Scales of Fire* is released. You'll also have first access to preview chapters and pre-release editions of the story, in addition to being automatically added into the draw for giveaways.

Acknowledgements

To everyone who backed the *Scales of Fire* Kickstarter campaign – you absolutely made this possible!

Before successful funding of the project, I wasn't sure that the *Five Furies* books were all that enjoyable for readers, but your belief has changed my mind :)

Thanks once more to the following legends:

Ryallen ~ William C. Tracy ~ C. Allan ~ Jennifer L. Pierce ~ J Mills ~ Carl Spitzer ~ Wilfredo J. Villafañe Ortiz ~ C.Wilson ~ Kupo ~ Stephen Ballentine ~ C.Niehot ~ Balazs Oroszlany ~ Heiko Koenig ~ Gee Rothvoss ~ Seamus Sands ~ Matthew Monagon ~ Brian ~ Grace Hoffman ~ Liam Dotson ~ Ellen Pilcher ~ NosivadWerdna ~ Scott Freisthler ~ konstance ~ Brian Griffin ~ Steven White ~ Vickie Grider ~ Jeff Lewis ~ Jon Auerbach ~ Kaitlin James ~ Robin Hill ~ Henry Neilsen ~ Elisha ~ Amanda Balter ~ Ben Mariner ~ Axel Kallesøe ~ Harrison Tu and **Virginia McClain.**

I'm also in debt to Amanda and Brooke for always finding ways to make my stories better – and perhaps above all, I owe Marcel Mosqi for the amazing cover art and Christina P for the text design!

Ashley Capes

Book of Never – a Free Prequel Story

A nameless rogue. A priceless treasure map. An abundance of bad choices.

The rogue Never wants two things – his blood curse lifted and to know his true name. He's hunted down every relic and clue only to end up empty-handed. Until he hears of a treasure map to a sunken city full of potential answers.

Getting his hands on the map might prove to be Never's most dangerous heist yet. When the city is invaded in the middle of his caper, Never trades stealth for brute force to save the map before it burns along with the city.

But his violence has consequences. As he makes an enemy of the invading commander, can Never survive long enough to secure the map as well as his getaway, or will he go down in flames?

Never: Prequel to The Amber Isle is the thrilling prequel novella to the epic fantasy series The *Book of Never*. If you love charming rogues, daring heists, and epic quests, steal a glance at *Never: Prequel to The Amber Isle*!

www.ingramcontent.com/pod-product-compliance
Lightning Source LLC
Chambersburg PA
CBHW030806210726
48290CB00002B/449